NANCY A. COLLINS

Right Hand Magic

A Novel of
GOLGOTHAM

ROC
Published by New American Library, a division of
Penguin Group (USA) Inc., 375 Hudson Street,
New York, New York 10014, USA
Penguin Group (Canada), 90 Eglinton Avenue East, Suite 700, Toronto,
Ontario M4P 2Y3, Canada (a division of Pearson Penguin Canada Inc.)
Penguin Books Ltd., 80 Strand, London WC2R 0RL, England
Penguin Ireland, 25 St. Stephen's Green, Dublin 2,
Ireland (a division of Penguin Books Ltd.)
Penguin Group (Australia), 250 Camberwell Road, Camberwell, Victoria 3124,
Australia (a division of Pearson Australia Group Pty. Ltd.)
Penguin Books India Pvt. Ltd., 11 Community Centre, Panchsheel Park,
New Delhi - 110 017, India
Penguin Group (NZ), 67 Apollo Drive, Rosedale, North Shore 0632,
New Zealand (a division of Pearson New Zealand Ltd.)
Penguin Books (South Africa) (Pty.) Ltd., 24 Sturdee Avenue,
Rosebank, Johannesburg 2196, South Africa

Penguin Books Ltd., Registered Offices:
80 Strand, London WC2R 0RL, England

First published by Roc, an imprint of New American Library,
a division of Penguin Group (USA) Inc.

First Printing, December 2010
10 9 8 7 6 5 4 3 2 1

PUBLISHER'S NOTE
This is a work of fiction. Names, characters, places, and incidents either are the
product of the author's imagination or are used fictitiously, and any resemblance
to actual persons, living or dead, business establishments, events, or locales is
entirely coincidental.

The publisher does not have any control over and does not assume any re-
sponsibility for author or third-party Web sites or their content.

Dedicated to the memory of my mother,
Marilynn Willoughby Collins
1936–2009

Acknowledgments

The author would like to acknowledge the following source materials as having been instrumental in bringing the neighborhood of Golgotham to life:

The Gangs of New York: An Informal History of the Underworld by Herbert Asbury (Paragon House); *Low Life: Lures and Snares of Old New York* (Vintage Books) and *Evidence* (Farrar, Straus and Giroux) by Luc Sante; *The Worm in the Bud: The World of Victorian Sexuality* by Ronald Pearsall (Penguin); *Abandoned Stations* by Joseph Brennan (www.columbia.edu/~brennan/abandoned); *Lost City* (http://lostnewyorkcity.blogspot.com); *Jeremiah's Vanishing New York* by Jeremiah Moss (http://vanishingnewyork.blogspot.com); and *Old Streets of New York: A Guide to Former Street Names in Manhattan* by Gilbert Tauber (www.oldstreets.com).

She would also like to acknowledge the amazing work of Andrew Chase (www.andrewchase.com) and Jeremy Mayer (www.jeremymayer.com) as having provided the inspiration for Tate's metal sculptures.

Right Hand Magic

Chapter 1

The flyer on the bulletin board at Strega Nona's Pizza Oven read "Room for Rent: $750 per Month." At the bottom of the page was a line of tear-away slips bearing a handwritten phone number, several of which were already taken.

I happened to be at Strega Nona's that particular day because I was looking at a loft in Tribeca. Since I was nearby, I decided to grab a slice. Located at Broadway and Perdition, on the border of Golgotham, it's one of the best pizza joints in the city.

Sounds too good to be true, I thought to myself as I tore off the next tab in line.

Housing at that price, just for a single room in a larger apartment, was hard to come by. I knew this because I'd been hunting for a new place for several weeks, without any luck. Even though I had a tidy quarterly income, courtesy of robber baron ancestors, I still had to watch my budget. The materials used in my work were far from cheap, and the last thing I wanted was to have to go to my parents, hat in hand, halfway through a project, and beg for an advance on my next trust fund payment.

The reason behind my need to relocate was that the management of my so-called artist's loft in SoHo, where I both worked and lived, had recently informed me that the amount of noise I generated creating my metal sculptures was in violation of their most recent tenancy rules and that I was to cease immediately or face the termination of my lease. Apparently the investment bankers and junior-level stockbrokers who lived on my floor didn't appreciate the sound of twenty-gauge steel being hammered into twenty-first-century art.

I decided it was far easier to move in toto than to either argue the point with the condo board or find separate studio space elsewhere in the city. As it was, there were some unpleasant memories associated with my current digs, all of them involving a certain ex-boyfriend, that made relocating attractive to me.

I checked the time on my cell phone as I shoveled a slice of pepperoni-and-andouille-sausage into my mouth. I had a meeting at three with Derrick Templeton, a Chelsea gallery owner interested in showing my sculptures. Since there were no subway stops in Golgotham, I had to walk either to Chambers or Wall Street if I wanted to catch a train uptown.

After all, time and gallery owners wait for no woman.

Two and a half hours later, I left Templeton Gallery with a smile on my face and a handshake from the owner, who had agreed to feature my metal sculptures at his next show. And my parents said I was wasting my time pursuing a career as an artist. Ha!

I wanted to call them up and tell them the good news.

Well, good as far as I was concerned, anyway. That would rub it in nice and hard. Take *that*, Mom and Dad!

As I fished the cell phone out of my purse, my fingers closed about the slip of paper I'd taken from the pizzeria. I stared at the numbers printed in a neat, almost-calligraphic hand for a long moment, and then punched them into the phone.

I'm probably too late. Still, what's the harm in trying? The worst they can tell me is that it's already rented out.

The phone rang four times before someone picked up. "Hello? Who's this?" The voice on the other end was definitely male.

"Hi, I'm calling about the room for rent? Is it still available?"

"Yes, it is. Would you like to look at it?"

"Sure!" I replied excitedly. "When's a good time?"

"How about now?"

As I scribbled down the address on the back of an old takeout menu, I marveled at my good luck. Finally, after weeks of dead ends and near misses, I had not only landed a gallery show, but was now hot on the trail of an apartment.

"I'll be there as soon as I can," I said. "I'm in Chelsea right now."

"Just make sure to knock real loud when you get here. Sometimes I can't hear the door if I'm in the kitchen."

"Taxi!" I raised my arm as I stepped off the curb. A cab swerved out of the stream of traffic and pulled up alongside me. The driver leaned out of the window, eyeing the tattoos on my arms and the stainless steel piercing adorning my right brow.

"Where to, lady? The Village?"

I shook my head. "Golgotham."

The taxi took off without another word, leaving me

standing in the gutter. I gave the fleeing cabbie the finger, for all the good it did me, and resumed walking in the general direction of downtown.

After three more hacks left me standing at the curb, I finally got a driver who was willing to take me most of the way there. The cabbie was a powerfully built West African, with tribal scarring on his cheekbones that resembled the waves of the ocean.

"I take you as far as Gate. No farther," he informed me solemnly.

"I'll pay you double the meter if you take me to the exact address," I offered as I slid into the backseat. I held up a fistful of bills so the driver could see I wasn't bullshitting him.

"No. Gate only," the cabbie responded firmly, shaking his head.

"Very well." I sighed, dropping my shoulders in surrender. I learned long ago there was no arguing with a New York City cab driver.

Fifteen minutes later the taxi reached the Gate of Skulls, one of the city's most famous landmarks, right up there with the Statue of Liberty and the Empire State Building.

Actually, "the Gate of Skulls" was something of a misnomer since it wasn't really made of numerous craniums, but was simply fashioned to resemble an extremely large one. It stood thirty feet high, and twice as wide, carved from a single slab of white marble. Over the decades, the smooth surface had become pitted and stained from exposure to the elements, giving it an increasingly realistic appearance. Each tooth lining the Gate's upper jaw was the size of a paving stone, and its eye sockets were lit from within by a flickering green light that burned day and night.

That last bit was a relatively new touch, added by the Golgotham Business Owners' Organization (GoBOO) back in the 1970s, in order to help promote tourism. Sensationalistic flourishes aside; the Gate of Skulls, straddling the east corner of Broadway and Perdition Street like the remains of some fallen giant, was an eerie sight, warning the unwary of the dangers ahead.

I couldn't wait to walk through its gaping maw.

Chapter 2

The address I was looking for was at the very top of Golden Hill Street, between Perdition and Beekman. Unlike the rest of the surrounding city, there had never been an attempt to turn Golgotham into flat, orderly squares. Because of this, the basic layout of the neighborhood had changed very little since the early eighteenth century.

I stared up at the house before me. If ever there was a perfect example of Golgotham architecture, this was it. With its twin turrets and ornate lightning rod perched high atop its peaked roof, it looked like an escapee from a Charles Addams cartoon. There was even a gargoyle poised atop the cornice, bat wings folded tightly against its humped back. Marshaling my nerve, I strode up the granite steps, grabbed the brass door knocker shaped like a coiled asp, and knocked as loudly as I could.

After a few moments, there came a squeal of rusty hinges as the heavy door swung open. Although I was half expecting Dracula, I was pleasantly surprised to discover the person on the other side was a very handsome young man, no older than twenty-five, with the lean, muscled body of a skater. He was dressed in a T-shirt, with SUPER FRIENDS printed on the front, skinny jeans, and had a pair of scuffed Chuck Taylors on his feet. His hair was shoulder length and unruly, as if it couldn't decide whether to be straight or curly, and deep purple in color, with pale blue highlights.

He tilted his head quizzically to one side, fixing me with golden eyes that had cat-slit pupils. I noticed with a slight start that he gripped the edge of the door with six fingers instead of five. It was only then I realized I was face-to-face not with just another Lower East Side boho hipster, but with an actual flesh-and-blood Kymeran.

I had seen Kymerans on television and in movies, and read about them in books and on scandal Web sites, but I had never actually laid eyes on the real thing before. A part of me was surprised that the extra finger wasn't like the rigid fake plastic pinkies sold at Halloween costume shops, but actually curled and flexed like the others on his hand.

"Yes? What is it?" he asked with a hint of irritation. He had noticed me staring at his hands.

"We, uh, talked on the phone earlier," I replied, color rushing to my cheeks. "I've come about the room."

"You got money?" he asked bluntly, eyeing my own tattered jeans. "I don't care how hot you look; I'll not have a lubbard under my roof."

I had no idea what a "lubbard" was, but it didn't sound complimentary. "I can pay three months in advance, plus deposit, if that answers your question."

He studied me for a long moment, as if trying to decipher something written on my forehead that only he could see, before finally stepping aside. "The room's on the second floor."

As I entered the house, I caught the scent of used jockstraps boiled in potpourri. Well, that probably wasn't what it actually was, but it sure smelled like it. I automatically wrinkled my nose in disgust.

"Sorry about the stink," he said, closing the door behind me. "I was in the middle of mixing something up when you knocked. Give me a moment—I need to take the cauldron off the boil."

He hurried down the hallway to the back of the house. Unsure of what to do, I followed him. As I tagged along, I glimpsed a double parlor with an adjoining dining room and what looked like a study on the ground floor.

The kitchen was large with plenty of counter space, every available square inch of which was littered with glass vials and containers. Sitting atop the old-fashioned gas stove was a large cast-iron vessel, the contents of which bubbled and gurgled like a pool of lava waiting to erupt. As I watched, he pulled on a pair of oven mitts and lifted the heavy cauldron from atop the burner ring as if it were a pot of spaghetti.

"Careful! Hot soup!" he said as he crossed the kitchen and placed the steaming container on a circular slab of marble covered in arcane symbols. "I have a little side business as a nimgimmer," the landlord explained, noticing the puzzled look on my face. "I have a client with a fondness for fauns, so to speak, and he's picked up an unfortunate case of orf."

"Uh-huh." I tried my best not to let on that I had no clue what the hell he was talking about.

"It's a form of knob-rot passed along by livestock," he explained with a wry smile.

"*Oh!*" I lowered my head and coughed into my fist so he couldn't see me blush.

"You're new to Golgotham, aren't you?" he asked, not unkindly.

"Is it that obvious?" I winced.

"Just a tad," he replied. "So what kind of psychic are you? Clairvoyant? Telekinetic? Dowser?"

"I'm none of those," I explained, slightly baffled by the question. "I'm an artist."

He stopped what he was doing, a surprised look on his face. "Really? I would have figured you for a medium, myself. Normally psychics are the only type of humans who look to make their home in Golgotham. What brings you here?"

"Rent, for the most part. I'm looking for a place where I can live and work in the same space. The raw materials for my art are expensive. I need all the help I can get. Plus, I've always been fascinated by this part of the city. It's so . . . *real*."

"I've never heard it described quite like that before," he laughed.

Kymerans are known for giving off natural perfumes, as opposed to body odor, and now that the noisome concoction in the cauldron was off the boil, I finally noticed the landlord's personal scent. When he brushed by, I caught a hint of citrus, moss, and leather. It was definitely a masculine aroma, and one I found quite attractive.

As we headed up the stairs to the second floor, I looked around for signs of other tenants. "Do you live here alone?"

"Hardly!" he laughed. "I have another boarder right now, but I doubt you'll have occasion to see him. Assuming you want the room, that is."

"I hope you don't take this the wrong way—but aren't you kind of young to be a landlord?" I asked.

"I inherited the job," he explained. "The house has

been in the family for two centuries. When I told my mom I wanted to try my hand at lifting for a living instead of going to thaumaturgical college, she insisted I take over things here. It's worked out pretty good, so far."

Just then something small and close to the ground ran past me, brushing against my leg before disappearing into the shadows at the top of the stairs. Whatever it was didn't have fur.

"What the hell?!?" I yelped.

"Oh, that was just Scratch," the landlord laughed. "Don't mind him. He's always like that with strangers."

"Scratch is a . . . pet?" I asked uneasily.

"Something like that." He turned and addressed the darkness gathered at the second-floor landing. "Scratch! Come out and meet our guest!"

There was the sound of claws scrabbling on hardwood, followed by a flapping noise. Something resembling a house cat, save that it was utterly hairless with bat wings growing out of its back, leaped out of the shadows and made a perfect four-point landing on the second-floor balustrade.

"Dear God!" I clapped my hand over my mouth, but it was too late to hide my shock.

The winged, hairless cat fixed me with an eye as red as murder. "Who's the nump?" it sneered. "Another looky-loo?"

"Scratch! Where are your manners? Be nice. Or at least nice-*ish*. I'd like you to meet Miss . . . ?" The landlord gave me a smile that pinned me to the spot like a butterfly. "I'm afraid I did not get your name earlier . . . ?"

"Just call me Tate."

"Scratch, this is Miss Tate."

"Humph," Scratch sniffed, clearly unimpressed.

"Pleased to meet you, uh, Scratch."

"As well you should be," the flying cat replied curtly.

"Scratch is my familiar. I'm sure you've heard about such things from books and movies." As the landlord stroked the winged cat's back, Scratch butted his forehead against him, just like any other tabby would. "He is also my rent collector."

"Yeah—I eat the deadbeats!" The familiar grinned.

"Honestly, Scratch. You're such a liar. You're not allowed to take more than one bite, and you know it. Come along now, Miss Tate. . . ."

I nervously glanced over my shoulder at the winged cat still perched on the banister; the creature's eyes glowed like hot coals in the dim light. My mouth went dry as paper. Maybe moving to Golgotham wasn't *that* great an idea after all. . . .

"Ah! Here we are!" The landlord held up an old-fashioned key that looked better suited to unlocking a pirate's treasure chest than a door. He slid it into the keyhole and gave it a quick turn. The door swung open, revealing only darkness. He crossed the room and pulled aside the heavy velvet draperies that covered the windows facing the street. "Let's get some light in here."

As the late-afternoon sunlight spilled into the room, my trepidation about living among witches, demons, and things that go bump in the night instantly disappeared. The space was easily two thousand square feet—twice the size of the SoHo loft I currently called home—and outfitted with antique oriental carpets, a marble fireplace decorated with satyrs and nymphs, and a fifteen-foot vaulted ceiling.

"It's much bigger than I expected," I gasped in amazement.

"Yes, that's one of the unique features of this house.

It was designed by my great-uncle Jack. He was a Mason of Hidden Degree, famous for utilizing a form of geometric origami that allows you to occupy more space than is physically available."

"That's amazing! How many rooms are there?"

"I'm not exactly sure. Some of them only manifest during certain astronomical convergences. This floor is relatively stable, but you should never go upstairs by yourself. That's how we lost Uncle Jack."

"You mean something up there killed him?" I asked, trying to control the alarm in my voice.

"Heavens and hells, no! We just lost him, that's all. He's still wandering around up there somewhere," he said, gesturing to the ceiling. "So, do you want the room or not?"

"I'll take it," I said as I pulled out my checkbook. "Who do I make this out to?"

"The name's Hexe, with an extra 'e' at the end," he replied, returning my smile. "And welcome to Golgotham."

Chapter 3

I was really buzzing by the time I returned to my Crosby Street loft, without having taken a single drink or having indulged in any illicit substances. Landing a gallery show *and* a kick-ass apartment in one day? It looked like the gods were smiling on me, after all. Yet, as exciting as those two developments were, I found myself thinking more about my handsome new landlord than my recent good fortune. There was something about his golden eyes with their catlike pupils that intrigued me. My good mood abruptly ended, however, when the elevator door opened on the ground floor of my building, revealing Roger Price.

He had a boyishly handsome face, soulful brown eyes, a shock of carefully mussed dark hair, and an eternal case of five o'clock shadow that played up his strong chin. He also had a fondness for black Armani T-shirts and designer jeans that showed off his body to its best advantage. He worked as a graphic designer at an advertising company, and we'd met eighteen months ago at a gallery opening for a mutual friend. Our relationship had been extremely intense, both physically and emotionally, before it turned to utter shit.

"*There* you are." Roger smiled. "I just left a note on your door, since you're ignoring my calls. . . ."

"What the hell are you doing here?" I growled.

"Don't be like that, Tate," he said, trying to make it sound, as usual, as if I were the one being unreasonable. "I realize you have every right to be upset, but I really want to try and work things out between us."

"There's nothing to 'work out,' Roger," I said flatly. "You cheated on me. Now get out of my building."

"That's just it," he said, smirking as if he'd pulled a particularly clever move. "It's my building now, too."

"What do you mean?" I frowned.

"I just signed a lease on a loft on the next floor up from yours. We're going to be neighbors!"

"That's great, Rog," I laughed. "You're more than welcome to take my place as the token 'artist' in this so-called artists' loft."

Now it was his turn to look nonplussed. "What are you saying?"

"I'm moving out of this place," I explained, entering the elevator as he exited it. "The condo board doesn't appreciate me, and I certainly don't appreciate them. But that's okay—I found a place better suited for me."

"Where are you going?" The look of consternation on his face as he realized his attempt to woo me back was beginning to tailspin perked me back up. "Tribeca? Williamsburg?"

"Golgotham."

I really should have tried to take a picture of Roger's face as I told him the news, but the elevator doors closed before I could get my cell phone camera ready.

*   *   *

Two weeks later the movers arrived at my old apartment early in the morning and carried everything I owned into a van. The supervisor in charge of the load-out assured me that his crew would arrive at my new apartment by noon.

As I was sweeping out the corners of the emptied loft, there came a knock. I looked up to see Roger standing on the threshold of the open front door, holding a bouquet of roses in one hand and a bottle of wine in the other. I sighed and put aside the broom.

"What do you want?"

"I saw the moving van earlier," he said sheepishly. "I just wanted to say good-bye before you left for good."

"Thank you, Roger," I said as I placed the flowers and wine on the kitchen counter. I had to admit that his going away present actually made me smile a little bit. If there was one thing Roger excelled at, it was making the romantic gesture. "That was very thoughtful of you."

"We had something really good going on, didn't we?" he asked, staring at his feet as he scuffed the toe of his shoe against the floor. He was playing the mawkish schoolboy card—his favorite way of getting around me, and one that usually worked, despite my better judgment.

"It was good for a while, yes," I agreed. "But then it fell apart, Rog. You know that."

"I really don't know what to say, Tate, except I'm sorry," he said. "I feel like I'm the one responsible for your leaving, and that's tearing me up. . . ."

"I'll admit that what you did made giving up my loft a

lot easier, but you're not the reason I'm moving, Roger,"
I replied. "Believe it or not, this wasn't all about you."

"I'm just worried about you," he said, apparently
shrugging off that last little dig. "Are you sure you'll be
okay living there? Golgotham's a pretty sketchy neighborhood."

"I appreciate the concern, but I'll be fine."

"Just do me a favor, as a friend, and watch your back,
okay? What with all the freaks that live there . . . You
don't know whom you can trust."

"So far I haven't had to worry about Kymerans
double-crossing me," I said pointedly. "Now, if you don't
mind—I need to finish cleaning up so I can be at my new
apartment in time for the movers."

"Promise me if anything goes wrong and you end up
needing help, you won't hesitate to call."

"I'll keep that in mind, Roger," I lied as I closed the
door behind him. "Thank you for stopping by."

Once he was gone, I was free to turn my attention to
tidying up the kitchen one last time. After I finished, I
took the bouquet and bottle of wine and placed them
inside the refrigerator, as my gift to whatever yuppie
would end up moving in after me.

I looked out the window of my new apartment, searching the street in vain for some sign of the moving van.
I then checked my cell phone for the tenth time in as
many minutes. It was after three o'clock. Even giving
the crew time for lunch and possible traffic tie-ups, there
was no excuse for such a delay.

"Triple-A Aardvark Moving Company," the receptionist announced cheerfully. "We're number one in the
book. How may I direct your call?"

"I need to speak to Vinnie."

"One moment, please."

The receptionist's chirpy voice was abruptly replaced by that of Vinnie, who talked as if everyone around him were slightly deaf.

"Yeah, whaizzit?" the mover growled.

"Vinnie, this is, uh, Tate. . . . You picked up my stuff this morning?"

"Yeah. Whattaya want?"

"I was calling to find out when your guys are going to show up? You said they'd be here by noon. . . ."

"Oh, yeah! About dat . . ." I could hear him riffling though papers on the other end of the line. "I'm afraid dere's been a *problem* with yer delivery."

The schadenfreude in the mover's voice made my guts cinch. "What *kind* of problem?"

"My guys ain't bringing yer stuff."

"*What?!?*" I screamed into the receiver. "Why the hell not?"

"You see, when my driver plugged the address you gave 'im into his—whaddaya call it?—GPS, it came up Golgotham."

"Yeah? So?"

"Well, we ain't licensed to make deliveries to dat part of town. The streets down dere are too narrow to accommodate movin' vans."

"Why wasn't I informed of this earlier?" I asked as I massaged the throbbing veins in my forehead. "The sales rep from your company didn't say a thing about any of this!"

"Dat guy?" Vinnie chuckled nastily. "He ain't workin' here no more. Listen, lady, I don't know what he told ya, and it don't matter what he said, 'cause we don't deliver dere. Never have, never will. If ya want yer stuff delivered, yer gonna hafta arrange for a second movin' company to pick it up at da Relay Station over dere on South Street near da Brooklyn Bridge."

"Then where's my stuff? If it's not on the way here, where the hell is it?"

"Don't you worry. Everything's sittin' here in our warehouse, safe 'n sound. We'll be storin' it for ya until ya gets someone t'take it where it needs t'go. After dat, we'll be happy t'drop it off at da Relay Station. Of course, we gotta charge ya storage fees...."

"What about the money I paid you to move my things in the first place?" I asked heatedly.

"Storage is different from movin', lady." Vinnie's voice was as cold and blunt as a lead pipe. "Or wouldja rather we left yer stuff sittin' out on da coib?"

As much as I wanted to give that smirking cretin a piece of my mind, I knew it would only turn a bad situation into a horrible one. I sighed in resignation. "Very well, I'll see what I can do."

"Yeah, ya do dat. Oh, and by th' way—we charge for storage by th' day. Have a nice day, and t'ank youse for usin' Triple-A Aardvark Movin'. We're number one in da book."

"Damn it!" Since I didn't have anything to throw except my cell phone, I had to be satisfied with hopping up and down in a rage. "That no-good, lousy, stinkin' son-of-a-bitch ...!"

"Hey! What's going on in here? The chandelier downstairs is swinging like a pendulum."

I looked up to see Hexe standing in the open door of my very empty apartment, watching me with a bemused look on his face.

"I'm sorry," I replied sheepishly. "I didn't mean to jump that hard. It's just—damn it! The movers are holding everything I own hostage. My bed, my clothes, the tools I use in my work—*everything!* They're holding my entire life for ransom!"

Hexe raised a purple eyebrow. "Who did you use?"

"Triple A ..."

"Let me guess the rest of the sentence—Aardvark Moving?"

"You know about them?"

"Yeah, I know about them," he replied sourly. "They're 'number one in the book.' They're also notorious rip-off artists. They pull the same crap on everyone who moves to Golgotham. You didn't pay them up front, did you?"

"I gave them half. They were to get the rest after they delivered my belongings."

A thoughtful look crossed Hexe's face. "I know a fellow in the moving business who can help you. He's very good at what he does, but I warn you—he's not cheap."

I sat down on the window seat in my room to ponder the options open to me: either resign myself to being screwed over, talk to my landlord's friend in the moving business, or call Daddy's law firm and have them sue Vinnie's back brace off.

But as rewarding as that latter option sounded, I couldn't bring myself to go through with it. I was determined to strike out on my own, without relying on the family name and connections. And doing something like that would definitely be cheating.

"I'll pay whatever it takes to get my stuff back." I sighed. Since this move was already costing me more than expected, I decided I might as well see what Hexe's friend could do. "Those douche bags are holding my sculptures hostage."

"Then grab your coat. You'll have to meet with him face-to-face."

"Where are we going?" I asked as I slid into my jacket.

"You moved here to experience Golgotham's unique atmosphere, right? Well, I'm taking you to the Rookery. It doesn't get more atmospheric than that."

Chapter 4

With its narrow, twisting streets and alleyways, Golgotham was a world apart from the orderly grid-pattern and towering glass skyscrapers that made up the rest of Manhattan. Most of the buildings that lined the streets were tenements that dated back at least a century, the ground floors of which housed various commercial businesses. While the corner markets were no different from ones found in the rest of the city, the herbalists and alchemical supply stores clearly catered to the neighborhood's unique inhabitants.

Hexe wound his way through the crowded sidewalks of Golgotham with the speed and certainty of someone who knew the route by heart. I followed in his wake, trying not to stare as we passed a trio of leprechauns sitting at a sidewalk patio. While the little men were all dressed in green, the clothes they wore were designer labels, and each had the latest Bluetooth headset affixed to his pointed ears.

One of the leprechauns noticed me looking in their

direction and gave me the finger. I blushed and hurried to catch up with my native guide.

"When we first met, you said something about being a lifter—what is that, exactly?" I asked.

"A lifter removes curses for a living."

"But I thought Kymerans only laid curses?"

Hexe shot me a sharp look from the corner of his golden eyes. "Not *all* of us. I don't inflict curses on people. I refuse to practice Left Hand magic."

"I'm sorry if I offended you. I didn't mean—"

"I know you didn't," he said, waving away my apology. "Some of us work only Left Hand disciplines, and some work only the Right Hand. Truth of the matter is most Kymerans are jugglers, meaning they practice both Left and Right Hand magic. I'm what's called a dexter— Right Hand only."

"That's commendable."

"I'd make more money if I were willing to perform ligatures and mix up love potions for date rapists," he replied with a humorless laugh. "That's why my mother insisted on my taking over the boardinghouse—at least I'd have a place to sleep and a reliable income to fall back on. She doesn't have the greatest faith in my career choice."

"I can relate to that. My parents were less than thrilled when I told them I wanted to be a sculptor."

Hexe gave me another, softer look, accompanied by a warm smile. "Nice to know we have something in common besides the same roof over our heads, Miss Tate."

"Forget the whole 'Miss' business. Call me Tate, please."

His smile grew warmer still. "Very well . . . Tate it is."

*   *   *

The Rookery was located at the crooked crossroads where Skinner Lane intersected with Ferry, Vandercliffe, and Hag streets. Standing five stories tall and occupying an entire city block, it had once, centuries ago, been a brewery. After the original business closed up shop, the mammoth building became an indoor bazaar where Kymeran spellcasters, charm peddlers, potion pushers, and assorted oracles, of both the Right Hand and Left, gathered to offer their services to the human community.

The interior of the building had long been gutted of its machinery, and each floor was subdivided into smaller makeshift chambers. Some were the size of two-room apartments, while others were no bigger than a broom closet. While some had proper doors affixed to them, others were partitioned by a scrap of tapestry or a curtain of beads. It was here that those seeking to thwart a business rival, win the heart of an unwilling paramour, or punish a straying spouse sought their respective remedies.

The different floors were accessible only by a latticework of rickety wooden stairways and ladders that looked like the work of a drunken carpenter trying to re-create a spiderweb. I stared in awe as the inhabitants of the Rookery clambered back and forth on the hodgepodge network of tottering stairs like so many mountain goats.

The original beams and rafters met high overhead, and stray fingers of sunlight stabbed downward into the hazy darkness through breaks in the roof; otherwise the only light inside the building came from balls of blue-white witchfire that burned in a series of braziers on each floor. The air inside the converted brewery smelled of incense, smoke, and the unique, heady musk generated by hundreds of Kymeran bodies crammed into the same enclosed space.

"Come along." Hexe motioned to me as he mounted a stairway that looked as though it should lead to a child's tree house. "Faro does business on the third floor."

The steps groaned mightily, as if on the verge of giving way, as I followed his lead. I held my breath and did not take another one until I reached the relatively sound footing of the third floor.

Double rows of rooms stretched from one end to the other, with narrow, winding passageways threaded throughout. Everywhere I looked I saw Kymerans, easily recognizable by their bizarrely colored hair. I'd never seen so many hot pink, electric blue, and bright green coiffures outside of a rave.

As my eyes became adjusted to the dim light, I realized the majority of those coming and going from the different shops and stalls were, in fact, humans. Most of these visitors to the Rookery kept to the shadows, their collars pulled up and heads pointed down, purposefully avoiding eye contact with those around them for fear of being recognized. No doubt a good number of the Rookery's regular clients worked at nearby City Hall and did not want to be seen going about whatever business they were on. Attitudes toward consorting with Kymerans had changed a great deal in the last century, but it was one thing to get a promotion or win an election through the natural course of events, quite another to arrange it via sorcery.

After leading me through a series of confusing turns, Hexe came to a halt in front of a small room only slightly larger than the average office worker's cubicle. Sandwiched between a magic candle peddler and a crystal ball pro shop, it didn't even have a real door, just a flap of old tapestry with a business card pinned to it. The card read FARO MOVING: IF I CAN'T MOVE IT, IT'S NOT YOURS.

"You can't be serious?" I groaned as I eyed the threadbare covering over the doorway. "I came all the way for this?"

"I know how it looks," Hexe replied, sotto voce, as he ushered me inside, "but looks are deceiving in Golgotham. Trust me, he's the best in the city."

The scores of maps covering every inch of the aged walls were the first thing I noticed upon entering Faro Moving's minuscule "office." Most were of the city and the triboroughs, but there were also various different maps of the state, the country, the world, and even the moon.

Sitting behind a tattered old desk was a Kymeran male with spiky blue hair. His eyes had the same cat-slit pupil as Hexe's, but they were emerald green instead of gold. He was dressed in frayed jeans and a vintage Black Sabbath T-shirt, his sneaker-clad feet resting in an open drawer as he thumbed through a Rand McNally atlas. The only light in the small room was from a ball of witchfire that bobbed above the desk like a child's toy balloon.

"If you're lookin' to fuck somebody up or make somebody fuck you, you're in the wrong place," the blue-haired Kymeran said without bothering to look up from his reading.

"Is that any way to greet an old friend?" Hexe chided.

The blue-haired Kymeran laughed and set aside his reading material. "Heavens and hells! Hexe! It's been dogs' years! I thought you worked out of your house? What brings you to the Rookery?"

"I'm bringing you some business. Faro, this is Tate. She's my newest lodger, and she's in dire need of your services."

"Pleased to meet you, Miss Tate," Faro said as he got

to his feet, offering me his hand. "Any friend of Hexe's is a friend of mine."

"Thanks, Mr. Faro," I replied, trying hard not to think about how weird the Kymeran's sixth digit felt in my palm as we shook hands. Instead, I focused on his scent, which was a pleasant mixture of oakmoss, citrus, and the deep woods.

"Just call me Faro. So, what can I do ya for?"

"I was supposed to move in today, but the company I hired to handle it is refusing to deliver to my new address. . . ."

Faro cut me off before I could finish. "Triple-A Aard-vark, right?"

"I take it you're familiar with them?"

"Like the back of my hand." Faro sighed. "Normally I charge about a grand for an in-city move, but seeing how you're renting from Hexe, I'll cut you a deal. How does five hundred sound?"

"It sounds pretty damned good, at this point." I reached into my purse and took out five crisp one-hundred-dollar bills. "I had this money on me so I could pay the movers, but I might as well pay you instead."

"Excellent! That saves us a trip to the ATM on the second floor." Faro grinned as he slipped the money into his own pocket. "Let's get right to it, eh?"

He walked around the desk and stood in front of me, the witchfire following him like a loyal pet. He fished what looked like a monocle out of his pants pocket and screwed it into place in his right eye, and then looked me up and down as if measuring me for a wedding dress.

"Good—you have a very strong, extremely distinctive aura. It'll be no problem at all."

I wasn't sure what my aura had to do with moving my belongings out of storage, but I decided it was best to remain silent. Faro went back to his desk and took a handheld GPS device out of one of the drawers and entered an address, all the while muttering under his breath in a language I'd never heard before. He paused only to glance up in Hexe's direction.

"Which floor?"

"Second," Hexe replied. "The front room that overlooks the street."

"Gotcha." A couple of seconds later, the GPS made a beeping noise, and Faro nodded his head in approval. "Okay. Everything's taken care of." With that he returned the GPS to its hiding place.

I glanced around, unsure of what had just happened. "When can I expect your guys to show up?"

"What 'guys'?" the Kymeran snorted. "I'm the proprietor and sole employee of Faro Moving."

"But—what about my stuff—?"

"It's already been delivered."

"How's that even possible? You haven't left my sight!"

"All the same, your belongings are waiting for you."

Hexe stepped up and took my arm, squiring me out the door. "Thanks for the help, Faro!"

"Always a pleasure, dude," Faro called after us. "And give my best to Lady Syra."

The moment we were out of the cubicle, I yanked my arm free of his grasp. "What the hell just happened in there—? Did you bring me here just to get ripped off again?"

"Of course not," he replied indignantly. "Look, things are done differently in Golgotham—a *lot* differently. Faro's one of the most respected movers in not just this city, but the entire world. If he says it's taken care of, it's taken care of."

I was suddenly aware that I was staring deep into Hexe's golden, catlike eyes, which seemed to shine with an inner light. They were unlike anything I had ever seen before. I quickly looked away, fearful that I had offended him yet again.

"I'm sorry if I sounded angry. But after everything I've gone through today, I'm kind of leery of movers, human or otherwise," I explained.

"It's okay," Hexe assured me as we headed back through the Rookery. "You have every right to be skeptical."

I heaved a sigh of relief. So I hadn't screwed things up—at least not yet, anyway. "So, why did Faro ask you to say hello to Lady Syra?"

"Because she's my mother," he said matter-of-factly, as if talking about the weather.

"No way!" I grinned, my surprise momentarily overcoming my need to seem cool. "Lady Syra, 'Witch to the Stars,' is your mom?"

"Could you say that a little louder?" Hexe winced. "I think there's a deaf granny in Hoboken who didn't hear you."

My face flushed bright red and my ears started to burn. "I'm sorry. I didn't mean to, you know, get all fangirl on you."

"That's okay." He sighed. "I'm used to it."

As we exited the Rookery, Hexe waved down one of the neighborhood's trademark cabs. A blue roan centaur, dressed from the waist up in a black cutaway coat, stopped at the curb, tipping his top hat in greeting.

"Evening, Hexe."

"Good evening, Kidron. Here's that salve for your hooves." Hexe took a jar from his coat pocket and handed it to the cabbie. "Use it first thing in the morning and again before bedding down, and it should keep the tenderness at bay."

"Thank you." Kidron smiled. "Where to? The ride's on me."

Hexe turned to face me. "Look, I have some personal errands I need to run. Why don't you go back to the house and see things with your own eyes? That should put your mind at ease. Kidron, could you give my friend here a lift to my place?"

"No prob," the centaur replied, bobbing his head in assent. "Hop in, ma'am." He gestured to the open door of the hansom cab he was harnessed to.

"Thanks, man, uh, dude, uh . . . "

"The word you're looking for is 'stud,'" Hexe whispered helpfully into my ear, the warmth of his breath raising goose bumps along my neck.

"Yeah, thanks, uh, stud," I said, involuntarily blushing as I spoke.

"Don't mention it, ma'am," Kidron replied with a toss of his plaited dorsal mane. "Any friend of Hexe's is a friend of mine."

As the two-wheeled carriage pulled away into traffic, I turned to watch Hexe as he crossed the street. I managed to keep my eyes on him until Kidron rounded the corner. I dropped back in my seat and smiled to myself.

Lady Syra was the most prominent Kymeran in the city, if not the whole country. Her clientele included names like Astor, Vanderbilt, and Carnegie, not to mention movie and rock stars, as well as numerous politicians. Yet here was her son, trying to establish himself on his own terms, without flaunting his family name and connections.

No wonder I liked him.

Chapter 5

"Here you go, ma'am," Kidron said as he pulled up to the curb in front of the boardinghouse.

While the carriage horses in Central Park might appreciate a nice apple or a lump of sugar, the same could not be said of their centaur counterparts. As I climbed out of the hansom, I fished a five-dollar bill out of my purse and handed it to my cabbie.

"Thank you for the ride. Here's something for your trouble."

"No trouble at all, ma'am." The centaur smiled as he pocketed the money. "But your graciousness is most appreciated." He reached up and plucked a business card from the band of his top hat. "If you ever need a ride anywhere in Golgotham, please give me a call. I'm licensed outside the neighborhood, so I can take you as far as Tribeca or the Battery, if necessary. The last thing a beautiful young lady wants to do is ride in a rickshaw pulled by a satyr."

I nodded my understanding, at the same time fighting

the urge to pat him on the rump and say, "good horsey." As he trotted away in search of a fare, I dropped Kidron's card into my purse and retrieved my keys.

As I stepped inside, I was startled to find Scratch sitting in the foyer, glowering at me. I realized this was the first time I had ever been alone with him. While Hexe was home, he kept Scratch out from underfoot, but whenever his master was away, the familiar had free run of the house.

"Oh. It's you," he said, disgust dripping from every syllable. "Where's Hexe?"

"He, uh, had some errands to take care of," I replied, careful not to look directly at the familiar. However, it was impossible to avoid smelling him, as Scratch reeked of equal parts brimstone and cat. The familiar unnerved me in a way that centaurs and leprechauns did not. I was not at all used to winged cats, hairless or not, and I *certainly* wasn't accustomed to ones that talked.

As I headed for the stairs, Scratch leaped in front of me and blocked my way by spreading his batlike wings. "What *kind* of errands?" he asked suspiciously.

"Don't you know that curiosity killed the cat?" I snapped, no longer bothering to hide my irritation.

"I can't be killed," the familiar sneered as he moved out of my way. "Don't *you* know that? Oh, that's right— you're a nump. Numps don't know anything."

"What is a nump, anyway?"

Scratch laughed, and it was as snide as you would expect a cat's laugh to be. "A nump is an uncouth, smelly fool who knows nothing about everything. You know—a *human*."

Stepping past him, I continued up the stairs, muttering curses under my breath. I was determined not to let the familiar get under my skin. After all, I told myself, I had better things to do than hang around and be insulted by a flying, bald cat.

Despite Hexe's assurances as to Faro's abilities, I fully expected to find my room as empty as I had left it earlier. However, as I unlocked the door, I could only open it halfway, as something was blocking it from the other side. Peering around the jamb, I saw stacked throughout the room all of my earthly possessions, the same ones that Vinnie and his gang had loaded onto the Triple-A Aardvark van earlier that day.

"Faro, my man, I'm sorry I ever doubted you!" I shouted in delight as I squeezed past a jumble of boxes marked "kitchen."

Outside of a canopy bed, an easy chair, and a battered old armoire, the only real furniture I owned was a set of bookcases and my workbench. Once I had these furnishings properly situated, I began opening boxes. I was especially relieved to discover that my welding equipment and finished sculptures had made the journey intact. I was so engrossed in sorting through my belongings, I lost track of time. It wasn't until I heard a polite cough behind me and turned around to see Hexe standing in the doorway that I realized I'd been working nonstop for several hours.

"I hope I'm not intruding," he said. "I just stopped by to see how you're settling in. It looks like you've been very busy."

"I'm trying to make up for lost time. After all, the sooner I get unpacked, the sooner I can get back to work."

"Indeed." Hexe arched a purple eyebrow upon catching sight of the welder's helmet and oxyacetylene torch resting atop the workbench. "I'd like to find out more about the art you make. By the way, you must be famished—perhaps you'd like to join me for some dinner?"

I hadn't really thought about it beforehand, but once Hexe brought up the subject of food, I was suddenly aware of just how hungry I was. I hadn't eaten since early that morning, and the thought of dinner was enough to make my belly growl like an angry puppy.

"Sounds good to me," I admitted. "Give me a couple of minutes to get ready."

"I'll be waiting for you downstairs."

"Do you invite all your boarders out to dinner?" I asked as he turned to leave the room.

Hexe paused on the threshold, his hand resting on the doorknob, and favored me with another of his warm smiles.

"Only the ones I find interesting."

The moment the door closed behind him, I launched myself at my armoire in search of something halfway decent to wear. After a couple of minutes, I decided on a black twill pencil skirt, a red V-neck cardigan sweater, and a pair of black leather wedges. I made a quick visit to the bathroom to check my hair and apply some lipstick and mascara, then hurried downstairs. I found him waiting for me in the parlor, thumbing through that day's edition of the *Herald*.

"You look nice," Hexe said, lifting a purple eyebrow.

"It's not too much, is it?" I asked nervously.

"No, I think it's just enough," he replied with a smile.

"So where are we going?"

"There's a place not far from here that serves up some decent grub—it's a favorite haunt of mine. It's called the Two-Headed Calf. Trust me, it's better than it sounds."

*   *   *

The restaurant was located on Morder Lane, a couple blocks over from the boardinghouse, between Nassau and Horsecart Street. It was a three-and-a-half-story, gambrel-roofed Georgian brick building, with four ground-floor bay windows. Above the entrance swung an old-fashioned wooden pub sign depicting the establishment's namesake. The calf head on the left looked more than a little drunk, with its tongue hanging out of the side of its mouth, while the head on the right contentedly munched on a daisy.

"Here we are," Hexe said. "It's something of a land-mark. The Calf was first open to the public in 1742. That makes it America's oldest restaurant in continuous ser-vice. Of course, because it serves Kymeran cuisine and is located in Golgotham, it gets overlooked by the record books. But that's okay, because that way we don't have to worry about looky-loos ruining the place."

Upon opening the door, we were greeted by the sound of laughter, music, and the smell of tobacco. Just to the left of the entrance was an open, semicircular oaken bar with a copper sheet-metal top, behind which stood several ornate beer pulls and a mirrored shelf with an impressive array of liquors. The stools that lined the bar were supported by cast-iron poles and fastened to the floor. The rest of the seating on the ground floor consisted of stall-type booths, some of which were out-fitted with privacy curtains.

The bartender, a towering Kymeran with wiry, ketch-up red hair and a matching beard that hung halfway to his belly, nodded in greeting as Hexe steered me toward one of the booths.

"Who's that?" I asked.

"None other than the owner of this fine establish-ment. We went to school together."

As I looked around the comfortingly cramped interior of the Two-Headed Calf, it suddenly occurred to me that I was the only human in the pub. Everyone else was either a Kymeran or a member of some other supernatural race. All of them were socializing over whiskey, ale, and tobacco—lots and *lots* of tobacco.

Since Kymerans can't contract cancer, they tend to ignore the state and federal guidelines concerning smoking in public places, which makes them no different than Parisians, I suppose. Still, I was unprepared for the pall of secondhand smoke that hovered above the room. As I discreetly coughed into my fist, I noticed a couple of Kymerans glare in my direction.

One thing I can say for sure is that Hooters' waitstaff has nothing on that of the Two-Headed Calf. The barmaid who came to take our drink order was not only a dead ringer for a young Sophia Loren, she was dressed in the classic chiton of the ancient Greeks. The outline of her voluptuous body was clearly visible through the diaphanous material, save for the portion hidden by the leopard skin draped over her left shoulder.

"Evening, Hexe. Drinks or dinner?" the maenad asked, plucking the pencil from the wreath of ivy and grapevine that adorned her dark head.

"Evening, Chorea. Dinner. How long before a table opens up?"

"Table?" I frowned, puzzled by the statement. "We're already seated."

Chorea rolled her eyes in open contempt of my ignorance and pointed with her pencil at the wooden staircase at the back of the room and the arrow-shaped sign that read in big block letters DINING ROOM UPSTAIRS. Although she didn't say "nump" out loud, I knew she was thinking it. My face turned as red as my cardigan.

"Shouldn't be more than a ten-minute wait," Chorea said. "Fifteen, tops. How about a drink to pass the time?"

"I'll have a barley wine," he said.

The maenad nodded as she scribbled the order down on her pad, and then glanced at me. I thought about ordering a light beer, but changed my mind at the last moment. I didn't want to come across as any more of a nump than I did already.

"I'll have the house red."

Chorea's eyes lighted up, and she favored me with a smile that would have made a satyr blush. "*Excellent* choice, ma'am."

As our waitress headed to the bar to place our drink order, I leaned across the booth and whispered, "Is she for real?"

"As real as it gets," Hexe assured me. "I've known her for some time. She's a good person, when she's sober. Hell of a mean drunk, though. Sadly, there aren't many places Dionysian cultists feel comfortable nowadays, save for bars and strip clubs."

I looked up and was startled to find the bartender looming over us. He stood nearly seven feet tall and wore a pair of battered bib overalls and a plaid work shirt, the sleeves of which were rolled back to reveal swarms of tattoos on both arms. I don't know if it was his personal scent, or a result of working in a restaurant, but he smelled of corn dogs, tobacco, and bananas Foster.

"Thought I'd come over and say hello," the bartender said as he placed our drinks down in front of us. "Who's your friend?"

"Tate, this is Lafo. Lafo, I'd like you to meet Tate,"

Hexe said, nodding in my direction. "She's my new tenant."

"Taking on a human lodger, eh?" The burly bartender lifted a bristly red eyebrow in surprise. "What does old Esau have to say about that?"

A look of distaste flickered across Hexe's handsome face. "I don't give a shit what he says—even less for what he thinks."

"Always the diplomat!" Lafo said with a throaty laugh and a twinkle in his sapphire blue eye. He thrust a large six-fingered hand in my direction. My smaller five-fingered one fit inside his palm with room to spare. "Nice meeting you, Miss Tate. Welcome to Golgotham."

"Thank you, Mr. Lafo," I replied.

"Just call me Lafo. I'm not much for formalities."

"Lafo it is—and, please, call me Tate."

"Will do. FYI, when you get upstairs, I recommend the blackbird pie. I made it fresh this afternoon." With that, Lafo returned to his post behind the bar, pouring drinks for his thirsty customers.

"Who's Esau?" I asked as I sipped my house wine.

Hexe made a sour face, as if the very mention of the name were somehow painful to him. "He's my uncle."

"I take it you two don't get along?"

"That's a polite way of describing it." He sighed. "Esau is my mother's older brother, and therefore family . . . but there's no love lost between us."

"I understand. You don't have to explain. I'm sorry I brought him up."

Hexe waved his hand, dismissing my apology. "You'd find out about him sooner or later. This way, at least, you're forewarned. Uncle Esau is a terrible misanthrope."

"He hates humans, I take it?"

"Only slightly more than he hates me."

"You're exaggerating, I'm sure."

"I wish I were. And it's not as if I've given him any reason to be so ill disposed toward me. The old fecker has despised me since I was in diapers. I suspect it's because his father—my grandfather—disinherited him in favor of my mother."

I was tempted to tell him that his family sounded suspiciously like my own, but I didn't want to come off sounding either glib or proud of being dysfunctional.

"I hope your boyfriend won't take offense by my asking you out to dinner," Hexe said as he drank from his tankard of barley wine.

"I don't have a boyfriend," I replied.

"I find that hard to believe, what with your being such an intelligent and lovely young woman." He smiled.

"Well, I am just getting out of a relationship," I admitted.

"Oh?"

"The breakup was my idea," I explained. "It's part of the reason I moved. I decided I needed a change of scenery to get my head straight."

"I can understand that." He nodded.

Now that Hexe had finished his little fishing expedition, it was time for me to start mine. "How about you?" I asked. "Is your girlfriend cool with our dining together?"

"She'd have to exist, first," he laughed. "I'm not much of a catch, I'm afraid."

"Now that *I* find hard to believe," I replied.

A second maenad, this one a blond Brigitte Bardot clone, tapped Hexe on the shoulder. "Your table is ready, sir."

As we followed the hostess to the dining room above, I paused to look at a few of the framed photographs of famous celebrities arranged along the narrow staircase. Some were human, such as Charlie Chaplin, Oscar Wilde, and John Lennon; others, like Houdini, Bowie, Marilyn Manson, and Picasso, were long rumored to be either half-breeds or full-blooded Kymerans surgically altered in order to pass.

"That's my great-great-grandfather," Hexe said, pointing to a steel engraving depicting three men posed in front of the horseshoe-shaped bar. They were dressed in colonial-era clothes, complete with buckled shoes and tricorn hats, and wore Freemason aprons about their waists. I recognized the men on either side of Hexe's ancestor as George Washington and Thomas Jefferson. "My family's been coming here since Lafo's great-great-grandmother first opened the doors."

The dining room was one large open room with a coffered ceiling and dark weathered wood. Save for me, everyone seated for dinner was a Kymeran. As we wended our way to our table, I was keenly aware of being watched. When I dared to challenge the stares aimed at me, most looked away, but one or two continued to glower in my direction, letting me know my presence was unwelcome.

Once we were seated, our waiter—a young Kymeran with mango-colored hair who smelled of herbal tea and vetiver—handed us a pair of menus. It was then I discovered that Lafo's parting comment about the blackbird pie wasn't a joke.

I'd always assumed that the stories about Kymeran cuisine were born of ignorance and cultural bias. As I stared at the listings for owl soup, soaked cod, pork brains in milk gravy, and blood dumplings, I realized that all stereotypes have to get their start somewhere. I wondered if I would have to resort to a stomach pump before the evening was over.

"What will the lady be having this evening?" the waiter asked. I couldn't help but notice a hint of malicious amusement in his voice.

"I'll try the blackbird pie," I replied, trying to sound more confident than I felt.

"One house special—very good! And you, sir?"

"I'll have the same, with a Cynar aperitif."

"Excellent choice."

"What's Cynar?" I asked after our waiter hurried off to the kitchen.

"It's a liqueur made from artichokes. Would you like to try some? It tastes like copper pennies. . . ."

"No—! Thank you," I replied quickly. "Not tonight."

Hexe leaned back in his seat, a quizzical look on his handsome face. "Tell me—how much do you know about my people?"

"Not a whole lot. We studied the Unholy War in school, of course. . . ."

"*We* call it the Sufferance," he corrected politely.

"Of course. Forgive me." I dropped my gaze to the table, embarrassed by yet another faux pas on my part.

"You needn't be so apologetic. I don't view you or any other human alive today as personally responsible for what happened a thousand years ago. However, there are a few Kymerans who do hold grudges against humankind, such as my uncle Esau. They resent encroachment on what they view as their territory. As you've noticed, there's a lot more to Golgotham than what's printed in the tour books. I am happy to volunteer my services as your native guide—assuming you'll have me."

As I looked into his golden, catlike eyes, I felt myself getting light-headed. I wasn't sure if it was because I was feeling something exciting and new, or because I hadn't eaten all day. In any case, I hoped I didn't look like, well, like a nump.

"I'd be honored," I said, returning his smile.

Just then our waiter returned, placing the blackbird pie on the table with a flourish usually reserved for the finest cuisine. To both my delight and surprise, it smelled delicious.

Maybe I wouldn't need that stomach pump, after all.

Chapter 6

"What made you decide to become an artist?"

We were walking back to the house when he asked me that. I paused in midstep, forcing Hexe to turn and look back at me as I spoke.

"I've always had a creative bent, even as a toddler. At least that's what my nanny claimed. The first time I realized I wanted to be an artist was in middle school. My school took a day trip to the Guggenheim. I was fascinated by the exhibits—enough that I went back on my own every weekend for nearly three months. When we studied sculpting in art class, I tried to re-create this statue I'd seen there called *The Dying Gaul*, in modeling clay, no less. It was awful, of course, but there was something about creating something from nothing, using only my hands and will, which was very—gratifying. After that, I was hooked.

"As you may have guessed, I grew up rich. Filthy, stinking rich. All that was expected of me was to grow up, marry someone else who grew up filthy, stinking rich, and have a couple of filthy, stinking rich kids to inherit the family fortune. I knew so many brats with Roman numerals behind their names who had no reason or desire to make anything of themselves besides what they were the minute they were born, it was disgusting. The last thing I want to do is add to that 'tradition.'

"The trouble with that lifestyle is this: Hanging around doing nothing while waiting for an inheritance is boring. So many of my old schoolmates got fucked up on drugs and alcohol, mainly out of boredom. I swear, half of the girls in my graduating class in high school developed eating disorders simply to have something to do! The sick thing is, my mother wouldn't have any problems with my being an anorexic—after all, that's *expected* from someone of my background."

"I take it your parents don't approve of your career choice?"

"They like to call it a 'phase' I'm going through, like I'm the moon. I guess they think I'll eventually grow out of it—kind of like baby teeth. They keep saying they don't want to see me get my hopes up and end up hurt, which is another way of saying they're expecting me to fail—at least, that's what they're hoping for."

"Isn't that a bit harsh?"

"You haven't met my mother," I grunted. "What about you? What made you decide to practice only Right Hand magic? You said so yourself, you could make a lot more money if you used both hands."

"A lot of it has to do with family, and what's expected of someone like me," he explained, his voice taking on a bitter edge. "Humans tend to view my people as no better than drug dealers and pimps. If you want to destroy somebody's life, just line a kymie's palm with silver, am I right? We're the rapist and the murderer's best friend, are we not? My people are, for the most part, good-hearted. But a lifetime of good can be undone by a single evil act. I wanted to prove that it's possible for a Kymeran to make a living without resorting to the Left Hand Path."

"Do you? Make a living at it, that is?"

"I'm renting out rooms, aren't I?" he replied with a depreciative laugh.

"That doesn't mean anything. Most of the musicians signed to labels in this city still have their day jobs. Do *you* think you're doing okay?"

"I have some steady clients," he admitted. "I rely a lot on word of mouth. And word is getting around that I'm *very* good at what I do. . . ."

"Gardy-loo!"

Hexe broke off in midsentence and turned to look in the direction of the voice. A Kymeran with bright orange hair came staggering out of the Highlander Tavern across the street, closely followed by another warlock whose hair was the color of lime sherbet. Both looked extremely inebriated.

"*Gardy-looooo!*" the orange-headed Kymeran shouted drunkenly, his voice echoing down the street. "I'll show *you* who's the fastest slinger in Golgotham, Oddo!"

"Bloody abdabs!" Hexe groaned. He grabbed me by the arm and pulled me into the nearest doorway.

"What's going on?"

"Looks like we're caught in the middle of a pissing contest."

"A what contest?" I grimaced.

"It's when wizards get into a duel with each other," he explained, then added, as an afterthought, "when they're drunk."

"What's he yelling 'Gardy-loo' for?"

"It means 'Look out.' It's kind of like shouting 'fore,'

when you play golf. Except instead of getting hit by a golf ball, you're likely to be set on fire or turned into a lamppost."

The orange-haired Kymeran drew back his left hand, like a baseball player winding up for the pitch. A tongue of flame suddenly burst to life in his palm, rapidly growing in size and intensity until it looked like a snowball made of fire. With a drunken shout, he hurled it at the other Kymeran's head.

The warlock with the lime sherbet hair, the one called Oddo, raised his right hand and made a dismissive gesture, as if waving off a bothersome fly. The fireball abruptly changed trajectories, flying across the narrow street and striking the fire escape of a nearby tenement building. It flew apart in a shower of white-hot sparks, which cascaded downward, sizzling as they made contact with the sidewalk below.

"Don't let any of it touch you," Hexe warned, pulling me even closer to him. "Those projectiles are made of hellfire. It burns hotter than natural fire, and once it gets on you, it burns clean to the bone."

"Is that the best you can do, Zack?" Oddo sneered, drunkenly pushing up the sleeves of his shirt. "I'll show you some real slingin'!"

Suddenly the wail of an approaching police siren could be heard. The drunken warlocks exchanged worried looks, their reason for their duel forgotten.

"Some fecker called the PTU on us, Oddo!" Zack exclaimed, genuinely surprised that someone might take offense at his hurling balls of molten death in public.

The drunken wizards linked arms and lurched up the sidewalk in an attempt to escape before the Paranormal Threat Unit arrived. They had barely managed to stagger a dozen yards before a black paddy wagon, a flashing blue light on top and pulled by a centaur outfitted in a PTU flack jacket and riot helmet, rounded the corner at a dead run.

The paddy wagon came to a halt and a half-dozen uniformed PTU responders, a mix of human and Kymeran law enforcement agents, jumped out of the back, spells and riot gear at the ready.

"Hands behind your backs! Hands behind your backs!" a Kymeran officer shouted. "Put your hands where I can't see 'em!"

The fleeing drunks did as they were told, dropping to their knees as they placed their hands in the small of their backs.

"It's safe to go now," Hexe said, stepping out of the doorway. "The PTU have it under control."

"Does that happen a lot around here?" I asked.

"Not as often as it used to. The Paranormal Threat Unit does a good job of keeping the duels off the street. Some resent their interference, viewing it as humans trying to force their ways on our culture, but it's what has kept the NYPD out of the neighborhood so far."

"What'll happen to those two?"

"They'll take them to the Tombs to sleep it off, then fine 'em for public dueling. Which means Zack will be knocking on my door tomorrow, wanting his usual hangover cure. Speaking of which, I need to harvest some herbs from my garden. Would you care to join me?"

"You have a garden?"

I was genuinely surprised. Open green space in New York City is a rarity, especially in the older neighborhoods like Golgotham. Hexe's only response was to smile mischievously at me.

Although the boardinghouse stood in the middle of the block, there was a long, narrow passageway between it and the building next door. Hexe ducked down the alleyway. I had to turn sideways to follow him. After about thirty feet, the passageway widened enough for us to move normally, although still in single file.

After another fifty feet, he came to a halt in front of a metal door. As I looked up, I realized the brick wall ended six feet over my head. I glanced back the way we came and saw the back of the boardinghouse looming over us. Hexe fished his jangling key ring out of his pocket and inserted a green key into the lock.

Like the house itself, Hexe's garden was far larger than it appeared from the outside. Just inside the entrance was an undulating walk, bordered by monkshood, verbena, and hydrangea bushes that led to thyme-covered steps that ended at a bed of lavender. Moonflowers as big as my hand wound about pieces of classical statuary, interlaced with honeysuckle vine that filled the night air with its sweet perfume.

"Hexe, this is incredible!" I gasped. "This belongs to you?"

"It belongs to the house," he replied. "I wouldn't dare claim it as mine. Uncle Jack originally designed it. . . ."

"The one who went upstairs?"

"And didn't come back. Yes, that's him." Hexe stepped inside a small wooden shed built next to the garden wall and returned a moment later with a pair of work gloves and some pinking shears.

"Cool." I stared in open amazement at the neatly trimmed hedge maze at its center. "Gardens are like works of art. They're meant to be experienced, not just looked at. You can't create a garden without its revealing a basic truth about you. He must have been, uh, must *be* an interesting man. Still, you must have a doozy of a green thumb!"

"Not really. I grow herbs and other organics necessary for my salves and unguents, but most of the gardening is handled by a hamadryad that lives in that tree over there." He pointed to a stately sycamore that stood in the far corner. "She's pretty shy around strangers, so I doubt we'll see her tonight."

We walked down a winding pathway past strange-looking plants, some of which seemed to rustle and move of their own volition. Hexe knelt and clipped a double handful of sage.

"Since you're a tenant, you're allowed access to the garden," he explained as he stood up. "So feel free to explore—however, steer clear of the maze. Humans were never meant to navigate it."

"Is it dangerous?"

"It can be, if it has a mind to."

Before I could ask any more questions, Hexe turned and headed in the direction of the house. "It's been a long day for you. I'm sure you must be exhausted."

"I'm doing okay," I lied. As excited as I was about my new surroundings, I was pretty much running on fumes. Still, I didn't want to admit my weariness, just like when I was a little girl and would protest being put to bed, even though my eyelids were so heavy I could barely keep them open.

Hexe went up the porch stairs and unlocked the back door, ushering me inside. Sitting on the kitchen table like a Halloween centerpiece was none other than Scratch.

"About time you got home!" the winged cat meowed. "I'm *staaaarving*!"

"Bloody abdabs, Scratch! You know you're not supposed to be on the table!" Hexe snapped. "We have to eat on that, you know."

"The nerve!" the familiar sniffed as he leaped onto

the floor. "Here I am, practically skin and bones, and all you do is insult me."

"Poor you, you're so mistreated," Hexe snorted as he rinsed off the sage in the kitchen sink. "If you're so clever, why don't you pour it yourself? Oh, that's right—thumbs."

"It's not that I can't feed myself; it's that I refuse to," Scratch said defensively. "Why should I, when I can get you to do it for me?"

"All right! All right! Quit your bellyaching!"

Hexe opened the pantry door and dragged out a fifty-pound bag of Purina Familiar Chow. Scratch's eyes grew larger and took on an even stranger gleam than usual. Hexe opened the bag and withdrew an aluminum scoop, which he used to ladle out the dried demon kibble into a food bowl the size of a mop bucket. Hexe glanced up at me as he dumped a second heaping portion into his familiar's dish.

"You really don't want to be in the same room when Scratch feeds," he said meaningfully. "He can get . . . carried away."

As I could see a long strand of drool hanging from the corner of the demon's mouth, I decided that was as good a time as any to say my good-nights and retire to my room.

Chapter 7

I don't know what else is in blackbird pie, but I do know it will make you thirstier than you've ever been in your life a few hours after you've eaten it. I was dragged out of a sound sleep around three thirty in the morning by my body's need for water. I smacked my lips, trying to work up enough spit to swallow, but no luck.

I stared blearily around at my surroundings, momentarily disoriented, until I woke up enough to remember that I was no longer living in SoHo. I also remembered seeing a watercooler next to the fridge downstairs. Since my rent included kitchen privileges, I lost no time pulling on a T-shirt and my yoga pants and heading downstairs.

As I slaked my thirst with a glass of cold spring water, it suddenly occurred to me that this was the first time I was able to experience the house without either Hexe or Scratch being nearby. If the gothic romance novels I'd read in middle school were anything to go by, this would be the time I'd expect to hear mysterious noises and see spectral figures flitting across the lawn.

I tilted my head and listened to the sounds the house made late at night. Instead of rattling chains and ghostly moans, all I heard was the slow, steady grind of the electric clock over the stove, the gurgle of the watercooler, and the muffled rattle of the ice maker inside the fridge. So much for the sisters Brontë.

As I turned to rinse my glass in the sink, I glanced out the window and saw something flit across the backyard. At first I thought it might be Scratch, but whatever it was seemed larger than the familiar, and I was pretty sure it had hair.

I am a sucker for animals in distress. Always have been, always will be. It doesn't matter if it's a duckling or a wildebeest; if it's limping, lost, or hungry, I'll try to nurse it back to health, find it a home, or feed it. And although I had caught only a fleeting glimpse of whatever it was, the way it moved told me it was hurt.

I unlocked the back door and stepped out onto the porch, peering into the shadowy garden. "Don't be afraid," I called out softly as I headed down the steps and crossed the yard. "I'm not going to do anything bad to you."

A rustling sound came from deeper in the garden. The moon was a third full, and its distant light limned everything in silver and shadow. I could make out the tops of the shrubbery shaking as something pushed through it.

"It's okay, boy," I whispered, patting the side of my leg in hopes of calling the animal into the open. I eased my way down the path, the gravel crunching under my slippered feet. "C'mere, boy. . . ."

My desire to help a poor, hurt animal was suddenly replaced by a sliver of fear as whatever was in the bushes moved to circle behind me. It was too big to be a house cat, of that I was sure. My heart began to race. I took a step backward, only to freeze when I heard a growl coming from a nearby elder bush. As I looked into the shrubbery, I saw a pair of yellowish green eyes set two feet from the ground staring back at me. I realized then that what I had seen running across the garden lawn wasn't a dog, either.

Now that I knew precisely where to look, I had no problem seeing a cougar with a shock collar about its neck crouched in the shadows. I stared at the creature for a long moment, trying to decide whether it was better to flee or stand my ground.

"*Thaaaat's* a good kitty," I said like an idiot. "I'm not going to hurt you. I'm a friend...."

As it stood upright, the cougar revealed the torso and lower body of a man. Although I had never seen one in the flesh before, I recognized the creature as one of the bastet, a species of shape-shifter that took the form of various big cats—in this case, a mountain lion.

The were-cat's fangs flashed in the moonlight as it hissed at me. I screamed and fled in what I thought was the direction of the house. I glanced back and saw the bastet in hot pursuit. It ran with a strange, rolling gait, as if hobbling. No doubt that was the only reason I wasn't cat food already.

Hoping I wasn't making things worse than they were already, I ran in the direction of the hedge maze. At that moment I decided it was better to chance whatever dangers might lie inside it to the certainty of being torn limb from limb by a ravening hell-beast.

The moment I entered the maze, its living walls shot upward, until they towered over me like evergreen monoliths, sealing off the sky. All I could see wherever I looked was tightly grown shrubbery, broken here and there by arch-shaped openings. Not sure which way to go, but fearful of stopping, I dodged through a passageway on my left.

As I crossed the living threshold, there came a sound like the rustling of a thousand crinoline skirts. I turned and saw the opening behind me seal itself shut. The hedge abruptly shook, knocking a few leaves free on my side of the wall, as the were-cat collided against it on the other side.

The were-creature tried to push its way through the dense growth, but it could not pass. I could hear it sniffing the ground, less than three feet from where I stood. I was too terrified to scream, much less move. My heart was beating so fast it felt like I was swaying in time to phantom music.

My paralysis was broken by the sound of the were-cat shrieking as it caught my scent. I turned, raw terror spurring on my weary body, and headed down the narrow passageway that opened up before me like Alice's rabbit hole, sending me even deeper into the living maze.

My lungs ached from running, and my face and arms were bleeding from scratches inflicted by the maze, which plucked at my hair and clothing with grasping twigs like a mischievous child, but I dared not stop for even the briefest moment.

Although I could not see it, I knew I was being stalked like a deer in the wilderness. What at first had seemed a godsend—the ever-changing maze—now heightened my fear even more, for I realized that I could run headlong into the creature at any moment without any warning.

After what seemed an eternity of twists and turns, I finally stumbled into the clearing at the center of the maze. Once more the moon overhead was visible, as was the boardinghouse. Still disoriented, I looked around the open green space and saw a group of people standing about, talking to one another. I called out as I ran toward them.

"Help! Over here! I'm being chased—"

My momentary sense of relief died as I realized I was looking at a collection of statues. There were four of them, gathered around a small reflecting pool, arranged so that they appeared to be holding a conversation. Three of the statues were male, one female, each from very different periods of history. One was dressed like an Egyptian queen, another wore a toga and laurel wreath, a third was dressed in the chain mail and helmet of a knight, while the last one wore a tricorn hat.

The sound of snapping branches grabbed my attention, and I turned to see the were-cat stumble free of the maze, pieces of twigs and leaves still stuck in its coat. The moment it saw me, a feral grin spread across its face. Now I knew how Bambi must have felt. I wished I had my welder's helmet and oxyacetylene torch handy. I'd probably still end up dead, but at least the bastard would know he'd been in a fight.

The man-cougar dropped into a crouch and began to advance, staring at me with these horrible, burning eyes. I knew that the moment I turned to flee, it would be on me, so I did the only thing I could do—I stared back.

Suddenly a shadow slid across the heart of the maze, one so large it covered not only me, but my attacker as well. The were-cat looked up, its growl turning into a hiss, and I thought I saw fear in its eyes.

The next thing I knew, something big swooped down, striking the shape-shifter with enough force to take it to the ground. The bastet screamed like a house cat hit by a car and, idiot that I was, I automatically felt sorry for the damned thing.

However, although I was glad the were-cat was no longer a threat to me, the sight of my rescuer did nothing to calm my fears because standing before me was a hairless, dragon-winged saber-toothed tiger with a long, scaly tail that looked like it belonged on a crocodile. The creature's skin was olive in color, with glowing red eyes, and it had long, downward-curving fangs. It also smelled strongly of brimstone and cat—*big* cat.

"Scratch?" It came out more like a squeak than a question.

"Yeah, it's me," the familiar growled. "You okay, nump?"

"I think so," I replied. As soon as I spoke, my head started to swim, and I sat down heavily on the ground. The dew from the grass soaked through the seat of my yoga pants.

Scratch turned his attention back to the wounded were-cat squirming under his front paws. "You picked the wrong garden to trespass in, Garfield," he snarled, licking his fangs with a serpentine forked tongue. "I eat trespassers. It's what I do. Me, I like to start with the head...."

"Scratch! Stop that right this minute!"

Hexe was hurrying toward me, dressed in nothing but a pair of jeans. Although I was going into shock, I still noticed he looked damned good without a shirt on.

"Can't I take just a *teensy* bite?" the familiar grumbled, his crocodilian tail swishing back and forth in consternation.

"No!" Hexe replied sternly. "Not even a nibble—and that includes the ears!"

"You're no fun."

Hexe knelt beside me, peeling back one of my eyelids to study my pupil. "Are you okay?" As he reached to take my pulse, he noticed the bloody scratches on my arms. "You weren't bitten, were you?"

"I'm all right," I assured him. "Just scratched up, that's all."

"Thank goodness. Bites from shape-shifters can be worse than those from a rabid animal for humans. I'm glad you're unhurt." He looked genuinely relieved I was okay. I hoped it wasn't simply because he'd have to find a new tenant if I'd been eaten alive.

As Hexe helped me back onto my feet, I felt a tiny thrill of excitement brushing against his naked chest. I was expecting him to put a solicitous arm about my shoulders and escort me safely back to the house. No such luck. Instead, he sprinted over to the pinned-down were-cat.

"It's okay, boy," he said soothingly as he inspected the creature's wounds. As he knelt beside the were-cat, the beast tried to squirm free of Scratch's talons. "Nobody here's going to hurt you. . . ."

"Speak for yourself, buddy," Scratch growled.

After a cursory inspection of the bastet's hind paws, Hexe stood up, a disgusted look on his face. "He's been hambled. The balls of his feet have been cut out."

To my surprise, I saw something like sympathy flicker in Scratch's eyes. "Poor bastard," the familiar grunted.

From the pocket of his jeans Hexe removed a copper tube the size and shape of his sixth finger. He placed it to his lips and a puff of fine white powder jetted forth, coating the were-cat's muzzle like a French Market beignet. The creature struggled for a moment; then its eyes rolled back and it went limp.

"Is it dead?" I whispered.

"No, only sedated. And he's a 'he,' not an 'it.'" Hexe turned and spoke to his familiar. "Take him to the house. Put him in the spare room on the second floor and keep an eye on him."

"As you wish," Scratch said, bobbing his head in ritual obeisance. Without another word, the demon picked up the unconscious shape-shifter the same way a mother cat moves a newborn kitten, and, with a single beat of leathery wings, soared into the air.

"Are you nuts?" I exclaimed in disbelief.

Hexe frowned, genuinely puzzled by my reaction. "Beg pardon?"

I was so mad I could barely see straight. It was all I could do to keep from taking a swing at him. "You're actually bringing that thing into the house? After it did its best to try and turn me into a chew toy? What is a were-cat doing in New York in the first place? Don't they live on the wildlife preserves?"

"I don't know why a were-cougar would come to the city," Hexe replied. "But not all of them live on the preserves. All I know is what was done to him once he arrived in this city is a crime. That 'thing,' as you put it, is an innocent victim, I can tell you that much. He is also badly injured. I am a healer. I can not turn him aside simply because of what he is. I understand your being scared—but Scratch and I have things well in hand. Now, are you ready to come back inside? Or do you need me to refund your deposit?"

"No, that won't be necessary," I grumbled. "I'm upset, but I'm not *that* upset."

"Good. Because I already spent the money on bills," he said wryly. "C'mon—let's get back in the house. I'm getting cold."

"So I noticed," I said, nodding to his bare chest. His nipples were standing so erect they looked like little pink pencil erasers.

"Same here," Hexe laughed, returning my nod.

I glanced down and noticed my own chest made it look like I was trying to smuggle candy corn out of the country, two at a time. I quickly crossed my arms over my breasts. I wanted to say something clever and flirty, but I decided trying to sound like James Bond wasn't the smartest move—especially if I ended up coming off more like Roger Moore than Sean Connery.

As we headed out of the maze, I fixed Hexe with a curious look. "How did you know I was in trouble? And how did you know where to find me?"

"It's simple, really," he replied. "Phoebe told me."

"Phoebe?" I frowned. "Who's she?"

Hexe pointed to the sycamore that stood in the far corner of the garden, overlooking the hedge maze. In its uppermost branches, which were too frail to support anything but the slightest of sparrows, crouched a young woman.

The hamadryad was incredibly beautiful, by human definitions, with long hair the color of grass and large, gray-green eyes. She wore a simple shift made of stitched sycamore leaves, and her exposed skin blended in with the bark of the tree. I lifted a hand in greeting to the nymph, who smiled shyly and waved back.

Hexe spent the walk back to the house reassuring me that the were-cat in the spare bedroom down the hall from me was in no way a danger. I told him that I believed him and trusted in his ability to keep things under control.

I then returned to my room, changed out of my dew-soaked clothes into something drier, and pushed the armoire in front of my door. Then I went back to bed.

It had been a long first day in Golgotham.

Chapter 8

I woke up the next day feeling as though someone had been using me for batting practice. I staggered to the bathroom at the end of the hall and took a shower in the cast-iron lion-footed tub. I'm not sure which woke me up more, the brisk shower or the stinging of my scratches. After changing into clean clothes, I headed downstairs in search of coffee. I found Hexe at work in the kitchen.

"Good morning." He smiled as he dropped three cinnamon sticks and six cloves into the saucepan sitting on the front burner. "Or, should I say good afternoon?"

I glanced up at the electric clock hanging over the stove—a quarter past twelve.

"Crap. I didn't mean to sleep this late."

"You were up late," Hexe said with a shrug as he added a large lump of brown sugar to the pan. "And you had something of a rough night."

"That's an understatement," I grunted. "By the way— I thought were-cats came out only during the full moon?"

"You're thinking of werewolves," he replied as he broke off a chunk of Baker's Chocolate and added it to the mix. "The bastet can shape-shift anytime they like. So can werewolves, for that matter. That full moon stuff is just in movies."

"So why did this one attack me?"

"That's something I'm hoping to find out," he said, stirring the melting chocolate with a wooden spoon.

I didn't know what he was concocting, but it smelled yummy. My curiosity got the better of me. "What's that you're making?"

"You could call it a restorative," he laughed as he poured coarsely ground coffee into the saucepan. "The Aztec king, Montezuma, would drink a version of this every night, before visiting his harem. The Mayan priests made theirs with vanilla beans, honey, and chile peppers. . . ." He retrieved a mug from a nearby cabinet that had WITCHES' BREW printed on it in a comical font and set it on the kitchen counter.

"Who's it for? One of your clients?"

Hexe lifted the saucepan from the burner and poured the steaming contents through a small steel mesh sieve into the waiting mug. "No, it's for you," he replied. "I knew you were up because I heard the shower running, and I figured you'd be in the mood for a pick-me-up after last night. You can add milk to that, if you like. Let it cool down a bit before you drink it, though."

I stared at the steaming cup apprehensively. "What does it do?"

"It wakes you up. It's coffee," Hexe replied sarcastically. "Not everything I make is a magic potion, y'know. I got the recipe off the Internet. It's called Mexican clay-pot coffee. Normally it's made in a Mexican clay pot, hence the name, but since I didn't have one handy, I decided to improvise."

I blushed. Numped again. It seemed like every time I

scored a point with the warlock, I said or did something totally uncool. I felt like I was taking one step back for every two steps forward. Luckily, Hexe didn't seem to be holding my ignorance against me.

I took the carton of nonfat milk I'd bought the other day from the fridge and added a dollop to my coffee. The concoction was rich and fragrant, and it shot through my weary system like a jolt of electricity.

"Mmmm! It's delicious. Thank you for making this for me. It was very thoughtful of you."

"My pleasure." He smiled. "Oh, by the way—our new houseguest has been asking for you."

I nearly choked on my drink. "You mean he can *talk*?"

"Of course he can talk. He's not feral."

"What does he want?" I asked nervously. Hexe might be so used to supernatural creatures that he considered shape-shifters to be no more worrisome than raccoons, but I had seen one too many horror movies to act so blasé.

"He says he wants to apologize. You really ought to go see him, Tate. He's quite contrite about the whole thing."

The thought of coming face-to-face again with the creature that had pursued me the night before made my head swim. I took another gulp of the coffee, hoping it might fortify me further.

"That's . . . nice, I guess. Can't you just tell him I accept his apology?"

Hexe shook his head. "He insists on doing it himself. Bastet are very proper, in their own way."

"It's not that I want to be rude. . . ." I glanced away, trying to control the ill ease steadily growing inside me. "But don't you think it's a little soon? I mean, he tried to murder me only a few hours ago. . . ."

"If you're going to live in Golgotham, you can't let one bad experience color your understanding of an individual, much less an entire species. You have nothing to fear, Tate. He's completely harmless."

"Are you sure about that?"

"Scratch is under orders to bite his head off the second he tries something. Does that make you feel safer?"

"Yeah, it does, actually," I conceded. Funny how my earlier apprehension regarding the familiar miraculously disappeared once he saved my life.

The were-cat's recovery room was on the second floor, on the other side of the communal bathroom. The knowledge that my would-be killer was only a few yards away from where I slept did little to soothe my nerves.

As Hexe opened the door, I steeled myself for the sight of the shape-shifter as I'd last seen him, sitting in bed, propped up on pillows, like a feline version of the Big Bad Wolf after he'd gobbled down Little Red Riding Hood's granny.

Instead, what I saw was a teenaged boy, around sixteen years old, dressed in a pair of ill-fitting *Star Wars* pajamas. The fear and apprehension I had about confronting my attacker face-to-muzzle instantly disappeared.

I turned and stared at Hexe in disbelief. "You've gotta be shitting me—he's a kid?"

"You must be Tate," the teenaged were-cat said, struggling to sit up.

Scratch, once more in his winged house cat form, was curled up at the foot of the bed. He lifted his head and growled a warning at the shape-shifter.

"Allow me," Hexe said, defusing the situation by arranging his patient's pillows.

I stepped inside the room and closed the door behind me, unable to take my eyes off the young were-cat. He was lean, with the build of a track star, unruly sand-colored hair and a fairly impressive unibrow. If I hadn't known he was a were-cougar, my only thought upon seeing him would have been that he was in desperate need of a brow wax and a sandwich.

"I'm Lukas, son of Evander and Valentina. And I am *so* ashamed of what I did to you," the were-cat apologized. "My parents raised me better than that. Please forgive me, ma'am. I was not myself last night. They pumped me full of drugs to make me fight. I was still under the influence when you stumbled across me. . . ."

"Fight?" Suddenly things started to make a horrible kind of sense. "How old are you, Lukas?"

"Sixteen, ma'am."

"Where are you from?"

"My clan lives on the Dannemora Preserve. My people make their living as trappers."

Hexe sat down on the edge of the bed. "What are you doing in the city?"

"I saw it on TV."

"You saw it on TV?" I was unable to hide my surprise. It suddenly occurred to me that what little I knew about shape-shifters came straight from Hollywood and even less reliable sources.

"Not all of us sleep in dens and eat raw meat," Lukas pointed out defensively. "Some of us live indoors, cook our food, and have satellite television."

Good, at least he's housebroken, I thought to myself.

"I spent my entire life on the preserve, just like my father, and his father before him. But I always knew there was something more, something better. I felt hemmed in. I wanted to sniff trees that weren't already marked, you know? Once I saved up enough money, I snuck off the preserve and bought a bus ticket to the city. I knew enough to wear a cap and pull it down low enough to keep humans from noticing my brow. . . ."

"Perhaps it would be easier if you showed us your story, rather than told it to us," Hexe said. He reached into his pocket and withdrew a crystal the size of a goose egg. After polishing it on his shirtfront, he offered it to the young were-cat. "Here, take a deep breath and exhale it onto the scrying crystal, then hold it up between your thumb and forefinger. We'll be able to see into your past," Hexe explained, "but I'm afraid we won't be able to hear anything."

Lukas did as he was told and breathed onto its surface. As he held it up, I could see dozens upon dozens of tiny black-and-white figures moving around within the crystal. After a second I realized I was looking at the interior of the Port Authority bus terminal.

I spotted Lukas among the swirling mass of humanity, looking lost and confused. Suddenly he was approached by a man with long, dirty blond hair pulled back into a greasy ponytail, dressed in a black leather jacket and matching jeans.

"Who's the bus station pimp?" I asked.

"That's Phelan," Lukas explained, his voice growing cold. "He's shaved an open patch in his brow, but I could tell he was a werewolf by the way he moved. He told me he could take me to a den in the city, where there were other weres like ourselves, and I could bed down and get fed, free of charge." He gave a bitter laugh. "At the time I couldn't believe my luck! Normally I wouldn't have anything to do with a werewolf, but I didn't see any reason in holding grudges."

I watched as Phelan led Lukas out of the bus terminal into the streets of Times Square. I could see Lukas staring in awe and trepidation at the traffic surrounding him on all sides. Times Square is intimidating enough for kids raised in the suburbs; I could only imagine how daunting it might seem to someone raised in a forest. Suddenly the side of a black panel van parked in the loading zone rolled open and a big Kymeran with a faux-hawk jumped out.

Hexe frowned. "A Kymeran? Working with a were-wolf?"

Lukas nodded. "Yeah. He was the first one of your kind I'd seen in the flesh. You can't tell by looking at this, but he has pink hair."

The big Kymeran raised his hand to his mouth and blew a whitish powder in Lukas's face, just like Hexe did the night before, with the same result. Phelan and the pink-haired guy then dragged Lukas into the van. The moment the door slammed shut, the picture became scrambled, like an old television signal.

By the time it cleared up, I could see Lukas was in a room somewhere, possibly a basement, judging from the exposed pipes. He was strapped to some kind of medical gurney. A figure stepped forward—a tall, thin Kymeran dressed in a long white coat with dried blood-stains all over it. For some reason my blood ran cold.

"That's Dr. Moot." Hexe more spat the name than spoke it. "He used to be a surgeon—until they found out he was doing unnecessary surgeries to harvest body parts for the black magic market. What is he saying to you, Lukas?"

"He's telling me my new owner needs to have a few 'adjustments' made to me. He needs me to put on my cougar skin. But I refuse. He says it doesn't matter because he can *make* me change, whether I want to or not."

I watched as the Dr. Moot inside the scrying crystal filled a syringe with some kind of liquid and jabbed it into Lukas's arm. The captive bastet started to convulse, transforming into his were-cougar aspect. Dr. Moot then turned to a tray of surgical instruments laid out beside the table. He picked up a scalpel and held it to the light, turning it so he could study its blade.

Hexe leaned forward, peering deep into the crystal. "Is that a silver scalpel?" he asked.

"Yes." Lukas nodded sadly.

"What's he doing?" I asked, a sick feeling rising in my gut.

"Moot's hambling him," Hexe replied grimly. "It's a stroke of evil genius, really. Not only does it keep a beast fighting in the pit from being physically able to back away, basically forcing it to fight, it guarantees they won't try and run away."

"Why's that?"

"If any of us were to return to our preserves as a cripple, it's practically a death sentence," Lukas replied. "Some of the older weres who end up in the kennel simply lie down and die after they realize what's been done to them."

Mercifully the image inside the crystal grew fuzzy and distorted as Dr. Moot took the scalpel to Lukas's hind legs. When the picture cleared back up, I could see Lukas, once more in his human skin, lying on a pile of dirty straw inside a large metal cage. He was dressed in nothing but a pair of track pants, with filthy, bloody bandages wrapped about his feet. There was a shock collar fastened around his throat. I watched, my heart nearly breaking, as he dragged himself across the grimy floor to a metal bowl to try and get a drink of water.

Suddenly Lukas looked up and saw a figure sitting in

the cage next to his. It was a young man slightly older than he, with scruffy hair, dressed in a tattered pair of jogging pants with a shock collar around his neck. I could see a scar going from his left brow up into his hairline.

"Who's that?" I asked.

"That's Rufus," Lukas said sadly. "He was from the Embreeville Preserve. We became friends. He was the one who told me that all the werewolves and other shape-shifters in the kennel belonged to someone called Boss Marz—and the only way I could hope to stay alive was by fighting to the death in the pit."

"I should have known Boss Marz was involved." Hexe scowled. "Leave it to the Malandanti to traffic in something barbaric."

I felt a little flower of panic blossom in my belly. I might be a nump, but even I knew about the Kymeran version of the Mafia. Gambling, drugs, smuggling, prostitution, theft ... If it was illegal and going on in Golgotham, the Malandanti had a six-fingered hand in it.

They first emerged during the Unholy War, where they offered protection to fellow Kymerans and other supernaturals—for a price. After the Divine Intervention of 1111 put an end to the wholesale persecution of nonhumans, the organization went underground, infiltrating supernatural ghettos worldwide.

"I realize shape-shifters have a bloodthirsty reputation in the human world, but among our own kind there are only two situations where fighting to the death is acceptable—mating and protecting our families," Lukas explained. "Anything else is an unpardonable sin. You must understand that what we were being forced to do was an abomination."

The picture faded out for a second. When it returned, I saw the henchman with the fauxhawk who had drugged Lukas unlocking the were-cat's cage. He had a buddy with him, and they were both laughing at something. The one with the fauxhawk pushed a button on this gadget that looked like a universal remote. Suddenly Lukas fell to the ground in convulsions. The bastards tormenting him laughed and jolted him at least two more times before fixing a leash onto his collar.

They took him out of his cage and led him, still in his human form, out of the kennel and into some kind of tunnel. At the end was a door. Next to it stood the werewolf Phelan.

"They're taking me to my first fight," Lukas explained, his voice oddly flat. "I could hear people shouting and laughing on the other side of the door. I could also smell sawdust and blood. Lots of blood."

Phelan grinned at Lukas and held up a hypodermic. The werewolf then shoved the needle into Lukas's arm and opened the door. The two Málandanti threw Lukas across the threshold like bouncers kicking out a drunk, then slammed the door shut behind him. By the time the boy hit the sawdust, he was already changing into his were-cougar aspect.

Lukas stood at the bottom of a pit fifty feet across, with wooden sides twenty feet high, topped with bales of razor wire. Beyond the pit were bleachers full of spectators. Some were human, some were Kymerans, but all of them were waving handfuls of money. I could tell they were shouting at the top of their lungs, even though there was no sound.

Of all the faces peering down at Lukas, one in particular caught my attention. It belonged to a heavyset

Kymeran with slicked-back hair. He was wearing an expensive suit and had gold rings on every finger.

"Who's that?" I asked, pointing to the figure in the gazing glass.

"That's Boss Marz," Lukas said, a mixture of hatred and fear in his voice. "I knew it was him the moment I smelled him. He's the alpha, for sure."

A panel in the wall on the other side of the pit slid open. I couldn't see what was on the other side, but I knew it had to be big and pissed off from the way the spectators overhead started shaking more handfuls of money at one another. The picture suddenly went haywire, and when it reappeared I saw Lukas, still in his were-cat form, roaring in triumph, his fur sticky with blood. The crowd overhead was even wilder than before. Then I realized Lukas was straddling a disemboweled African lion. I don't know if Boss Marz caught it in the wild or if he bought it from a circus, but I could tell from its ribs that he had starved it before setting it loose.

"I don't really remember much about the fights themselves," Lukas explained. "The drugs that force the change also trigger a blood rage that makes rational thought almost impossible."

The picture inside the gazing crystal blurred and refocused itself long enough to show a glimpse of Lukas in his were-cat form battling first a jaguar, then a grizzly bear, and finally a gryphon.

"Bloody abdabs!" Hexe gasped upon seeing the eagle-headed lion. "Those things are on the Endangered Species List. And that son of a bitch uses them for pit fighting?"

The image in the crystal resolved into that of Lukas

being taken from his cage and led down the tunnel yet again. Phelan gave him the same shot, just like before, and then sent him into the pit. But this time his opponent wasn't a beast, or even a half-beast. It was a werewolf.

"That's Rufus." Lukas's eyes shone with unshed tears as he stared at his friend's image, trapped within the crystal. "Every one knows that once the lunacy is upon a werewolf, it can be slaked only by blood, and that the only thing that can kill a werewolf, besides silver, is another shape-shifter." He lowered his head in shame, unable to continue.

Inside the crystal, Lukas and Rufus battled to the death as the heartless bastards who took delight in their suffering wagered handfuls of money on which friend would die. In the end it was Lukas who was triumphant, tearing out Rufus's throat in a single bite.

"It's not your fault," I assured him, hoping to assuage the agony the poor kid was feeling. "It's not as if you *wanted* to kill him. And he would have killed you, too— you said so yourself. It was self-defense."

"I know." Lukas's voice was a ragged whisper when he finally spoke. "But I should have tried to escape before they made me fight him. I might not be able to run, but I can walk, sort of. I should have attacked one of the croggies and forced them to kill me. But I didn't, and now I have Rufus's blood on my claws, because I was afraid to fight back."

As the guards escorted Lukas back to his cage, it was obvious they were too busy talking to pay proper attention to their prisoner. Suddenly Lukas lashed out, launching a surprise attack on the one holding the zapper. Lukas grabbed the arm holding the remote and twisted it until it came out of the guard's shoulder like a roasted chicken wing. The severed arm was still holding the remote control in its hand as it hit the ground. Lukas picked up the zapper and smashed it to bits on the floor.

The second guard just stared in shock at his pal who was writhing at his feet, clawing at the bloody stump where his arm used to be. Lukas took him down with a quick snap to the throat. After that the picture got blurry again. There were glimpses of Lukas running through an underground complex full of caged creatures, both natural and supernatural, followed by partial images of street signs and what looked like the wall surrounding Hexe's garden.

"I don't remember much after attacking the guard. Just a dim recollection of wandering the streets, sniffing the air in hopes of catching the scent of grass, dirt, plants . . . something of nature. That's how I ended up in your garden. I simply followed my nose." Lukas turned toward me, a heart-stricken look on his young face. "I behaved like an animal toward you, Miss Tate. Can you possibly forgive me?"

"Of course I forgive you, Lukas!" No one was more surprised than I to hear those words coming out my mouth, but I figured the poor kid had enough on his conscience already—the least I could do was make him feel better about trying to kill me while under the influence of mind-warping drugs.

"So, now that you know the whole truth—are you going to hand me back over to Boss Marz?"

"Of course not!" Hexe replied. "I'm going to do exactly what I said I'd do—nurse you back to health, and then make sure you're returned to your people. You don't have to be scared anymore, Lukas." He patted him on the head, ruffling his sandy hair. "You are among friends now. Get some rest."

"Aren't you scared of Boss Marz?" Lukas asked in surprise.

"No, I'm not."

"You should be," the were-cougar said darkly.

Chapter 9

It was a couple of days after my misadventure in the garden maze, and I had gone out to buy art supplies. While standing on the front step, fishing around in my purse for my house keys, I heard someone behind me cough. I looked over my shoulder and saw a paunchy, middle-aged stranger with thinning hair standing on the stoop. Oh, yes, and he was wearing a kilt. That, in and of itself, would not have seemed too odd, save that from the waist up he was wearing two-thirds of a three-piece business suit. As I stared at him, it suddenly occurred to me that he was the first human I'd seen in Golgotham outside of the Rookery since I'd moved here.

"Excuse me," the man in the kilt said, without the faintest hint of a Scottish burr. "Are you Hexe?"

"Not even close," I laughed, wiggling the fingers of my free hand.

The stranger's face turned beet red. "Oh, I'm sorry. I didn't realize—"

"You're at the right place, though," I assured him as I unlocked the front door. I quickly checked the foyer

to see if Scratch was standing guard, but he was still upstairs, keeping an eye on Lukas.

"Hexe!" I shouted at the top of my lungs. "There's
someone here to see you!"

Hexe emerged from the back of the house, drying his
hands on an embroidered dish towel. He didn't bat an
eye at his visitor's sartorial splendor.

"Yes, sir. How may I be of service?"

"The name's Ottershaw. Wallace Ottershaw. You
come highly recommended by a friend of mine—Louis
Feldspar?"

Recognition sparked in Hexe's golden eyes. "Ah,
yes! Mr. Feldspar! His estranged wife cursed him with
dysmorphophilia."

"Dysmorpho-whatsit?" Ottershaw scowled.

I silently heaved a sigh of relief that someone else,
for once, was willing to play the nump, because I didn't
know what the hell it was, either.

"It's a compulsive preference for ugly sexual partners," Hexe explained dutifully. "Mr. Feldspar was most
relieved when I succeeded in lifting the curse."

Ottershaw eyed Hexe, taking in his purple hair and
the faded CBGB's logo on his T-shirt. "Louis said you
were good. Are you?"

"At the risk of sounding immodest, Mr. Ottershaw, I
am *very* good." Hexe gestured to the open door of his
study. "Please step into my office and tell me what your
problem is. Oh, before we start, I trust you won't mind
that I include Miss Tate on the consultation?"

Ottershaw gave me an uneasy look. "Is it absolutely
necessary that she be involved?"

"I will need her help in preparing a potion," Hexe
replied with the utmost seriousness.

This was news to me, but I didn't argue the point.

I had always wondered what kind of services Kymerans provided for their human clients, and now I had a chance to find out firsthand.

I followed Ottershaw into Hexe's office, which resembled a cross between a law office and P. T. Barnum's rummage sale. Bookshelves crowded the walls, extending all the way to the ceiling, from which hung a stuffed crocodile. While some of the shelves housed leather-bound books, others were crowded with religious reliquaries, pickled pathology specimens, carnival sideshow memorabilia, and, in one case, a tableaux depicting taxidermy squirrels playing poker. In the middle of the room was a desk covered in drifts of arcane ephemera, on which sat a Tiffany-style lamp with a shade made from an armadillo's shell.

"Please be seated," Hexe said, gesturing to the easy chair opposite the desk.

Ottershaw hesitated as he tried to figure out a way to sit down without flashing everyone in the room, before finally tucking the kilt between his milk white legs like a diaper. He sat down, wrapping his hands protectively across his knobby knees. The only way he could have looked more uncomfortable was if he set his hair on fire for good measure.

"The reason I came to see you is . . . I can't wear pants."

"I take it you're not Scottish, then?" Hexe said with just a hint of a smile.

"I was born in Scarsdale, for crying out loud. My mother's grandfather was from Aberdeen, though. This is his kilt I'm wearing. It's an heirloom," Mr. Ottershaw explained, shifting about uneasily. "And it's as scratchy as hell."

"So I see. Now, what makes you believe you can't wear pants?"

Ottershaw's cheeks turned crimson. "It's not that I *can't*. It's just that whenever I *do* put on a pair of trousers, I, uh, well, you see—I have this uncontrollable urge to go."

Hexe frowned. "Go where?"

Mr. Ottershaw's blush climbed all the way to his bald spot. "You know—*go*."

Hexe's eyes suddenly widened. "Oh! I see! Would that be Number One or Number Two?"

"Number One," Mr. Ottershaw said as he glanced at me, a look of utter humiliation in his eyes. Admitting to wetting yourself in front of an attractive young woman is the last thing any man wants to do—unless he's into that kind of thing; but that's a whole other story.

"I see," Hexe said as he jotted something down on a notepad. "So, what makes you think this condition is supernatural in origin?"

"As long as I'm not wearing trousers, I'm fine. But the moment I pull up a zipper—bam! Just like Old Faithful. I've ruined every pair of pants I own! Business, casual, formal, jeans, shorts . . . all of them, completely destroyed! You can't tell me this is natural!"

"I agree. It sounds to me that someone has inflicted micturition upon you."

"Mickey-what?"

"It means that you have been cursed so that you will urinate while wearing pants."

"Ugh! That's *disgusting*!" I exclaimed, forgetting my role as silent observer.

"Tell me about it," Mr. Ottershaw grumbled.

"Be grateful for small favors—at least you weren't inflicted with imbulbitation. That involves Number Two," Hexe explained, seeing the blank look on his client's face. "Still, let's not be too hasty—I said it sounded like micturition. I need to confirm if that is, indeed, the case."

He opened a drawer in the desk and removed a large crystal the size and shape of a goose egg. Stepping forward, he motioned for Ottershaw to stand up. Holding the crystal between his thumb and first forefinger, Hexe squinted through the scrying egg as he passed it up and down the length of his client's body.

"Hmm. Very interesting. Yes, I was correct—you have been crossed. Luckily, the curse is a relatively simple one to turn widdershins."

"Widder-what?"

"It'll be easy to reverse." Hexe sighed. "Tell me, Mr. Ottershaw. Do you know of any reason why someone might want to inflict a curse upon you?"

"No, of course not," Mr. Ottershaw said indignantly.

"No troubles at home, I take it?" Hexe prodded.

"I'm not married," Mr. Ottershaw replied.

"I see. How about your place of employment? Any friction with your coworkers?"

Mr. Ottershaw thought for a moment. Suddenly a light came on in his eyes. "Wait a minute! I'm supposed to give a presentation to the shareholders later today. If it goes well, I'll be promoted. You don't think that has anything to do with this, do you?"

"It's very likely. Workplace rivalries are the second-highest cause of curses, right after sexual jealousy."

"Of all the underhanded, sneaky, backstabbing . . ." Mr. Ottershaw's eyes flashed with anger. "Can you tell who did this to me?"

Hexe shook his head. "I can only identify the type of spell, and who might have cast it. Some wizards have more distinctive means of spellcasting than others. However, I cannot see who paid to have it done."

"Do you know who cast the spell on Mr. Ottershaw?" I asked; utterly fascinated by what I was hearing.

"I recognize the signature as belonging to a juggler by the name of Bozz who slings spells out of Witch Alley. He does slapdash work that tends to be crude but effective."

"I bet Boyland's behind this," Mr. Ottershaw muttered. He seemed to be paying more attention to his own thoughts than to what Hexe was saying. "That two-faced bastard! I wouldn't put it past him to try and scuttle my promotion!" He scowled at his bare knees and then looked up at Hexe. "I want you to get back at the asshole who did this to me. Give him really bad flop sweat, or make him fart really loud every time he sees a pretty girl. . . ."

Whatever sympathy I felt for Mr. Ottershaw abruptly evaporated. I was creeped out by how, within the space of a few heartbeats, the cursed businessman had gone from comical milquetoast to someone bent on revenge. "But you don't even know who's responsible for laying the curse on you!" I protested.

"That's okay; The more I think about it, the more I'm pretty damned sure it's Boyland," Mr. Ottershaw insisted.

"I don't care if there's a video of him paying for it on YouTube; I refuse to curse him, or anyone else," Hexe said sharply. "I practice Right Hand magic only, Mr. Ottershaw. That's why my lifting powers are so strong. I don't dilute them by practicing any Left Hand magic. If that's what you really want, you can take your money and go elsewhere!"

"I'm sorry; I didn't mean to insult you," Mr. Ottershaw said, unnerved by the outrage in Hexe's voice. "Go ahead and get rid of this curse, spell, whatever the fuck it is. Assuming you can fix it, that is."

"Are you asking if I can lift the curse?" Hexe sniffed. "Of course I can."

"How much?"

"Five thousand dollars."

Ottershaw's eyes looked as if they were about to leap from their sockets. "Five thousand! That's outrageous!"

"If you say so." Hexe shrugged. "You're welcome to go elsewhere. However, I doubt you'll be able to find anyone willing to do it any cheaper. And if you *did* find someone who could underbid me, I doubt they could reverse the spell in less than two days."

"Two days?!?" Mr. Ottershaw wailed. "But my presentation is this afternoon!"

"All the more reason to get started, then," Hexe said pointedly, folding his arms across his chest.

"Okay! Okay! You win! Five thousand it is!" Ottershaw snapped. "It's not as if I have a choice in the matter, is it?"

"No, you don't," Hexe agreed as he reached inside the desk and removed a wireless handheld credit card terminal. "Will that be credit or debit, sir?"

I blinked, taken aback by the sudden intrusion of modern technology in the middle of a conversation about curses, sorcery, and the casting of spells.

"Credit," Mr. Ottershaw replied as he fussed with the clasp of the horsehair sporran hanging from the front of his kilt. "Give me a second. . . . It's somewhere in this damned fuzzy purse. . . . Is MasterCard okay?"

"I take everything except Diners Club."

"So . . . are most of your clients like this guy?" I asked.

Hexe laughed without looking up from the cauldron he was stirring. We had withdrawn to the kitchen, leaving Mr. Ottershaw to ogle the pickled monkey's paw and other oddities in the study while we concocted the potion needed to counteract the curse. I say "we," but in reality Hexe was the one doing all the work. All I did was hand him jars full of dried herbs and less identifiable items when he asked for them.

"He's pretty typical. Most curses are more embarrassing than deadly—more like elaborate practical jokes, really. For example, an angry wife makes her cheating hubby's junk look like a balloon animal; a jealous man inflicts horrendous bad breath on his romantic rival; someone arranges for the coworker in the cubicle beside him to develop Tourette's. Hand me that jar of dried frog feet, will you? Thanks.

"These curses might be socially awkward, but, in the end, they're far from life threatening. They're also the curses easiest to lift, because they're normally cast by jugglers—Kymerans who use both Left and Right Hand magic. Because the caster is ambidextrous, the curse is rarely dark enough to do any real damage.

"But I also get victims of genuinely malevolent curses—where they vomit up sharp objects, like pins and needles, or are compelled to bite themselves or murder their own children. Those cases are extremely difficult to turn widdershins. Hand me that jar of fly agaric, please. . . .

"The reason those are harder to lift is because the caster is usually a necromancer. They practice nothing *but* Left Hand magic, and because of that, their curses tend to be very dark, and very, very strong.

"Luckily, Mr. Ottershaw's enemy—whoever he or she might be—was only interested in hindering him, not harming him. I suspect he or she simply nicked down to Witch Alley during lunch and paid fifty bucks to have him 'inconvenienced.' I need the peppered lark's tongue—no, not that bottle, the one next to it."

"And you're charging five thousand to lift a fifty-dollar curse?"

"I *was* going to charge him a thousand, but then he asked me to curse someone. Now he qualifies for the douche-bag rate."

"So why did you tell him you needed me to sit in on your 'consult'?"

Hexe shrugged his shoulders. "I have clients coming in and out at all hours, and I thought it might be good if you got an idea of what I do for a living."

"Really? You mean you didn't do it just to impress me with your wizardly ways?"

"How is keeping a man from pissing his pants going to impress you?" he laughed.

"Hey, I'm easily amused."

Mr. Ottershaw was standing in front of a glass-fronted bookshelf, frowning at a shrunken head that bore an uncanny resemblance to Elvis. He jumped as we returned to the room.

"Here—drink this," Hexe said, handing him a ram's horn cup full of the potion. "Drink it fast, while it's still warm. You're going to want to throw it up—don't. As bad as it is going down, it's even worse coming up."

Mr. Ottershaw stared dubiously at the viscous grayish green liquid. He did not look happy. "What's in it?"

"If I told you, it would just scare you."

Steeling himself, Mr. Ottershaw took a deep breath, closed his eyes, held his nose, and tossed back the potion. He gagged and hurled the ram's horn to the floor.

"Mother of God! That's the filthiest crap I've ever

had to drink in my life!" he moaned. He pointed a trembling finger at Hexe. "If this doesn't work, Kymeran, I want my money back!"

"It'll work," Hexe assured him. "Of course, it'll be two or three hours before it takes full effect...."

"Two or three hours?" Mr. Ottershaw glanced at his wristwatch. "My presentation is in an hour and a half! I can't show up wearing a kilt!"

"I have good news for you, Mr. Ottershaw. I'm willing to throw in a pair of magic pants that you can wear without fear of micturition, at no extra charge."

"*Magic pants?* You've got to be fuckin' kidding me," Ottershaw groaned.

Hexe pulled a small wooden sea chest from one of the bookshelves. From it he removed a pair of men's trousers unlike any I'd seen before. They were made of purple velvet and decorated with countless tiny mirrors.

"Are you nuts?" Mr. Ottershaw yelped. "I'm not wearing that monstrosity! At least with the kilt I just look like I'm Scottish, not a freaking disco ball!"

"Granted, they are somewhat unconventional," Hexe agreed. "But the mirrors that cover the pants are enchanted. Not only do they deflect the curse that was inflicted upon you, but once you put them on, those around you will only see what they expect to see—in your case, a nice pair of conservative suit trousers, nothing more. You'll be protected from fouling yourself, and your junk will no longer be at the mercy of updrafts."

"What the hell—at this point, I'm willing to risk it," Mr. Ottershaw said, snatching up the mirrored pants. "This kilt chafes like a bear!"

*   *   *

After a quick visit to the powder room under the staircase, Mr. Ottershaw emerged dressed in his glorious magic pants. The myriad mirrors caught and refracted the low light from the armadillo lamp, bouncing it back upon itself until I had to avert my gaze. When I looked again, I was surprised to see a pair of staid, slate gray trousers with a razor-sharp pleat in their place.

"Wow!" I breathed. "They really work!"

"Of course they work," Hexe said proudly.

Mr. Ottershaw checked his watch again. "I'd better leave—I have to get back to the office in time for that presentation."

"Good luck, sir. And I appreciate your business today," Hexe said, sliding a card into Mr. Ottershaw's pocket. "Please don't hesitate to recommend me to your friends and colleagues."

"Yeah, sure," Mr. Ottershaw replied uneasily.

"Allow me to see you to the door. . . ."

As Hexe and I watched Mr. Ottershaw leave, it occurred to me that if he was trying to get back to the financial district, he was headed in the wrong direction.

"Where's he going?" I asked.

"If I had to guess, I would say he's headed for Witch Alley," Hexe replied. "No doubt in search of someone willing to curse the unfortunate Mr. Boyland on the cheap."

"You're right," I grunted. "He *is* a douche bag."

"That's probably why someone cursed him in the first place." Hexe sighed wistfully. "I suppose I should have mentioned that the enchantment on those pants is good for only two hours at a time. Oh, well—he'll find out for himself."

Chapter 10

Although I was no longer frightened of Lukas, it was still kind of weird living under the same roof as a were-cougar. I've had unsavory neighbors before—this *was* New York, after all—but knowing your housemate changes into a bloodthirsty hell-beast is a lot different than suspecting the dude down the hall from you sells X.

Instead of dwelling on being murdered in my own bed, I opted to throw myself into my work. I had a show coming up, and I needed to finish the last two pieces on time. Being killed by a were-cat would be a walk in the park compared to dealing with an irate gallery owner—especially one as influential as Derrick Templeton.

I work in metal, sculpting fully articulated, life-sized human figures out of electrical conduit, transmission parts, plumbing pipe, and twenty-gauge steel. Unlike conventional sculpture, they're fully poseable. I landed the show in Chelsea on the strength of my prototype, *The Dying Gaul*.

I suspect my parents' dislike of my being an artist had more to do with the discipline I chose than an intrinsic distaste for the medium itself. After all, my father wrote sizable checks to the Guggenheim and the Whitney every year. There might even be a wing with his name on it at MoMA, come to think of it.

Had I chosen to become a painter or a photographer, they might have been willing to accept my decision, but being a sculptor was simply beyond the pale. What with my oxyacetylene equipment, steel-toe boots, overalls, and welder's helmet, I might as well have been a blue-collar worker. At least that was my mother's opinion. Then again, she also thought Roger was suitable son-in-law material simply because his father was a cardiologist and his mother a psychiatrist.

The last time I went to dinner with her, she actually called me "Rosie the Riveter." That was my mom: always on the cutting edge of culture. I'm surprised she didn't throw in a "twenty-three skidoo" for good measure.

I was in the middle of crafting a hip joint from a Dodge transmission when I heard a loud thump outside my door. I turned off my torch and flipped back my helmet in time to hear a string of profanity coming from the hallway.

I opened the door to find Lukas sprawled on the floor outside the bathroom. Although I should have been concerned to see a were-cat near my door, I couldn't muster even the tiniest amount of dread. Frankly, it's impossible to fear someone dressed in *Star Wars* pajamas a half size too small.

"Oh, my God!" I exclaimed as I hurried to his side. "What are you doing out of bed, Lukas?"

"I just wanted to go to the bathroom by myself, instead of using the bedpan," he explained. "I managed to get there on my own ... but coming back ... my legs gave out from under me. . . ."

"Let me help you up," I said, sliding my arm behind his back. "Are you able to stand?"

He nodded weakly. "I think so . . . but I feel dizzy. . . ."

"Come into my room and sit down—I'll go fetch Hexe."

"No, don't bother him," Lukas insisted. "I'm a nuisance enough as it is."

"Don't be silly," I said as I guided him to the easy chair on the "living" side of my space, safely removed from my workbench and tools. "Why would you say such a thing?"

"Because it's *true*." The young were-cat sighed. "I'm taking Hexe away from his paying clients. And I don't know why you're being so nice to me, either, after I traumatized you in the garden. . . . "

"I'll admit you scared the shit out of me." I smiled. "But I wouldn't go so far as to call myself 'traumatized.' Who told you that?"

"Scratch."

"Yeah, well, you really shouldn't give anything Scratch tells you too much credence. He says shit like that to everyone—that's just his style. I should know. You are *not* a nuisance, Lukas." I could tell from the look in his eye that the boy didn't believe me, so I decided to change the subject. "Anyway, I'm impressed that you made it that far on your own steam. That means you're healing. Maybe you'll be ready to go back home soon."

Lukas dropped his eyes to the floor. "Great," he mumbled.

"Is there something wrong?" I asked, surprised by his response. "Don't you want to go back home?"

"Of course I do." He sighed. "It's just that I don't think home wants me back."

"You're kidding, right? Your parents must be out of their minds with worry over you!"

"I doubt it. I'm sure they've forgotten they ever had a son by now."

It suddenly occurred to me that no one runs away to New York City just to see the sights, no matter what they say, even if they're a were-cat. "So the stuff you said about coming to New York to mark fresh trees, that was all bullshit, wasn't it?"

"Not all of it," Lukas admitted sheepishly. "But it's not the real reason I left the preserve. I love my family, and I love my people. But life on the preserve can be ... difficult.

"My father is an alpha. *His* father was an alpha, as was *his* father before him. Me? I am so not an alpha. I've always tried to live up to what my dad—and my mom, she's an alpha, too—expect from me. It's been hard, because I just don't have it in me, you know? Dad says I think too much, instead of relying on my instincts.

"There's this female in our village the same age as I am. Her name's Yvonne. We were cubs together. She's got the prettiest fur.... Anyway, we grew up together on the preserve. I liked her and she liked me. Then she went into season...."

"Girl trouble, huh?" I rolled my eyes. "I think I know where this is going."

"Suddenly Konrad comes sniffing about. He's big and stupid and treats everyone else like shit and ..."

"He challenged you for Yvonne?"

Lukas grimaced in disgust. "It was horrible. The only reason Konrad didn't tear out my throat is because I soiled myself first. After that, I was looked at as a submissive by everyone, including my father."

"I'm sure he'll get over it, in time."

"You don't understand. By my kind's rules, I've lost the right to mate," Lukas said mournfully. "My family's bloodline ends with me. I shamed my father and lost the one I love. I was forced to watch Yvonne become the mate of that thick-skulled bully. Everywhere I went, the others were mean to me because they knew I was weak. And every time I looked into my parents' eyes, all I saw was disappointment and disgust. That's when I decided I had to leave the preserve.

"I picked New York because I knew there were supernaturals living within the city. I hoped I could lose my past and reinvent myself here. So much for hope." He sighed, slumping down even farther into the easy chair.

"Don't you think your family misses you even a little?" I asked.

"What's to miss? I'm a failure—worse, than that, I'm an evolutionary dead end! My parents are young enough to try again and get it right with a new cub. I'm doing them a favor by disappearing, Tate.

"As it is, there's no way I can truly rejoin my people—I've killed a fellow were. Even though I had no choice, and Rufus was a lycanthrope and not a bastet, in the eyes of my people, killing a fellow were-being is worse than killing a human—sorry. No offense."

"None taken," I replied.

"I'm a pariah, now. Just like Phelan is a lone wolf."

"You're *nothing* like that creep!" I suddenly found myself angry—not at Lukas but at all those who had conspired to try and break this young boy's spirit and turn him into the monster they expected. "I don't want to hear you talking like that anymore. You're a good kid. You've just gone through a lot of shit, that's all. After listening to you, I feel like a jerk complaining about my folks."

"You have problems with your parents, too?" His eyes widened in surprise.

"Nothing on the order of what you're dealing with. Mine just don't like what I do, where I live, and who my friends are, that's all."

"What is it you do they do not like?"

"This," I replied, gesturing to the sculptures, both assembled and in progress, that crowded the "working" side of my space.

Lukas turned to stare at me, a look of amazement in his eyes. "Why would they not like this?"

Now it was my turn to shrug. "My parents simply disapprove on general principles. They think I'm wasting my time."

"They're wrong," he said, his voice surprisingly sure for one so young.

There was a quick rap on the half-open door as Hexe entered the room. "Sorry if I'm interrupting—but have you seen Lukas?"

I pointed to the easy chair. Lukas smiled wanly at Hexe and waved hello.

"There you are. I was afraid Scratch had made good on his threats and eaten you. You got all the way down the hall on your own—? I'm impressed."

"Don't be," Lukas replied. "The only reason I'm sitting in this room is because Tate picked me up off the floor."

"He fell down," I explained. "But he seems okay. We were just comparing family drama before you arrived."

Hexe nodded in understanding. "Well, in my experience, everyone has *two* families. The first is the one you're born into; the second is the one you create for yourself. So what if your first family doesn't want you around or understand you? Your second family does. As long as you have someone who cares, everything's right in the world. And that's how it should be. Being alone isn't healthy for shape-shifters *or* humans."

"You're a wise man, Hexe."

"I have my moments," he laughed. "But the real reason I came looking for you, Lukas, is that I want to take you to see a friend of mine named Dr. Mao. He's a healer."

"Aren't *you* a healer?" Lukas asked. "Why do I need to go see another one?"

"It's called a second opinion. Besides, I'm nowhere as skilled as Dr. Mao. He operates an apothecary on the corner of Pearl and Frankfort, on the border between Golgotham and Chinatown."

"Frankfort Street? There's no way he can walk that far!" I exclaimed.

"That's why I've arranged for Kidron to pick us up. But before we go anywhere, we need to camouflage our young friend," Hexe said, pointing to Lukas's forehead.

As I stared at the were-cat's telltale unibrow, I was struck by inspiration. "Stay right there—I've got just the thing!" I returned a minute later with a pink disposable razor, a small hand mirror, and a can of strawberry-banana-scented shaving cream. I squirted a dollop onto my fingers and daubed it on Lukas's brow, just above the bridge of his nose, then proceeded to scrape away the excess hair, creating the illusion of two separate eyebrows.

"Oww!" Lukas winced. "Not so rough!"

"Consider yourself lucky I'm not giving you a brow wax," I replied. "Now hold still." I stepped back and held up the hand mirror so Lukas could admire my handiwork. "What do you think?"

"I feel naked." The were-cat frowned as he gingerly rubbed the freshly denuded space above his nose.

Hexe's BlackBerry rang. He fished it out of his pocket and peered at the caller ID. "It's Kidron. He's waiting for us outside."

As Hexe helped Lukas to his feet, the young bastet looked in my direction. "Tate—aren't you coming with us?"

"Well, I was hoping to get some more work done on this sculpture. . . ."

"Pleeeease?"

I glanced at Hexe. "I don't want to get in the way. It's a doctor's visit, after all."

"The more the merrier, I always say," Hexe said. "Besides, I think you'll find Dr. Mao very . . . interesting."

"Not in the Chinese sense of the word, I hope," I replied.

It took a little doing, but we managed to rustle up enough clothes for Lukas to go out in public without calling too much attention to himself.

Hexe loaned him a pair of jeans that were an inch too short, as well as an old hoodie sweatshirt, while my contribution consisted of a pair of scuffed-up old Vans.

Once he was dressed, Hexe and I escorted Lukas downstairs, careful to keep him sandwiched between us so he couldn't fall down. Walking the single flight was torture for the poor kid, but he put up a brave front, moaning only once.

Upon reaching the first floor, Hexe disappeared into his study and returned carrying a cane, the shaft of which was fashioned of ironwood and the handle made from a goat's horn.

"Use this," Hexe said, handing Lukas the cane. "The

handle's a scapegoat's horn. It'll absorb most of the pain while you're walking. Be careful with it, though—anyone who touches it after you've used it will be in for a nasty surprise."

As Lukas leaned his weight upon the charmed cane, I could see the pain drain from his face. He paused on the threshold of the open door, staring in wonderment at the buildings that crowded the streets.

"I've been in New York for weeks, but this is the first time I've really seen this city," he marveled.

"Believe me, the rest of New York looks nothing like this," I assured him.

Kidron was waiting patiently at the curb in front of the house. Instead of the two-wheeled hansom cab, he was hitched up to a closed, four-wheeled carriage.

"Good afternoon, Miss Tate," the centaur said, tipping his top hat. "Nice to see you again."

"Hello, Kidron," I replied as I opened the door of the cab. "It's nice to see you, too."

As I turned to help Lukas into the carriage, the shape-shifter eyed the centaur uneasily. Hexe stepped forward and patted his young patient on the shoulder. "There's no need to be scared, Lukas. Kidron is a friend. Isn't that so?"

The cabbie bobbed his head in agreement. "We all run in the same herd, do we not?"

After we situated ourselves inside the cab—Lukas and I side-by-side, Hexe seated opposite us—Kidron trotted off in the direction of Pearl Street. Hexe glanced over at Lukas, who was looking out the window of the moving cab, taking in the sights.

"Do you mind telling me why you hesitated before getting in the cab?" he asked. "Was it because you've never seen a centaur before?"

"No. That's not it." Lukas dropped his gaze in shame. "It's just that I—well, I fought one in the pit."

"Bloody-minded fecker!" Hexe spat in disgust.

Lukas flinched and lowered his head. Seeing his reaction, Hexe reached out and clasped the boy's shoulder.

"Please don't misunderstand—I'm not mad at you, Lukas. I realize you had no choice in what happened. Marz is the one I'd like to get my hands on. He's a vile piece of bad business."

It wasn't long before we arrived at our destination: a row of mixed-use tenement buildings facing the elevated Brooklyn Bridge access ramps. Dr. Mao's apothecary shop was on the ground floor, sandwiched between a plumbing supply shop and a tapas restaurant.

As Kidron pulled up to the curb, a one-armed pink-haired Kymeran dressed in an ill-fitting dark suit emerged from the apothecary. I glanced over at Lukas. The young shape-shifter was trembling like a malaria victim.

"That's him," he croaked. "That's the guard I attacked the night I escaped!"

"It's all right, Lukas," I said, patting his hand. "He didn't see you. You're safe."

"But what is he doing here?" Despite the cool weather, sweat stood out in beads along Lukas's brow and upper lip. I wondered, perhaps a little too late, if a panic attack could trigger shape-shifting in a bastet.

"There's no point in getting your tail in a twist before you know if it's a problem or not," Hexe said, doing his best to calm the boy. "Dr. Mao's a very good healer. I bet that croggy is simply one of his patients."

"You could be right," Lukas admitted. "But what are the odds of his being here, of all days?"

"Golgotham's a very small world, I'm afraid." Hexe sighed. "One that's getting smaller every day."

The interior of the apothecary shop was crowded, dimly lit, and smelled strongly of bitter herbs. One side was taken up by a long counter, behind which stood a wall full of antique cabinets, each drawer labeled in neat, Chinese script. Deer horns, still clad in their velvet, hung suspended from the dusty ceiling, along with goat horns, a narwhale tusk, and the ubiquitous stuffed crocodile.

Seated on a stool behind the counter was an elderly Asian gentleman dressed in a black silk shirt with a mandarin collar. As the bell over the shop door announced our arrival, the old man jumped to his feet with amazing speed, his head morphing into that of a tiger.

"I already told you. I don't know anything!" he snarled.

Once he saw Hexe, the black stripes faded back into the old man's skin and the bristling whiskers relaxed, becoming a long, drooping mustache. His gray eyebrow stretched across his forehead without a visible break.

"Forgive me, Hexe! I thought you were someone else."

"I can see that." Hexe smiled as the were-tiger came out from behind the counter to greet him. "You're looking good, you old rascal."

"The same is true of you, my friend." Dr. Mao smiled. He turned and shouted something in Chinese over his shoulder. The set of heavy curtains that partitioned the front of the store from the back parted, revealing a teenaged Asian girl dressed in a traditional mandarin silk gown. Where her father's unibrow was wild and bushy, hers had been waxed and tweezed into a delicate, pencil-thin line.

"Meikei! Prepare tea for our honored guest!" Dr. Mao said, briskly clapping his hands.

"Of course, Father," the young girl replied, bowing her head. As she left the room, she peeked over her shoulder and gave Lukas a teensy smile.

"She's beautiful." The young were-cat had a goofy grin on his face. Little cartoon cupids flying around his head were the only thing missing.

"Play it cool, kiddo," I whispered, giving him a quick nudge to the ribs. "You're drooling."

"Sorry," he muttered, wiping his mouth on his sleeve.

Hexe took me by the elbow, steering me toward the elderly were-tiger. "I hope you don't mind, but I've brought a couple of friends with me. Tate, I would like you to meet Dr. Mao."

"Most pleased to meet you, young lady," Dr. Mao said politely as he shook my hand. "You are human, yes? Are you a client?"

"Tate is my newest boarder," Hexe explained.

Dr. Mao raised his unibrow in surprise. "Does your uncle know yet?"

"No, he doesn't. And I'd like to keep it that way."

Dr. Mao nodded his understanding. He then turned to face Lukas. "It would seem by the way this one walks that he is in need of healing. Is that not so?"

"You are correct," Hexe replied. "Lukas—say hello to Dr. Mao."

As Lukas moved forward to greet the healer, Dr. Mao gasped and took a step back. For a brief second the tiger stripes swam back to the surface of his skin. The apothecary grabbed Hexe by the arm and quickly pulled him aside.

"That boy is a were-cougar!" Dr. Mao hissed in alarm.

"I'm aware of that," Hexe replied. "I didn't think his being a were-cat would matter to *you*."

"You don't understand, Hexe. The Malandanti are looking for him! In fact, one of them just left here."

"I know; we saw him. What did he have to say?"

"He said that Boss Marz is offering a cash reward for the were-cougar's return. They're checking with every healer and hedger in Golgotham. I'm surprised they haven't shown up at your door yet."

"I suspect it's only a matter of time." Hexe sighed. "How much money are they offering?"

"Enough," Dr. Mao said grimly.

"Does this mean you won't help us?"

"Of course not!" Dr. Mao exclaimed indignantly. "I am a healer above all else. I just want you to know what's at stake. The Malandanti may fear your mother, but that will not keep them from striking at you."

"I appreciate your concern, old friend." Hexe smiled, placing a hand on Dr. Mao's shoulder. "But I'm not afraid of Boss Marz, and I don't think you are, either."

"Marz!" Dr. Mao's face twisted in disgust, as if the crime lord's name were foul to the taste. "He can—how do the young ones say it? Ah, yes. He can kiss my butt!"

"I like you, Doc," I laughed. "You're not afraid to say what you think."

"I wish I could claim to be a brave man," Dr. Mao said, blushing slightly. "But the truth is I'm simply too old to care about what others think anymore." He motioned for Lukas to follow him. "Come along, young one. I must inspect your feet."

Lukas hobbled across the room and sat down in a traditional Chinese horseshoe armchair. Mao's daughter reappeared, carrying a tray with a blue-and-white celadon tea service on it. Placing the tray on a table next to the chair, she poured a measure of hot tea into one of the delicate cups and handed it to Lukas.

"Th-thanks," he stammered.

"Meikei, please prepare the young man's feet for inspection," Dr. Mao said matter-of-factly.

"Yes, Father," she replied dutifully.

Lukas's eyes widened as Meikei knelt before him and began unlacing his shoes. He reached out to stop her, his cheeks burning bright pink. "You don't have to do that!" he blurted.

"But I must," Meikei explained, smiling up at him. "I am my father's apprentice."

Lukas sat transfixed, staring down at the young girl as she removed his shoes and socks. Once she was finished, Meikei frowned upon seeing the untouched cup of tea still in his hand.

"Is there something wrong with the tea?" she asked.

"Oh! No!" Lukas assured her, shaking his head vigorously. "It's delicious!"

"But you haven't even tasted it," she pointed out.

Lukas quickly downed the contents of the cup and held it out for her inspection. "Yes, I have. See? It's delicious!"

"Enough silliness," Dr. Mao said, shooing his daughter out of the way. "And as for you, young man, stop ogling my apprentice and let me examine your feet."

The healer squatted down and cradled first Lukas's right foot, then the left, in his hands, as if weighing them. "Does it hurt when I push here?" he asked, probing the scarred flesh with long, nimble fingers.

Lukas winced in response and nodded his head.

"How about there?"

The wince became a grimace, and the were-cat involuntarily yanked his foot away. Dr. Mao leaned back and pensively stroked his long, drooping mustache.

"How bad is it, Doc?" Lukas asked nervously.

"I will not lie to you, my young friend. The damage is quite extensive. Fortunately, while silver might kill a shape-shifter in the form of a knife or a bullet to the heart, lesser wounds made by such weapons are not permanent. However, they *are* extremely slow to heal. I am going to prescribe a course of treatment requiring special ointments, plasters, and foot baths that should draw the silver from your wounds over the course of the next few weeks. You are to take the treatments in both your human and cougar aspects. I am also prescribing a special diet to help restore your strength. I will have my daughter deliver these medicinal meals every day, so no one will see you coming and going from my apothecary."

"Does that mean I'll be able to run again?" For the first time there was something like hope in the young were-cat's voice.

"Don't worry. We Children of Bast must stick together. I'll soon have you back on your feet," Dr. Mao said, stroking Lukas's head as he would a house cat's. "And you'll need all four of them in perfect shape if you want to escape beyond Boss Marz's reach."

Chapter 11

"Do you think she likes me?" Lukas asked breathlessly as we climbed back into Kidron's cab.

Barely an hour ago, the young were-cat thought life was barely worth living. Now his eyes gleamed with excitement for the future. Funny what a smile from a pretty girl could do.

"It certainly looks that way," I replied.

"I can't believe I'll get to see her every day!" The grin on Lukas's face was suddenly replaced by a frown. "I need to get some real clothes. I don't want her to see me in those pajamas."

"What's wrong with them?" Hexe asked. "They used to be mine."

"Did you ever score while wearing them?" I countered.

"Point taken," he conceded. Hexe glanced at the BlackBerry's screen as it began to ring. A worried look crossed his face. "I just got a text from Kidron. He says he thinks we're being followed."

"Followed? By whom?"

Lukas moved to stick his head out the carriage window, but Hexe quickly restrained him. "Don't look!" he snapped. "There's an easier way of finding out."

Hexe reached inside his jacket and retrieved a smaller version of the scrying egg he had used earlier on Mr. Ottershaw. He muttered something in Kymeran and exhaled onto it, fogging the crystal's surface with his breath.

Holding it between thumb and second ring-finger, he raised the egg so that we all could see the images inside. The figures were greatly reduced, and the reception limited to black-and-white, but it was obvious that a Malandanti goon—this one with two arms—was following thirty feet behind Kidron's cab, riding in a rickshaw pulled by a satyr.

"They know I'm here!" Lukas yelped. "They're coming to get me!"

"I don't think so," Hexe replied as he returned the scrying device to his pocket. "If that was true, they would have attacked us the minute we left the apothecary. No, I suspect Boss Marz has his men keeping an eye on any young male who goes to see any of the neighborhood healers."

"What are we going to do?" I asked.

"I have an idea. Give me a second." Hexe's fingers flew across the keyboard of his BlackBerry. "I don't want to lead Marz's man back to my place. I'll ask Kidron to make a detour. . . ." He glanced up from his texting and gave Lukas a reassuring smile. "Don't worry, kid. It's all under control. Look at it this way—you're finally going to get in a little sightseeing."

Lukas shifted about uneasily in his seat, fighting the urge to hang his head out of the moving vehicle. "I don't understand—what's so special about this place we're going to?"

"In 'ye olde' days, traffic between humans and Kymerans had more of a stigma attached to it than it does now," Hexe explained. "I'm not saying humans didn't seek out magic back then—far from it. They were just a lot more circumspect in how they went about it. That's why Kymeran ghettos, no matter what city they're in, are always within walking distance of the seat of power. It's all about easy access.

"In the 1800s there was a grand playhouse called the Park Theatre located on Park Row, just east of Morder Lane, which, at the time, was the farthest boundary of Golgotham. The theater overlooked what eventually became City Hall, and for several decades it was the only theater in the entire city. Every night the cream of New York society would go there to be entertained.

"Back then, Witch Alley was nothing more than the service lane for carriages bringing customers to the theater. The carriage drivers would drop their wealthy passengers off at the front door, and then park behind the theater to wait for the play to end. A few enterprising Kymerans started working the alley, offering good luck charms for sale to the drivers. Eventually the fine men and women who owned the coaches began sneaking out the back door during performances. Upstanding citizens who would never set foot in Golgotham proper had no problem ducking into Witch Alley to pick up a love potion or lay a quick curse on a rival.

"The Park Theatre burned down in the 1850s and was replaced by a block of storefronts, but by then Witch Alley had become its own destination. Since those days, it's become one of the biggest tourist attractions in Golgotham—and the street with the worst traffic. It's the perfect place to lose an unwanted tail."

"I *still* don't understand—" Lukas suddenly fell silent and cocked his head to one side, a quizzical look on his face. "What's that sound?"

A second later my human ears detected the buzz created by the voices of a large crowd off in the distance. As the cab made the turn off Beekman toward Morder Lane, the low hum developed into boisterous shouting, until at last the different cries became distinct, and the air was filled with the din of a thousand different voices all bellowing at once.

"Here potions! Charms and spells! Fine come-hithers!"

"Glad Eyes! Twenty spot a buy!"

"Who'll buy a potion for ten spot a dose?"

Witch Alley was a long, narrow street sandwiched between the unglamorous backsides of old crumbling buildings. Although a few doors opened onto the alley, no windows looked onto it, adding to the air that whatever transactions occurred there went unseen. Despite the close quarters, the alleyway was jammed from end to end with street sellers, purchasers, and tourists. The hubbub that accompanied the crowd was deafening, the Kymerans who worked the alley all crying their wares with the full force of their voices, each fighting to be heard over the next.

"Pick 'em out cheap! Three good luck charms for the price of two!"

"Charms for luck! Charms for love! Charms for money!"

"Goofer dust! Get your goofer dust here! You can't cross an enemy without your goofer dust!"

Despite being packed together like sardines in a can,

the occupants of Witch Alley parted before Kidron's cab, allowing it to enter the backstreet. The moment the carriage was completely inside the alleyway, the various street sellers surged forward, putting a wall of living flesh between the cab and the rickshaw following it.

I gazed out the window of the carriage, taking in the riotous spectacle. Over here was a charmer walking with a long pole slung over his shoulders, from which dangled numerous different amulets and good luck charms. Over there a potion pusher showed off her wares from a tray held in place by a leather strap about her neck. Next to the pusher stood a Kymeran dressed in a traditional patchwork coat playing a hurdy-gurdy, doing his best to draw the attention of passersby to his own selection of magical goods. Meanwhile, yet another competitor darted through the crowd, potion bottles jutting from his side pockets and layers of charms dangling from his hands and neck.

To my right was a secretary on her lunch break, her purse clasped tightly under one arm as she perused love charms laid out on a tray; to my left a businessman in a three-piece suit wiggled his way through the crowd, nervously avoiding eye contact. Stirred into the mix of buyers and sellers of quick, cheap magic were several dozen tourists dressed in I ♥ GOLGOTHAM T-shirts, happily snapping pictures of the chaos that surrounded them.

Hexe, a sad look on his face, gazed out at his fellow Kymerans as they strove among themselves to make a living. "Most who work the alley either have no steady clientele or can't afford the rent at the Rookery," he explained. "I don't begrudge them a living, but so many humans see us as nothing more than rapacious spell-slingers who'd curse their own mothers if the price was right. . . ."

Just then a tall, rangy Kymeran with a pistachio green

handlebar mustache, smelling strongly of citrus and spice, hopped onto the running board of the cab and thrust a bar of Fast Luck Soap under Lukas's nose.

"Need some luck, kid? Need it now? Just wash yourself head to toe and hey, presto! You're lucky for the day! Comes in Springtime, Ocean Breeze, and Regular! Ten spot a bar! Whattaya say, young sir?"

Lukas recoiled, unsure of how to react to the peddler's hard sell. Hexe leaned across the cab and gave the charmer a hard stare.

"He's not interested," he said firmly.

The charm peddler's eyes widened in surprise. "Please forgive the intrusion, Serenity! I didn't see you sitting there."

"It's quite all right, Bozz," Hexe replied. "I see you're still running a special on micturition. How's your mother doing?"

"Passing fair," Bozz said. "She'll be tickled you asked, Serenity." With that the peddler hopped back down and rejoined the throngs of Witch Alley.

"Perhaps we *should* have bought the soap," Lukas said. "Maybe if I bathe with it, it'll change my luck and Boss Marz will leave me alone?"

"I seriously doubt a bar of Fast Luck Soap would do much good," Hexe said with a shake of his head. "Once you start forcing good luck, the bad will follow on its heels—and it'll be even *worse* than normal because you've tampered with the order of things."

"What's with this Bozz guy calling you 'Serenity'?" I asked.

"It's nothing," he insisted. "Just a nickname."

"It sounded more like a *title* to me."

"We can discuss that later," he replied. "After we make our transfer."

I looked in the direction Hexe was pointing and saw another enclosed carriage, this one drawn by a beautiful sorrel centauride, headed our way down the opposite side of the alley. The female centaur was dressed in a halter top that looked like one of Madonna's bras, with a garland of daisies atop her auburn head and a Bluetooth headset clipped to one ear.

"That's Kidron's stablemate, Wildfire," Hexe explained. "She's our ride back home."

The alley was barely wide enough to accommodate one cab, much less two, but somehow the vehicles managed to pull up alongside each other, with barely three feet between them. Wildfire pulled a cord affixed to her harness, and the door of the empty cab swung open. A second later the door to our own cab swung open as well.

"Hurry up!" Kidron shouted over the din of the street sellers. "Before the rickshaw enters the alley!"

Lukas quickly leaped into the empty cab. I jumped in after him, closely followed by Hexe, so closely, in fact, that both of us were knocked to the floor of the carriage.

I rolled over to find myself pinned under Hexe, my limbs tangled with his, staring up into those amazing, catlike eyes. The feel of his weight resting against my body made my skin flush and other, less public, parts of me tingle. I looked down and realized a six-fingered hand was planted firmly on my right breast.

"Do you mind?"

"Oops! Sorry!" Hexe yanked his hand away as if my boob were a red-hot stove. "I didn't mean to, um, you know . . . um . . ."

"Cop a feel?" I suggested helpfully as I rearranged my clothes. I climbed off the floor and peered out the window after Kidron, who continued to forge through the congested alleyway. Ninety seconds later the rickshaw bearing Boss Marz's goon pushed its way past us in dogged pursuit of the empty cab. The rider didn't even glance in our direction. We were home free.

Morale was high as we returned to the boardinghouse. We joked among ourselves about how stupid the Malandanti following us had been. I could tell by the way he laughed that a great weight had been lifted from Lukas's shoulders. All of that came to a crashing halt the moment we arrived home and saw the one-armed man walking up to our doorstep.

"Oh, shit. Do you see what I see?" I hissed.

The smile on Lukas's face dissolved instantly. "That's it. I'm doomed!"

"Remember what I said about getting upset about things that haven't happened yet," Hexe said in a steady, reassuring voice. "Dr. Mao told me that the Malandanti were going to *every* healer in Golgotham looking for you. That would include me." He fished his BlackBerry out of his pocket and began typing. "I'm texting Wildfire to keep moving and let me out around the corner. She'll go around the block a couple of times until I get rid of him. Everything will be okay."

As we passed the boardinghouse, I could hear the one-armed man rapping on the front door. I realized for the first time that he was missing his right arm. I glanced over at Lukas. He looked worried but did not seem as fearful as before. I wondered if he was thinking about Meikei and if those thoughts were giving him newfound strength.

Wildfire rounded the corner and stopped to let Hexe out. Before exiting the carriage, he turned to address us. "I'll give this guy the brush-off as fast as possible. But if it turns out bad, I want you two to get out of here, you understand? Tell Wildfire to take you to my mother. You'll both be safe with her."

As I watched Hexe leave the cab, the thought of him confronting Boss Marz's goon on his own made my guts feel as heavy as a length of anchor chain. I was already out of the cab and halfway down the street before I realized what I was doing.

"Wait a minute—I'm coming with you."

Hexe stopped and turned to face me. I expected him to be displeased, but, instead, he merely smiled.

"Are you sure you really want to do this?"

"No. But I'm damned sure not going to be left behind just to worry about you."

"Very well," he said. He pointed to Lukas, who was watching us from the cab. "What about our young friend?"

"Lukas is a big boy. You can ride in a cab by yourself, can't you?"

The were-cougar nodded his head.

"And you know what to do if the shit hits the fan, right?"

Lukas shook his head and grimaced, an alarmed look on his face.

"Relax, kid," I whispered. "That just means 'when things go wrong.'"

"Oh! In that case, yes, I know what to do," Lukas replied with a sigh of relief.

As Hexe and I walked up to the house, the one-armed goon was still standing on the front stoop. He had taken a couple of steps back and was staring up at the second story. It both creeped me out and pissed me off that he was staring at the windows of my apartment.

Hexe took a deep breath and then plastered a smile on his face. It was the same one he had used to greet Mr. Ottershaw.

"Hello—!" he called out. "Are you looking for someone?"

The one-armed man turned to glare at us. The cotton-candy pink hair did nothing to soften the brutal lines of his face. The smell radiating from him was equal parts licorice and fish oil. I almost gagged.

"Are you Hexe?" he growled.

"Yes."

"Then I am looking for you."

Hexe nodded at the Malandanti's missing arm. "Have you come to me for healing?"

"I don't need healing from you," he replied curtly. "My name is Nach. I'm here in the service of Boss Marz."

"I see. And what does Boss Marz want from me?"

"He wishes to know if you have treated a young male were-cougar in the last few days."

Hexe raised an eyebrow in mock surprise. "What would a *were-cougar* be doing in Golgotham?"

"Just answer the question." Nach scowled. "Have you treated one or not?"

"No," Hexe lied. "I have not."

The Malandanti soldier reached into the breast pocket of his suit jacket and took out a business card. "If one comes to you, or should you hear of someone harboring such a creature, call this number," he said, shoving the card into Hexe's hand. "Boss Marz is offering a handsome reward for any information leading to the capture of the beast."

"And what if I elect *not* to call?" Hexe replied, holding the business card by its edge like a soiled tissue.

"You don't want to do that," Nach said grimly. "It

would be bad for you." He shot me a look that made me feel as though a hungry crocodile were sizing me up. "*All* of you."

The smile disappeared from Hexe's face as if Nach had slapped it off. "I don't like it when people threaten my friends," he said, his gaze as hard and menacing as that of Marz's goon. "Do you know who you're addressing?"

"The Malandanti fears no one in Golgotham, be they peasant or prince," Nach replied flatly as he pushed his way past us. "That includes you, Serenity. You would do well to remember that."

Chapter 12

After our visit to Dr. Mao's apothecary shop, Hexe kept the drapes pulled and warned Lukas against looking out the windows, day or night. The poor kid probably would have gone stir-crazy, if not for Meikei.

Every day the young were-tigress would arrive with a specially prepared medicinal meal designed to help purge the silver from his body and speed up his physical recovery. Sometimes she brought baby pigeon stew garnished with huang qi, or crocodile soup served with braised mutton, all washed down with Flowering Dragon Eye Tea. No matter what the ingredients, Lukas eagerly consumed each and every dish without a moment's complaint—as long as Meikei agreed to sit on the corner of his bed and watch him eat.

Being a proper young lady, Meikei insisted that the door to Lukas's room remain open the whole time and that they be overseen by a chaperone. Needless to say, Scratch was less than thrilled with having to play shepherd to their budding teen romance.

One day, after spending another lunch in the young

couple's company, the familiar sauntered into my room and hopped onto my workbench. When he wasn't guarding Lukas, the familiar would come into my room and watch me work. He claimed the sparks from my welding gear and the smell of hot metal reminded him of home.

"I hate watching Garfield and Hello Kitty make goo-goo eyes at each other," he grumbled. "It's enough to make me yack up a hairball."

"You don't have hair," I reminded him.

"I didn't say it had to be *my* hair, nump," the familiar replied, flashing me a toothy grin.

In the weeks since we first met, Scratch had become increasingly social toward me—although I wouldn't go so far as to call it "friendly," which is to say that while I no longer feared being eaten alive, he wasn't above insulting me.

"How long have you been with Hexe?"

"Since he was a child," Scratch replied, his tone suddenly cautious. "Why do you ask?"

"I was just wondering if you might know why the other Kymerans call him 'Serenity'?"

"Ask him yourself," the familiar replied curtly, and refused to say anything else for the rest of the day.

Although I was curious, I decided not to press the issue. It was clear from the way Hexe reacted to the charm peddler in Witch Alley that he was uncomfortable with whatever connotations the word held for him. I decided it would be better if I let him explain in his own time, instead of pressuring him. Since we lived under the same roof, I could afford to be patient.

One night I was working late on one of my sculptures for the gallery show. I was in "the zone"—where I focused so intently on what I was working on the rest of the world ceased to exist for me. When I was zoning, hours could pass by without my knowing it. In fact, the only reason I finally set aside my tools was because it felt like a bear was gnawing my belly. As I looked at the clock, I was startled to realize that it was well past midnight. No wonder my stomach was growling—I hadn't eaten since breakfast!

The house was quiet as I left my room and headed downstairs to raid the kitchen.

Hexe had left earlier in the evening to consult with a client, and had yet to return, while Lukas had long since turned in for the night, Scratch curled up at the foot of his bed.

I opened the fridge and carefully scanned the shelves. One of the first things I did upon moving into the boardinghouse was buy a bunch of plastic containers and write my name on them, so I could tell my food from Hexe's. While Kymeran cuisine was nowhere as bad as legend would have it, it *was* something of an acquired taste. I might have *joked* about being hungry enough to eat a horse, but that didn't mean I wanted to chow down on pony goulash.

I located a bag of deli meat, gathered up some condiments, dragged a loaf of whole grain from the bread box, and proceeded to slap together a sandwich on the kitchen counter. I stuck the finished product into the toaster-oven, in order to get the cheese all melty the way I liked it, and then headed back to the icebox to score myself a beer.

As I closed the fridge, bottle in hand, I had the weirdest feeling that I was being watched. I looked over my shoulder and was startled to discover that the door leading to the cellar was standing wide-open. I gasped in alarm, the beer slipping from my grasp, upon seeing the silhouette of a man at the top of the stairs. There was an angry hiss as the beer bottle's contents started to squirt from under the cap, spraying the linoleum with foam.

"I *knew* that was going to happen," the shadowy figure said, speaking with a doleful, midwestern drawl. "I'm sorry if I frightened you, ma'am. Let me clean that up for you."

I took a cautious step backward, unsure whether I should grab a kitchen knife or hand him a roll of paper towels. As I moved back, the stranger stepped forward, revealing himself to be an old, and I mean *old*, man.

"Who the hell are you?" I asked as I handed him the paper towels. "And what are you doing in my—I mean—Hexe's cellar?"

"My name is of little consequence," the old man replied. "I have been called Mr. Manto, in the past. You may call me that, if it suits you. As for what I am doing in the cellar: I live there."

As he spoke, I recalled Hexe's telling me that there was at least one other boarder in the house, one I would probably never have occasion to meet.

My fellow housemate was older than anyone I'd ever seen before, his long face weighted by heavy folds of wrinkles about the mouth and eyes. What hair he still had was the color of dirty snow, gathered about his ears and the nape of his neck. His exposed scalp was dappled with liver spots, as were the tops of his hands. It was clear from the way he stood, slightly stooped with rounded shoulders, that he had once been tall as a younger man.

He was dressed in a pair of baggy olive green trousers, held up by old-fashioned leather braces, and a plain, rumpled white shirt with a dark, narrow tie. Over this he wore a cable-knit cardigan the color of oatmeal, the elbows of which were sewn with well-worn brown suede patches. On his feet he wore a pair of tasseled leather house slippers.

As Mr. Manto soaked up the spilled beer with the paper towels, I stared at his hands and saw that his fingers were swollen from arthritis—I also noticed that there were ten of them instead of twelve.

"You're not a Kymeran." It was more an observation than a question.

"You are correct. I am, technically, human," he replied evenly. As he struggled to stand up, I grasped his elbow, helping him to his feet. "Although I may not be a witch or a wizard, I *am* a soothsayer. The last of a very long line, to be exact."

"You've been living in the basement all this time? How come I've never seen you before?"

"My apartment is self-contained. Everything I need is down there. It has its own entrance. In fact, this is the first time I have been upstairs in three decades."

"So what are you doing here, then?"

"Because you need your fortune told," he replied simply. "That, and I must borrow some cream. I seem to have run out."

I followed Mr. Manto down the cellar stairs to have my fortune told. The old man went ahead of me, carrying in one hand the carton of half-and-half I had given him. I didn't particularly want to know what lay ahead in my future, but there wasn't any point in arguing with the elderly soothsayer. He had seen a vision of himself reading my fortune, and, by damn, he was going to make sure it came to pass.

"You're not from here, are you?" I asked.

"Do you mean Golgotham or New York City?"

"Both."

"You are an astute young lady," Mr. Manto said with a dry chuckle. "I was originally born in Missouri, the 'Show Me' state; ironic, considering that I'm supposedly descended from Tiresias, the blind prophet of Thebes. I traveled quite a bit as a younger man, before finally settling here, but I consider Golgotham to be my home now."

Upon reaching the bottom of the stairs, I saw that the basement was divided into two sections. To the left was an old boiler that squatted in its corner like a household god, behind which lurked a mare's nest of fuse boxes and electrical wiring, some of which looked like it dated back to Thomas Edison. Opposite the boiler was a tall, narrow door painted a bilious shade of green, which led to Mr. Manto's apartment.

The elderly oracle gestured for me to enter ahead of him. Upon opening the door, I was greeted by the smell of moldering paper, yellowing newsprint, and fading ink. Mr. Manto's apartment was as large as my own, possibly even bigger, but it was hard to tell since virtually every square inch of space was given over to the printed word in all its various forms.

Bookshelves not only lined the walls but divided up the room, creating narrow corridors that zigzagged back and forth like livestock chutes in a stockyard. Every table and chair was covered by a jumble of old magazines, comic books, and newspapers. Stalagmites of stacked books as tall as a man dotted the remaining open floor space.

As Mr. Manto closed the door behind us, he called out in a surprisingly high-pitched, almost girlish voice.

"Daddy's back, my babies! Daddy brought you some delicious cream, just as he promised!"

There was the sound of books toppling and newspapers being scattered as the members of a horde of previously unseen cats emerged from their various hiding places within the overflowing shelves and teetering stacks. Mewling piteously, they hurried forward to greet Mr. Manto, running in and out between his shins like little furry eels. Within seconds, six felines were gathered at his feet.

"Now, now—don't be such a bitch, Isis," Mr. Manto said, wagging an arthritic finger at the Siamese as it arched its back and hissed at one of its fellows. "There's plenty for everyone." He turned to me and smiled apologetically. "Gracious! Where are my manners? Allow me to introduce you to my little family. These are the twins, Comus and Momus," he said, pointing to a pair of black Persians. "The tabby over there is Bacchus. You've already met Isis—that Oriental shorthair is her son by Bacchus, Endymion. . . ."

"So you named your cats in honor of the gods?"

"Gracious, no!" he laughed. "They're all named after Mardi Gras krewes. I lived in New Orleans for a while before relocating to Golgotham." He bent down to pat the head of the massive Maine coon rubbing against his leg. "And this fat rascal is Rex. Say hello to the nice lady, Your Majesty." The tomcat meeped in response, its voice surprisingly tiny for what had to be a thirty-pound feline. "Once I get you settled in the receiving room and feed my babies, we can get started with your reading."

As I followed Mr. Manto and his furry entourage, I glanced at the bookcases I walked past, curious as to their contents. I expected to find them lined with antique books bound in leather with metal hasps and gold leaf pages. Instead, the shelves were crowded with cheap paperbacks, cookbooks, self-help manuals, outdated encyclopedias, and top-ten bestsellers.

Eventually we reached what Mr. Manto referred to as his "receiving room," basically a couple of easy chairs arranged about a coffee table, the surface of which was lost under a drift of loose papers.

"Please make yourself comfortable, my dear," he said, gesturing to one of the chairs. "I'll be back in a minute." Mr. Manto promptly disappeared behind a chintz curtain that separated his kitchen from the rest of the living space, his cats following after him, their tails held erect in anticipation of a fresh treat.

I moved a pile of dictionaries out of the chair and sat down, staring at the stacks of books that surrounded me. If there was any system as to how they were shelved, it was beyond my ability to recognize it.

A few seconds later Mr. Manto returned carrying a tray on which rested a plain white ceramic teapot and a single cup. Seating himself in the chair opposite mine, he unceremoniously pushed the mound of paper off the coffee table and onto the floor.

"You may have noticed that my tea service has only one cup. I assure you it's not because I'm an absent-minded old man or a bad host," he said drolly. "It's because this particular tea is the trigger for my visions. It is brewed from diviner's sage."

"You have to trip to see the future?" I frowned.

"I am not doing anything unethical, I assure you. It has always been necessary for human oracles to be intoxicated before they prophesize," Mr. Manto explained. "Unlike Kymerans, human soothsayers cannot pierce the veil of the supernatural without help, no matter how great our Sight. The sibyls of Delphi breathed the ethylene fumes that arose from a crack in the temple floor and chewed laurel leaves in order to see their visions. I merely follow in the footsteps of my ancestors."

He lifted the teapot and carefully poured a greenish brown liquid into his cup. "I knew from my own vision that you would be coming, so I brewed some earlier."

"It must be handy to know things like that in advance," I said.

Mr. Manto looked at me over the rim of the cup, his eyes filled with unwanted wisdom. "Tell that to Cassandra," he grunted.

Having downed his special tea, the soothsayer leaned back in his chair. The deep lines about his mouth gradually relaxed as his eyes lost their focus and grew cloudy. He fished around in the pocket of his cardigan and pulled out a Nano in a bright pink Hello Kitty case, which he popped into a portable iPod dock sitting on the table. Within seconds Mozart's *Lacrimosa Requiem* filled the room.

As if on cue, Mr. Manto rose from his easy chair, eyes still fogged, and walked over to one of the bookcases from which he pulled out a paperback romance. He opened the novel without looking at it, ripped out a page, and then returned the book to the shelf. He then went over to another bookcase and grabbed a cookbook and did the exact same thing. He repeated his actions five more times, defacing a children's book, a porno mag, a back issue of *Cat Fancy*, a Stephen King novel, and a volume from a set of encyclopedias.

The soothsayer returned to his chair and tore the individual pages in half, then ripped the halves into quarters, and then tore them again into eighths. He dumped the shredded pages into a small metal wastebasket and stirred the contents with one gnarled hand.

Muttering under his breath, he closed his eyes and reached into the trash can, pulling out individual scraps of paper, which he placed on the recently cleared surface of the coffee table. After several minutes of arranging the bits of paper, his eyes still closed, he fell back into the arms of his easy chair, a look of exhaustion on his long face.

"Is it done?" I asked.

Mr. Manto nodded his head wearily.

"What does it say?"

The aged oracle fished a pair of horn-rimmed glasses from the pocket of his cardigan and slid them onto his nose. He leaned forward, peering down through his bifocals at the cut-up prophecy arranged before him.

"Rise shall a fire-born army forged of woman to the bestiarii free," he read aloud in a stentorian monotone. "Drown will the streets the usurped in blood no mercy for his flesh show. From two will be one turned three. The hand is in the mind."

"What the hell does *that* mean?"

The soothsayer looked up from his reading, a surprised look on his face. "You don't understand it?"

"Of course not! Why can't you just tell me what you saw?"

"It's not that simple, my dear." He sighed. "I can remember the visions that involve me, such as the one where I saw us meeting upstairs. But once the trance is broken, I cannot recall what I beheld in the future of others. Don't worry—I'm sure it will all become clear to you when the moment arrives. Whether you understand it in time for it to do you any good is another matter, though."

*   *   *

I bid the old soothsayer good night and left him to his cats. I returned to my room and went to bed, but I had a hard time getting to sleep. While I wasn't entirely confident in Mr. Manto's skills as a fortune-teller, I couldn't help but be concerned by the prophecy he had pieced together. I definitely heard him say "fire," "army," "drown," and "blood." Those were not words *anyone* wanted to hear in regard to his or her future.

Chapter 13

"Just hold that pose a couple of more minutes, and I'll be done," I said, glancing up from my sketchbook at Lukas. I was busy drawing my newest housemate au naturel—in his four-legged form, not the nude, that is.

Being chased through the garden maze by a humanoid cat hadn't simply been a traumatic personal episode and an unlikely introduction to a new friend. It had also proved a source of inspiration for my art.

I had finished two of the three new pieces I had agreed to deliver to Derrick for the opening. The first two were individual sculptures that combined to re-create Rodin's *The Kiss*. But when it came to the third sculpture, I found myself stumped. I *knew* I wanted it to be a female form, but I was leery of offering up yet another reinterpretation of the Venus de Milo.

After my midnight run through the garden maze, it occurred to me that I should do another "paired" sculpture, like *The Kiss*. This time, though, instead of simply doing two human figures, one of them would be that of an animal. That was how I came to re-create von Dannecker's *Ariadne on the Panther* using transmission parts, steel tubing, and sheet metal.

Lukas agreed to serve as my live model, as he saw it as a way to make up for the less than ideal circumstances under which we first met. I saw it as an unparalleled chance to get an up-close and personal look at the musculature of a big cat like a panther without dealing with zoo personnel or certain death. While watching Lukas transition from outwardly normal teenager to mountain lion and back again was unnerving at times, it was considerably less terrifying than having Scratch pose in his demon aspect.

"Okay, you can turn back now," I said.

Lukas grunted in relief and reared back onto his hind legs. He snatched up his house robe and wrapped it about himself before he finished his transformation.

"Let me see," he said eagerly. "I've never had anyone draw my picture before!"

"I'm not that great when it comes to line drawing," I explained as I showed him my sketchbook. "My real skill is with the welding torch. Wait until you see the finished product. You'll actually be able to move the hip joints, and the tail will be fully articulated. . . ."

"I think you draw beautifully," Lukas replied as he studied the sketches of his cat form.

"No offense, kid, but you've never seen *real* art before."

"That may be true," he admitted, "but it still doesn't change my opinion of your work. I can't wait to see the finished piece!"

"Me, too. But first I have to find the materials to make it. I normally order parts from this guy I know in Williamsburg who used to play in a punk band. I called him yesterday to put in my order, and I found out he's sold his auto repair business to go on tour. The new owner said it's going to take three weeks just to get the transmission. I can't wait that long."

I spent the next couple of hours making calls to various automotive supply houses, but kept running into brick walls. Most of them refused to deal with an individual, as opposed to a licensed mechanic, or they only handled rebuilds. I tried to explain that a rebuilt transmission was of no use to me, as I had to be sure it was in perfect working condition before I disassembled it for my own use. You could literally hear the crickets chirping on the other end of the line as I told them what I wanted to use the transmission for. I finally tracked down a supplier in Red Hook who was willing to sell me what I needed, but he balked when he found out it had to be delivered to Golgotham.

By the time I finished with that last call, I was so mad I could spit nails. I decided the only thing left for me to do was drown my sorrows in some ice cream. I stomped downstairs and took the brand-new half gallon out of the freezer and fished a tablespoon out of the dish rack. I contemplated spooning the ice cream into its own bowl, then said, "Screw it," and started eating it right out of the carton.

Hexe entered the kitchen a few minutes later, only to halt upon seeing me attacking a helpless carton of chocolate-strawberry-cheesecake.

"What's wrong?" he asked.

"What makes you think something's wrong?" I mumbled around the tablespoon in my mouth.

"You're eating ice cream. You eat ice cream only when you're pissed off."

"I've lived here long enough for you to notice that?"

I asked, surprised that he'd picked up on that particular quirk so quickly. It took Roger six months to make that connection.

"Time flies, doesn't it? So what's the problem?"

"I'm having trouble finding a transmission to use for my final sculpture. I put in a call to my previous supplier, but he's out of business and everyone else is either giving me the runaround or refuses to deliver to this part of town. I've got to get my hands on one ASAP."

"Have you tried the Fly Market?"

"Why would I go there?" I frowned. "It's just weird food, magical stuff, and tacky tourist crap."

"The Fly Market is more than a place to buy centaur tack and cow brain tacos. If you know where to look—and whom to ask for—you can find anything you might possibly need underneath its roof."

"I take it you know whom to ask?"

Hexe nodded. "His name is Quid. He's my go-to guy for some of the harder-to-find ingredients I need in my business."

"Do you think he can find a transmission?"

"Let me put it this way: If Quid can't find one for you, *no one* can."

Since Quid didn't usually offer his services to humans, and Hexe was running low on pukeweed and screech owl blood anyway, he offered to accompany me to the Fly Market and introduce me to his buddy. It was a beautiful autumn afternoon in the city—the sky was clear, the sun was out—so we decided to skip the hansom cab trip and walk there instead.

As we headed toward the East River, I found myself surrounded by romance. Not the kind you find in soppy love stories or Julia Roberts movies, but the genuine romance of old New York, with its narrow streets and dark alleys, old buildings, hidden cemeteries, and ancient pubs. Unlike the rest of the city, which had been gradually modernized over the centuries, it was still possible to walk the streets of Golgotham and be certain that what I was seeing remained unchanged since the War of 1812. I was steeped in history, no matter where I looked.

As we crossed Water, Beekman Street became Mariner Lane. With the change in name came a noticeable increase in foot traffic. Processions of wagons drawn by Clydesdale-sized centaurs, each one wearing a Teamsters cap, jammed the cobblestone street leading down to the river. As we drew closer, I caught the scent of the East River on the breeze; it was strong, fishy, and deep. Within seconds of smelling the river, I saw the market itself.

Despite the jokes, the Fly Market wasn't named after the insects that buzzed around the stalls; it was actually a corruption of the Dutch word for "valley." Although it had grown and mutated since it was first opened in the eighteenth century, it remained the oldest public marketplace still in operation in the entire city.

The Fly Market was housed in an industrial Gothic loggia fashioned of brick and iron that occupied an entire city block, stretching along the quay from Mariner Lane to Perdition Street. The Brooklyn Bridge loomed above it all in the near distance, like an arcane tower raised to appease some nameless river god.

Whereas other such open-air markets in the city offered meat and produce for sale, the Fly Market sold not only the freshest comestibles suited for the Kymeran palate, but it also provided the raw materials needed in the unique commerce practiced by the denizens of Golgotham. Need a new crystal ball? A fresh deck of tarot cards? Looking for mummy dust or powdered unicorn horn to complete a certain potion? Then the Fly Market was sure to have it. It was also the biggest tourist attraction in Golgotham. Every year hundreds of thousands of human tourists flocked there to experience a taste of the "otherworldly" and bring back a souvenir of their visit to "the strangest neighborhood in America."

We approached the market from the Mariner Lane side, ascended the steps, and passed across the corner, where bleeding sides of beef and split hogs hung alongside butchered camels and dressed-out ostrich. Then we descended into the cavernous gallery of the market's interior, which was uninterrupted by walls of any kind and open to the elements via huge, vaulted doorways big enough to drive a forklift through. Underneath its twenty-five-foot-high ceiling were thousands of individual stalls, each of which boasted some kind of garishly painted banner advertising its wares, reminiscent of the old Coney Island freak show. Above each booth hung a ball of witchfire suspended in midair, which provided the only illumination within the building, save for what natural light managed to filter in through skylights set high in the ceiling.

Everywhere I looked, business was being transacted at a furious pace. The aisles of the market were crowded with a mixture of locals and tourists, and the noise created by the endless shuffle of the crowd passing to and fro was as unceasing as the sound of surf crashing on a beach. Boxes and crates were wrenched open, their contents strewed about haphazardly while the stall keepers bellowed orders to their subordinates at the top of their lungs.

I hastily jumped out of the way as a spider the size of

a blue crab scampered along the concrete floor, only to be scooped up and dropped back into one of the many barrels lining the front of a nearby stall. Glancing inside, I saw a confused mass of writhing giant arachnids viciously attacking one another, and I quickly looked away.

As I walked past a booth crowded with charmed bits of bric-a-brac, a pair of little jade fu dogs set to either side of a glass-domed clock turned to watch me pass. Farther down the same aisle, I stopped to study the collection of bottled djinns available for sale. I picked up a pale hexagonal bottle with an elaborate ceramic stopper sealed in wax from a magic candle and stared at the elemental trapped within. The creature was made of flame, with blazing fingertips and sparks in its hair, dressed in a gown of blazing opaline. It capered about inside its container, like a puppy eager to find a new home. I shook my head and put the bottle back where I found it.

Another stall nearby displayed a miniature gravel garden where dozens of black chickens scratched for a living like so many investment bankers. Across from it was a booth with a banner that read LIVE BLACK GOATS FOR SALE. Farther down was a stall that sold beeswax for creating magic candles, while another hawked scrying-quality crystals in their uncut state. Another stall sold designer-label knockoffs scaled down to accommodate leprechauns and other members of the "wee folk."

A Kymeran woman, her face covered by a black lace veil sewn with occult symbols, sat in her booth and carefully applied the last coat of wax to the severed hand of a hanged man so that she could sell it as a Hand of Glory. As we passed, she paused in her work long enough to bow her head to Hexe, who nodded in return without slowing his step.

"Do you know that woman?" I asked.

"No," he replied.

"Then why did she nod at you?"

"Because *she* knows *me*."

I was about to ask Hexe what he meant by that last statement when the smell of deep-fried food brought me to a dead halt. I stopped to investigate the source of the delicious aroma, which proved to be a stall with a sign advertising GATOR ON A STICK.

The vendor, a Kymeran woman who smelled of lily, rose, and sandalwood and wore her lilac-colored hair in a towering bouffant, took a length of alligator sausage and rammed a ten-inch wooden dowel down its length and immersed it in corn-dog batter. Once it was thoroughly coated, she dipped the gator-on-a-stick into a fryer full of smoking oil for several minutes, until it was a deep golden brown. She then dropped it into a cardboard tray, accompanied by a packet of mustard, and handed it to me in exchange for a five-dollar bill. Upon biting into the crunchy coating that shrouded the reptile meat, I was reminded of spicy Cajun boudin—and chicken, of course. Delicious.

As I enjoyed my snack, I scanned the vast interior of the market, only to have my heart skip a beat upon catching sight of a familiar-looking head of cotton-candy pink hair. I looked again and saw the Malandanti called Nach slowly moving through the crowd. He was still dressed in the same ill-fitting dark suit, but this time the right sleeve of his jacket no longer hung empty. The goon was carefully studying his surroundings, glowering at stall keepers and passersby alike, as if on the lookout for suspicious activity.

"What's he doing here?" I asked, pointing in Nach's direction with what was left of my gator-on-a-stick. "And how'd he grow his arm back?"

"He's here as a bodyguard to Boss Marz." Hexe scowled. "Today must be tribute day."

I looked again and realized that Nach was walking a couple steps behind and to one side of a burly man wearing a duster-length camel hair coat dyed deepest black. I recognized Boss Marz from the glimpse of him I had seen in the scrying crystal, when Lukas had shown us his story. He was built like a bear walking on its hind legs and, like the bear, he moved with a heavy grace. His shoulders were wide and he had a barrel chest, as well as oxblood-colored hair, which he wore in a pompadour. The rings on all twelve fingers of his hands flashed like heat lightning in the glow from the witchfires.

Riding on the crime lord's broad left shoulder was a little squirrel monkey dressed in a tiny red velvet vest with an even tinier matching fez atop its head. Sucker that I am, I thought it was cute.

As I watched, Boss Marz strolled up to a stall that sold elaborately embroidered caparisons. The vendor, an older centaur with a dappled beard, smiled nervously and placed a manila business envelope on the counter between them. Suddenly the monkey riding Marz's shoulder gave a fierce screech and leaped down, sending the goods on display flying in every direction. The tiny primate snatched up the packet and scampered back to its master, who exchanged the envelope for a pistachio.

"The Malandanti own the waterfront of Golgotham," Hexe explained, not bothering to hide the disgust in his voice. "If you want to operate a business in the Fly Market or the surrounding area, you must pay a tribute to Boss Marz for the privilege of doing so. Come, I've already purchased what I need. Let's go see Quid."

The stall we were looking for was on the Perdition Street side of the market, and had a banner that boasted, in Renaissance Fair–style lettering, QUID'S PRO QUO: GETTING ANYTHING FOR ANYONE EVERY TIME SINCE 1989. Behind the counter stood a completely bald Kymeran with a pair of lime green eyebrows that resembled fuzzy caterpillars.

"Hello, Quid. How's business?" Hexe asked as he clasped his friend's hand.

"Passing fair, I don't mind saying," the vendor replied. "You just stop by to chew the fat, or you looking for something in particular?"

"It's not me," Hexe explained. "My friend here is the one in the market."

Quid studied me for a long moment as he thoughtfully stroked his right eyebrow. He smelled pleasingly of papaya, jasmine, and green tea, with eyes that matched what facial hair he had left. "Human, eh? Are you a psychic, my dear?"

"No. I'm an artist. Hexe said you might be able to help me, but I'm not so sure. . . ."

"Don't you worry about that! I assure you there's nothing ol' Quid can't hunt down."

"I need an automobile transmission. And it has to be brand-new. I can't use something that's been rebuilt."

Quid nodded his head, still stroking his eyebrow. "I see. Any particular make or model?"

"I just need it to be a passenger car transmission. As long as it's in perfect working condition, I don't care if it's for a Ferrari or a Hyundai. And I need it delivered within three days. Think you can do it?"

"Easy-peasy," Quid assured me. "As to the matter of my fee . . ."

"I'm willing to pay up to four thousand, cash," I said, reaching for my purse.

"You misunderstand me, Miss—?" Quid's left eyebrow crawled halfway up his head as he waited for me to supply the needed information.

"Tate."

"I do not traffic in goods, Miss Tate. As my banner proudly states, this is 'Quid's Pro Quo.' I am a dealer of favors." He tapped his temple with an index finger. "Inside my brain is a database of who owes a favor for what, for how long, and to what magnitude. Thanks to this bartering system, I have not paid hard coin for food, drink, clothing, or housing since I was a boy."

"Let me get this straight—you don't want money?"

"You are correct. Mine is a cash-free business."

"Then what do you want in exchange?"

"Are you a mechanic, perhaps?"

I shook my head. "No. But I'm a skilled welder."

"Excellent!" Quid said, clapping his hands in delight. "Do you have your own tools?"

"Of course."

That particular bit of news made him practically giddy. "Even better! You'll make an excellent addition to my phone tree. All I require is that should I call upon your services in the future, that you ask no questions and respond no matter what, even if it means rising up from your deathbed."

"I don't have to sign anything in blood, do I?" I asked cautiously.

"Of course not," Quid assured me, spitting into his palm. "We'll just shake on it."

"Agreed," I said, spitting into my own hand as I grasped his. His grip was oddly trustworthy.

"Now that everything's settled between us, let me put

in a couple of calls, and I'll be able to give you an exact delivery time." Quid pulled a BlackBerry out of his breast pocket and started paging through his contacts list in search of the right numbers.

"Are you sure this guy can come through with the goods?" I asked, whispering behind my hand so Quid wouldn't overhear.

"You've got nothing to worry about," Hexe assured me. "Quid is the only person I know who could loan someone a cigarette lighter at breakfast and end up owed a yacht by dinnertime."

Suddenly there was a distinctly sharp, metallic smell, like that of a scorched saucepan, accompanied by a voice that was deep and smooth, yet somehow threatening, like caramel poured over the blade of a knife.

"Good afternoon, Hexe. I did not expect to see you here today."

Boss Marz loomed over me, his shadow sending me into partial eclipse. Underneath his coat he wore a bespoke Armani suit, tailored to accommodate his prodigious frame. He had a sardonic smile on his face and was clearly taking sadistic delight in forcing Hexe to acknowledge his presence.

"Good day, Marz," Hexe said reluctantly.

"That's *Boss* Marz to you," Nach snarled, taking a half step forward.

Marz calmly held up a beringed hand and waved his bodyguard back. "Now, now, Nach! Since Hexe and I have known each other for a *very* long time, I consider us on a first-name basis." Suddenly his massive head swiveled in my direction, like a tyrannosaurus spotting a trembling mouse hiding amid the ferns at its feet. "Ah! And who might *this* lovely young lady be?"

"Never you mind," Hexe replied curtly, forcing the

crime lord's attention back toward him. "What do you want, Marz?"

"Want?" Boss Marz affected a wounded expression, as if Hexe's question had cut him to the quick. "Why, Bonzo and I merely wished to stop by and say hello. Isn't that right, Bonzo?" The monkey riding his shoulder nodded and clicked his teeth, as if attempting speech. "There's nothing wrong with that, is there?"

"I see your flunky seems to have grown his arm back," Hexe said, pointing at Nach. "Mind telling me how you managed to pull that one off?"

Boss Marz's nasty little smile returned. "Nach is a valued member of my organization. So I arranged for your uncle to construct a prosthetic. Dr. Moot handled the reattachment. Nach, be kind enough to show Hexe your new arm."

The Malandanti pushed the sleeve of his jacket past his gloved right hand, revealing a gleaming metal forearm that seemed to be composed of stainless steel scale mail as seamless as fish skin.

"Most impressive," Hexe said grudgingly, his curiosity momentarily overcoming his distaste. "My uncle has outdone himself, yet again. Is it functional?"

"See for yourself," Boss Marz replied.

"Good as new," Nach said as he rotated his wrist, clenching and unclenching his fingers. "Maybe even better."

"Nach lost the original to a crazed bastet," Boss Marz explained, watching Hexe's face as he spoke. "One that takes the form of a cougar. You wouldn't know anything about such a creature, would you?"

"Your croggy here already asked me about that," Hexe replied coldly. "The answer hasn't changed."

"So you say," Marz said evenly. "But I cannot help but notice that one of the packages you're carrying is marked 'pukeweed.' Isn't that used in poultices in order to draw silver from a wound?"

I swallowed hard, worried Hexe might respond to Boss Marz's prodding, but his demeanor remained outwardly frosty. I, on the other hand, was ready to plotz.

"Ma'am, I can get that to you by tomorrow afternoon. Where do you want it delivered?"

I turned to see Quid standing behind the counter of his stall, waiting for me to respond.

"Have them deliver it to my address," Hexe answered quickly.

This time the look of surprise on Boss Marz's face seemed genuine. "You've rented to a *nump*? Does your uncle know about this?"

"All the hells and all their devils can take my uncle!" Hexe snapped, his eyes flashing angrily. "And I certainly don't have to answer questions from *you*!" He grabbed my arm, hurrying me away as fast as he could. "Come along, Tate!"

"Too bad you have to leave so soon," the crime lord called after us, his deep voice booming across the marketplace. "Be sure to give your mother my love!"

Hexe didn't let go of my arm until we exited the Fly Market on the Perdition Street side. "Sorry about grabbing you like that," he apologized, "but I had to get us away from Marz as quickly as possible."

"I understand." I rubbed my forearms, trying to chase away the goose bumps that close proximity to Boss Marz had given me. "Man, is that guy creepy."

"He's not creepy—he's evil," Hexe said darkly. "Boss Marz is a parasite feeding on the Kymeran people—and anyone else who calls Golgotham home."

"Do you think he knows about Lukas?" I whispered.

"He suspects me on general principles." Hexe shrugged. "He knows I don't fear him."

We walked down the steps, passing the different stalls that clustered about the open square on the Perdition Street side of the market, most of which seemed to cater to the tourist trade instead of the locals. One stall sold the ubiquitous I ♥ GOLGOTHAM T-shirts. Another vendor hawked snow globe paperweights with tiny replicas of the Gate of Skulls inside. Yet another enterprising merchant had a centaur painted onto a wooden board with a hole cut out so tourists could stick their heads through and get their photographs taken for five dollars a pop.

As we walked past a booth selling various kinds of tarot cards, a woman's voice loudly proclaimed, "Look who the familiar dragged in! Where are you going in such a hurry, Serenity? Don't you have time to say hello?"

Hexe stopped and turned to face the owner of the booth, a well-endowed Kymeran woman with long, moss green hair coiled atop her head like a living turban. Her eyes were pale gray, and she smelled of bergamot, white orchid, and sandalwood. She was dressed in the female equivalent of the traditional "coat of many colors," a patchwork skirt stitched together from dozens of scraps of brightly printed fabric, which marked her as a Kymeran with magic for sale.

"Hello, Dori," Hexe said in a politely reserved voice. "I'm sorry. I didn't see you standing there."

"Of *course* you didn't," she replied sarcastically. "So, *that's* the reason you haven't been returning my calls?" Dori asked, giving a curt nod in my direction.

Suddenly everything I thought I knew about Hexe, and assumed about our relationship, disappeared out from under my feet. The last time I'd been caught so badly off balance was when I came back to my loft after visiting my grandparents in Florida and walked in on Roger banging some secretary from Jersey he'd picked up at a bar.

"You know perfectly well why I stopped taking your calls," Hexe replied coldly. "And it has nothing to do with my friend here."

"I'm not going to starve just so you can keep to your precious 'ideals,'" Dori sneered. "I don't have a rich mommy to underwrite my mistakes. I have to live in the real world, Hexe. And high-def flat screens aren't cheap. Not like your nump slut, here."

"*Dori!*" Hexe snapped, his eyes flashing. "That was completely uncalled for!"

"I—I think I'd better go," I stammered, backing away from the table.

"Yeah, you'd better run," Dori snarled, glaring at me like a hawk about to swoop down on a helpless rabbit. "But before you go, I'll give you a little magic advice: Stay away from our men, nump!"

I turned and hurried across the plaza, biting back tears as my cheeks burned bright red. As I looked around the market square, I realized there were almost as many humans wandering back and forth among the different stalls as there were Kymerans. After being the only human on my block, it was jarring to find myself surrounded by my own kind.

Most of them clutched cameras or had digital camcorders held in front of their faces. Those not recording every second of their visit openly pointed and laughed at the native Golgothamites going about their daily market as if they were sideshow freaks on display for their amusement. As a native-born New Yorker, I instinctively felt a certain amount of disdain for out-of-towners, but now it was mixed with embarrassment for my species.

"What a bunch of numps," I muttered under my breath.

"You shouldn't use the N-word."

I was startled to find Hexe standing at my elbow. I hadn't seen or heard him come up behind me. He reached out to touch my arm, but I drew away.

"You said you didn't have a girlfriend," I said accusingly.

"I don't. Not recently, anyway," he explained. "Dori and I dated for a while, but I broke it off when she started laying curses. She's free to do whatever she wants, but I refuse to be part of it. Besides, it's easier for her to deal with things if she thinks I simply left her for someone else, not because I found her . . . loathsome. But as far as Dori's concerned, a relationship isn't over unless she's the one who does the dumping."

I gave a humorless laugh. "I know the type."

"I'm sorry she said those things to you, Tate."

"Yeah, well, I'm sorry I reacted the way I did," I replied. "I have some trust issues from my last boyfriend that I need to work out. I don't like admitting it, even to myself, but he really did a number on me. Hey, you want to go look at the river before we go back home?"

"Sure. I think we could both stand to clear our heads," he agreed.

We headed down Perdition, dodging the trucks and wagons that jostled their way along South Street, and walked under the massive steel girders that supported the FDR Expressway. The constant thump and hum of the speeding cars overhead sounded like the rush of white-water rapids. On the other side was a paved promenade that looked out onto the wharves and warehouses of the waterfront, beyond which the East River sparkled in the waning afternoon like a stream of living jade.

"See that building over there?" Hexe pointed to a large warehouse located on one of the wharves. "That's the Stronghold. It's the Malandanti's headquarters. The underground kennel Lukas escaped from is probably nearby."

"I thought we were going to look at the river," I chided.

"You're right. I shouldn't let that bastard Marz ruin what's left of the day." He turned his back on the warehouse and looked out toward the river. "Isn't it beautiful?" he asked, leaning against the iron balustrade.

The warm, diffuse light of the setting sun—what photographers call the magic hour—gave his skin a lustrous glow and framed his head, pulsing like the corona that surrounds the sun during an eclipse. I wanted to reach out and touch his deep purple hair, to see if the halo was real, but I stayed my hand for fear I might get burned—in more sense than one.

"Yes, it is," I agreed.

Chapter 14

"I'm so bored, I could chew off my own foot."

I set aside the orbital buffer I was using to polish the chrome skin on my twenty-first-century upgrade of *Ariadne and the Panther*, and turned to face Lukas. The young were-cat was lounging in a nearby chair with Scratch curled up in his lap. The familiar was enjoying a doze while being stroked behind the ears.

The shape-shifter had become a regular visitor to my room, where he would alternate between modeling and watching me work. Sometimes he would ask me about the human world, and how it was different from what he had seen on TV. But his most frequent questions were along the lines of, "Don't you think Meikei's pretty?" and "Do you think she likes me?"

"Sorry I'm not more exciting. But I warned you going into this that watching a sculptor at work is one step up from watching paint dry."

"It's not that," the were-cat explained. "I find what you do fascinating. Truly I do. It's just that I've been cooped up in this house for weeks! I might as well be back in Boss Marz's kennel."

Scratch peeled open one eye upon hearing this. "Yes, this is *exactly* like being kept in a filthy, damp, unheated, underground kennel and forced to fight to the death. Poor you."

"You know what I mean." Lukas sighed in exasperation. "All I see are the same walls, day in and day out!"

"Huh! You think *you* have it bad?" Scratch snorted. "I'm actually *bound* to this house. If I try to leave the grounds without Hexe's permission, my body demateri- alizes and I'm sent back to where I'm from."

"Yeah, but you're a familiar. That's part of your con- tract. I'm used to running free in the forest. Now the best I can hope for is a walk in the garden. Can't we go out, just for one night?"

"You know Boss Marz is still looking for you," I re- minded him.

"Yeah, but he can't be hunting me *every* second of the day. Maybe he's finally given up by now? For all he knows, I could be dead."

"Anything's possible," I conceded. "But it's still dan- gerous out there."

"The nump's right, for once." Scratch yawned. Having finished what he had to say, the winged familiar stood up, stretched, and jumped down onto the floor, where he proceeded to groom himself.

"If you're going to come into my room and lick your balls in front of mixed company, could you at least have the decency to turn your back while you're doing it?" I grimaced.

"Prude," the familiar sniffed.

"How's everything going?" Hexe was suddenly standing in the open doorway of my room, leaning against the frame, hands in his pockets. I could have sworn he wasn't there a second ago.

"I'm making good time," I said, motioning to the mechanical nymph that was supposed to ride on the back of my spare-parts panther. "Everything should be finished for the opening."

"Does that mean you can take the night off without feeling guilty?"

"Maybe—why do you ask?"

He shrugged his shoulders. "I was planning on going out tonight—I was wondering if you might be interested in joining me?"

"I think I can squeeze it into my busy social calendar . . ." I replied, trying to seem blasé. "Where were you planning on going?"

"Nowhere special. I was thinking of hitting the Calf tonight—I've got a craving for scrambled pork brains in gravy. Lafo serves up the best in town."

"What about me?" Lukas asked beseechingly. "Can I come, too?"

Hexe rubbed his chin in thought. "I don't know, kid. . . . It's risky."

"But I'm healing up really good—you said so, yourself! I can walk without the scapegoat cane, now. I'm about to go loco from cabin fever! *Pleeeease?*"

"You're going to have to go leave the house sometime, I guess. This way you can figure out your way around the neighborhood, without running the risk of getting lost. Very well, you can go with us to the Calf. Where we're going should be safe—Lafo refuses to have any truck with the Malandanti, so they tend to steer clear of it. You have to promise me you won't do anything to call attention to yourself while we're out, understand?"

"I *promise*!" Lukas purred.

"Good boy. Go shave your eyebrow."

It was a pleasant late-autumn night as our little group walked the few blocks to the Two-Headed Calf. The air was crisp without being brisk, so I didn't feel the need to bundle up. Lukas was so eager to finally be on the streets, he kept getting ahead of us, like a child dragging his parents to meet Santa. As we drew near our destination, I noticed the street in front of the restaurant seemed unusually crowded.

"What's with all the motorcycles?" I asked, pointing to the line of Harley-Davidson Sportsters and Softtails parked handlebar to handlebar along the curb.

Hexe raised an eyebrow. "Looks like the gals are out on the town."

"'Gals'?" It was now my turn to look surprised. "You mean there's an all-female motorcycle club in Golgotham?"

"There are two, actually: the Maiden Lane Amazons and the Odin Street Valkyries. They used to be sworn enemies, until their respective leaders reached a meeting of the minds—and, uh, other parts."

"Do you think there'll be any trouble?" I asked uneasily.

"It depends on what your definition of 'trouble' is," Hexe laughed as he opened the door to the restaurant.

As I scanned the downstairs bar area, I recognized several familiar faces: Dr. Mao and Meikei were seated at one of the booths, accompanied by Mr. Manto; Faro was lounging at the bar, openly flirting with the maenad barmaid, Chorea; and to my surprise, Kidron and Wildfire were standing at the back of the room, chatting with an elegantly dressed Kymeran woman with very blue hair. Although I could not place when and where I might have met the blue-haired woman before, there was something extremely familiar about her.

"We've got to get out of here—" Hexe whispered urgently.

"What's going on?" I asked as he turned back toward the door. "Is something wrong?"

Suddenly Lafo stepped out from behind the bar, blocking Hexe's path. The towering chef folded his arms across his chest and grinned down at his old friend.

"Oh, no you don't! You're not getting away that easily!"

Hexe sighed and turned back around to face the crowd. Everybody in the room lifted their drinks in welcome and said as one, "Happy birthday, Hexe!"

Hexe glared accusingly at Lukas. "You knew about this the whole time, didn't you?"

"Of course." The young were-cat beamed. "Meikei told me about it when she brought my lunch today. I didn't want to miss out on the party."

"Why didn't you tell me it's your birthday?" I chided. "I would have gotten you something!"

"I was going to tell you, over dinner," Hexe muttered. "But somebody beat me to it." He glanced meaningfully at the well-dressed woman approaching us.

As she drew closer, I realized the reason the blue-haired woman looked so familiar was not because we had met before, but because I had seen her in the newspapers. I was in the presence of none other than Lady Syra, "Witch to the Stars," occult adviser to the wealthiest men and women in the city, if not the world.

Lady Syra carried herself with a self-assured grace that was both dignified and no-nonsense. Her perfectly coifed, shoulder-length peacock blue hair framed her translucent skin, wide forehead, strong cheekbones, and tapered chin to great effect. She was dressed in Dior, complete with black kid gloves especially designed for her slender, six-fingered hands, and she smelled of rose, vetiver, and jasmine.

"Happy birthday, darling." Lady Syra smiled as she embraced her son. I noticed that they shared the same golden eyes.

"You got me again, Mom." Hexe sighed resignedly, planting a kiss on his mother's powdered cheek. "But how could you be so sure I'd decide to come here for dinner?"

Lady Syra turned and pointed to Mr. Manto, who was engrossed in a game of Chinese checkers with Dr. Mao. "Aloysius was kind enough to tell me."

Hexe gently grasped my elbow and pulled me forward. "Mom—this is my new tenant. Tate, I would like you to meet my mother."

"It's an honor, Lady Syra," I said, bowing my head in recognition. "I've read so much about you in the newspapers and magazines!"

"Damned lies, all of it, I assure you!" she laughed, waving away my compliment with an elegant six-fingered hand.

"That's a lovely piece you're wearing," I said, pointing to an ivory necklace resembling a snake with its tail in its mouth. "Wherever did you get it?"

"You mean this?" She smiled, reaching up to touch her throat. To my surprise, the necklace opened its ruby red eyes and slithered onto Lady Syra's gloved hand, where it wrapped itself about her wrist and became a bracelet. "That's just Trinket, my familiar." To my surprise, Lady Syra took my arm, steering me toward one

of the booths. "Now come, sit with me, my dear. I want
to hear *all* about you—"

Hexe quickly stepped in, putting himself between his
mother and me. "Mom, please—you can monopolize
Tate some other time. Right now I'd like to introduce
her to some of the friends you were kind enough to invite to my party."

"Very well." Lady Syra sighed, relinquishing her grip
on me. "You *are* the birthday boy."

Hexe's eyes lit up as Lafo emerged from the kitchen
carrying a cake. "Ah! That's more like it. I could definitely go for a snack."

We followed the Calf's owner and head chef to the
back of the room, where he placed a triple-tiered cake
slathered in pale green icing on a buffet table that was
already groaning underneath the weight of a bewilder-
ing collection of hors d'oeuvres.

"It looks delicious." Hexe smiled. "In fact, everything
here looks incredible—wouldn't you say so, Tate?"

"Absolutely," I agreed as I eyed the candied sea
horses and deep-fried silkworm cocoons.

"Happy birthday, my friend," Kidron called out. He
and his stablemate were both wearing long, elaborately
decorated caparisons that covered their rumps and flanks
and hid the manure catchers slung under their tails. They
also wore down-filled mufflers on their feet to lessen the
sound of their hooves against the wooden floor. "Or
should I say happy anniversary?"

"Anniversary of what?" I asked.

"Our friendship," Hexe replied. "Kidron and I met at
my fifth birthday party."

"I was the pony ride," the centaur explained.

Suddenly a pair of large hands clad in fingerless biker
gloves clapped themselves onto Hexe's shoulders, freez-

ing him in his tracks. They belonged to a towering blond woman dressed in a black leather motorcycle jacket, matching leather jeans, and a waist-length chain mail tunic, her hair worn in Teutonic braids. She stood six foot nine, with a right eye as blue as a Nordic fjord, while the left was covered by a leather patch emblazoned with the Harley-Davidson logo.

"Where d'ya think *you're* goin', Birthday Boy?" the blonde thundered.

Before Hexe could answer, she spun him around and wrapped her muscular arms around him, lifting him off the ground.

"Hi, Hildy," Hexe squeaked as he was squeezed in a bear hug.

A six-foot-tall brunette wearing matching riding leathers stepped forward and gave the blonde a friendly slap on the ass. "Put him down, honey, before you break his ribs."

"Oops! Sorry, dude," Hildy said, setting him back down.

"Thanks, Lyta," Hexe gasped. After dusting himself off, he gestured for me to join him. "Tate, I'd like you to meet two very good friends of mine—Brunhilde and Hippolyta."

"Just call us Hildy and Lyta," the brunette said as she shook my hand. Instead of a chain mail tunic, she wore a black leather bustier, the right cup of which was conspicuously empty.

"I understand congratulations are in order," Hexe said.

"*Ja*," Hildy replied, nodding her blond head. "We've finally been given permission to consolidate our clubs. From now on we roll as the Golgotham Iron Maidens."

"That's wonderful." Hexe smiled. "I'm very happy for you."

"It's hard to believe we spent so many years fighting each other." Lyta reached up and lovingly touched her girlfriend's patch. "Remember when I took your eye?"

Hildy smiled and nodded. "The bike chain. Odin's beard, you marked me good that time! I think that's when I started to really fall for you."

Lyta took Hildy's huge hand and gave it a squeeze. "You're such a romantic."

While Hexe and the gals caught up with one another, I drifted over to Lukas, who was staring across the room at his own object of affection.

"I see Meikei's over there with her father," I said, stating the Blatantly Obvious.

"Yeah." Lukas sighed wistfully.

"Aren't you going to tell her hello?"

The young were-cat shook his head and shoved his hands in his pockets.

"Why not? I know you like her. You practically talk the poor girl's ear off every time she comes to the house."

"It's easy to talk to her at the house," Lukas explained. "But this is *different.* . . . We aren't alone. What if another male who's interested in her comes up and starts to talk to her?"

"Things are different here than it is on the preserve—well, kind of, anyway. You don't *have* to fight someone to the death simply because he's talking to your girl." I clapped a hand on his shoulder to reassure him. "Besides, as far as Meikei's concerned, you're the only male in this room."

Lukas's eyes were filled with hopeful surprise. "You really think so?"

"Kid, I *know* so!" I grinned. "So stop wasting your time and just go for it—it's that simple!"

"Okay, I will," the young were-cougar said. "But you have to promise me you'll do the same."

"What do you mean?"

Lukas rolled his eyes. "What do you *think*? I see how you act whenever Hexe is around. And I've seen how he looks at you. . . ."

"Like how?" I cringed even as the words came out of my mouth. I sounded like an insecure junior high student obsessing over her first crush.

Lukas shook his head in disbelief. "Haven't you noticed how he *always* smiles when you come into the room?"

"You *really* think he likes me?" I felt myself start to blush.

"Of course!" Lukas grinned as he headed off to join Meikei. "He's just waiting for you to show *you're* interested. All you have to do is take your own advice, Tate."

He was right. It was time for me to stop hemming and hawing and to let Hexe know how I felt. It was just that simple. *Yeah, right.*

After all I'd been through recently, I was still skittish about making myself vulnerable again. At one point I'd thought my relationship with Roger was strong enough to build into a marriage, but it had proved to be an illusion. What if I was misreading Hexe's intentions? He *was* from a different culture, possibly even a totally different species, come to think of it. What if he was just being polite and had absolutely no romantic interest in me? What if he viewed being involved with a human the same as bestiality? It was one thing to be rebuffed; quite another to be viewed as repulsive. I didn't know if I could handle that kind of rejection.

"Would you like to sit down and have a drink?"

I blinked, finally able to break free of the Möbius strip of self-doubt going on inside my head. I smiled gratefully at Hexe.

"You must have read my mind."

He escorted me to one of the booths and motioned for the barmaid to bring two tankards of barley wine. Then, to my surprise, instead of seating himself on the opposite side of the booth, he slid in alongside me. I was keenly aware of the heat from his body against my own, which sparked a separate fire deep inside me.

When Chorea brought our drinks, Hexe took my tankard from her and handed it to me himself. His leg was against my leg, his smell in my brain, as his fingers touched mine. I did not pull my hand away, nor did he remove his hand from mine. I looked into his face and found myself once more staring into those golden eyes, which were as compelling as they were dazzling.

He smiled, unoffended by the nakedness of my gaze, and like an acrobat falling from a high wire, I felt a sudden vertigo as disorienting as it was delicious. It was as if my heart were filled with helium and trying to escape my body. I almost expected to see it bobbing between the smoky rafters of the pub like a toy balloon.

Suddenly a man's voice thundered out. "Where's that chuffing dunderwhelp?"

The entire room fell silent as if struck collectively mute. From the look of dismay on Hexe's face, he knew the voice all too well. I craned my head, trying to see who it was who had brought the party to a screeching halt.

Standing framed in the doorway of the restaurant was a tall man dressed in a black wool caped coat. His shoulder-length hair and neatly trimmed goatee were dark indigo, liberally shot with streaks of ice blue. His face was gaunt, with cheekbones sharp enough to draw blood, and golden eyes that blazed with an inner fire, like stars from some cold and distant galaxy. Perched on the dark man's left shoulder was a raven with the bright red eyes of a familiar.

Lady Syra stepped forward, blocking the newcomer's path. "Esau! That's no way to speak about your nephew," she admonished. "And it's *certainly* no way to greet him on his birthday!"

"I'll call him worse than that, if what I heard is true," her brother snarled, glaring about the room. "So where is he?"

Hexe sighed wearily and let go of my hand. "I'm over here, Uncle," he said as he slid out of the booth. "I take it you didn't come here simply to wish me happy birthday."

Esau stalked across the room, coming to a halt before his nephew. The smell of leather, black moss, and brimstone radiated from the older warlock like heat from a summer sidewalk.

"Of course not," Uncle Esau replied. "I came to see if there was anything to the rumors."

"What rumors?"

"That you're renting rooms to numps." He spat the last word out like poison.

"I didn't rent a room to a *nump*—I rented it to a *human*," Hexe replied, with more than a little heat. "Besides, what difference is it to you whom I rent to?"

"I grew up in that house!" Uncle Esau retorted, stepping to within inches of Hexe's face. He pointed a long, nicotine-stained finger at me as he trembled with indignation. "I refuse to see it defiled by this nump!"

"Stop calling her that," Hexe snapped.

"Don't use that tone of voice on *me*, boy!" Uncle

Esau snarled, his golden eyes growing as dark as a storm cloud. "You're nowhere near sorcerer enough to threaten me."

"Are you so sure of that, Uncle?" Hexe retorted, squaring his shoulders.

"That's enough—from *both* of you!" Lady Syra said sternly as she wedged herself between her brother and son. "Esau, I invited you because you are family, not because I wanted to listen to another one of your antihuman screeds. Besides, it's a little late to be concerned about humans inhabiting the family homestead. Mr. Manto's been living in the basement for half a century now."

"It's bad enough Father allowed the oracle to take up residence," Uncle Esau grunted in disgust. "But at least *he* has a talent!" He jerked his head angrily at me. "This nump has no occult gift whatsoever! I told Father he was making a mistake allowing human psychics and mediums to take up residence in Golgotham. It was only a matter of time before the others would start to trickle in. Now I'm warning *you*, Syra—once you start letting garden-variety numps into the neighborhood, there's no stopping them!

"First it's the psychics and mediums. Then it's the 'artists,' and then trust fund numpsters. Next thing you know, we're surrounded by chuffing numpies, gobbing away on those accursed cell phones and putting a Starbucks on every other street corner. They'll gentrify us out of existence. Can't you *see* that?" he shouted, the bulging veins on his forehead threatening to burst through his skin. "You would think the humans would have been satisfied after they stripped us of our lands, slew our dragons, and scattered our people to the winds. But no! Still they hound us! Every day they do their best to destroy our culture with their damnable technology. Cell phones. Satellites. Microwave ovens. *Feh!* Soon our children will be as weak and slack-jawed as the numps' worthless brats. Our people were building citadels of living glass while humans were still throwing their dung at one another. If I had my way, the fires would burn again and the skies once more grow black with their ashes!"

"Esau! This is *not* the time or place!" Lady Syra said, doing her best to keep calm. "Since Father left the house to *me*, I'm the one who has the final say-so over who lives there. And I have no problem accepting Ms. Tate as my tenant."

"Sure, take up for him," Uncle Esau sneered. "That's what you *always* do, no matter how foolish his decisions may be. You've always coddled him, Syra. The boy can't even support himself. Everyone knows it's impossible to make a living Right Handed. He'll never amount to more than a jumped-up nimgimmer!"

"That's enough, Esau," Lady Syra said sharply.

"You know what I say is true, Syra! You can't stay blind to his weakness forever."

"I said that's *enough*, Esau!" Her tone was so cold you could almost see ice crystals hanging in the air. "I'm not speaking to you as your sister."

Esau raised an indigo eyebrow in surprise. "Ah. So *that's* how it is." He glanced at the raven riding his shoulder. "It would seem we have offended the royal ear, Edgar." The familiar cawed in agreement. Esau executed a formal bow to his sister, one hand placed above his heart. "In that case, I beg your leave, milady."

"You are free to go, sir," Lady Syra said with a curt nod of her head.

With a dramatic flourish of his coat, Esau marched

out of the pub, leaving nothing but embarrassed silence in his wake.

Lady Syra heaved a huge sigh as she watched her brother leave. "My. How very public that was." She turned and gave me a wan smile. "Please forgive my brother, Ms. Tate. He is a necromancer by trade, and I fear it has warped him. I assure you that I do not share his prejudice."

"Thank you. I appreciate your standing up for me."

Lady Syra turned to her son and gave him a peck on the cheek. "I hope you won't think ill of me, sweetheart, but I'm going to call it a night. It was a pleasure meeting you, my dear." She was smiling as she left, but I could tell that the confrontation with her brother had affected her greatly.

"I'm *really* sorry you had to see that," Hexe said as he returned to the booth. "But I warned you about Uncle Esau."

"He's rather, uh, opinionated."

"He's a racist asshole."

"I was trying to be polite."

"Why bother?" Hexe snapped. "He doesn't care what humans think about him. And it's obvious he doesn't care about alienating his family. I hate him for how he treats my mother! She bends over backward to incorporate him into family gatherings and celebrations, only to have him shit all over everything."

"Yeah, about your mother—why is she called 'Lady Syra'? I mean, it's not a stage name, is it, like 'Professor Azar' or 'Madame Lola'?"

Hexe looked down at his tankard of barley wine, avoiding my gaze.

"So, are you going to tell me the reason?" I prodded.

"I will," he replied. "But you have to promise me that it won't change things between us."

"What things?" I asked, my helium-filled heart suddenly racing.

"You know." He gestured at the empty space between us. "Our friendship."

"Oh." I tried not to sound disappointed. "Of course. Okay, I promise."

"My mother's family members are the direct descendants of Lord Bexe."

"The last Witch King? The one who signed the Treaty? *That* Lord Bexe?"

"One and the same." Hexe nodded. "Except that he wasn't really the last Witch King. The royal family didn't go away—we simply no longer have a standing army or hold court. My great-great-grandfather Lord Beke, the one I told you about, was responsible for bringing the Kymerans to this country and was the founder of Golgotham. His son, Elas, inherited the title of Witch King after him. He had two children, Jack and Eben. Jack was the heir apparent. . . ."

"The one who got lost on the third floor?"

Hexe gave me a smile. "Nice to know you pay attention. Anyway, my grandfather ended up having to take Jack's place. When the time came to pass along the title, he chose my mother over Esau, making her the Witch Queen. It was an unusual decision on Grandfather's part, but not unheard of."

"So that makes you . . . ?"

"Prince Hexe, heir to the throne of Kymera. Such as it is."

"So *that's* why they were calling you Serenity."

"It's an anachronistic form of address," he said with

a shrug. "It's not like being the Prince of Wales, or even the Prince of Monaco. My title and a dollar won't get me in the subway. But that's the real reason Uncle Esau is such a prick toward my mother and me. Of course, she feels guilty about it. I've told her time and again that it's his problem, not hers, but she still tries to find ways to make it up to him."

"Why were you afraid of telling me this?"

"Because being royalty—even fucked-up witch royalty—makes people act differently around you. When I was growing up, I was never sure if people liked me for myself. Take Dori, for instance. I always got the feeling she was more in love with my *title* than with *me*."

I leaned forward, dropping my voice into a conspiratorial whisper. "I realize this is going to sound completely fake, but I *totally* know how you feel."

Hexe was too polite to verbally respond, but the look on his face was openly dubious. I didn't want him to think I was one of those types that, no matter what the situation, tries to one-up whomever they're talking to. However, since he had finally come clean, I decided this was as good a time as any to reveal my own secret.

"You know that Tate isn't my given name, right?"

Hexe frowned. "But it's on your checks. I saw it when you paid the rent."

"Yes, but that's my *business* account. I'm actually incorporated as T.A.T.E. That's what my initials spell. It's short for Timothea Alda Talmadge Eresby."

Recognition dawned in his eyes "Eresby? As in Timothy Eresby? One of the richest men in the country?"

"That's my dad. But I understand exactly what you mean about people seeing you as *what* you are instead of *who* you are. My last boyfriend, Roger, attached a great deal more importance to my being an heiress than I ever have."

"You said your family was rich, and I knew you were a trust fund baby, but I never dreamed—" He caught himself in midsentence, a chagrined look on his face.

"That's okay, Hexe," I laughed. "I *am* a trust fund baby. It's the truth, after all. But I'm *not* a numpster."

"I wouldn't have rented to you if I thought you were." He leaned back and rubbed his hands together eagerly. "Now that we've revealed our secret identities to each other, what do you say we enjoy the party my mother was kind enough to throw for me? Just wait until you try Lafo's parsnip and prune cake. It's even better than his dark chocolate turnip bread."

"Yum," I said, forcing the corner of my mouth up into a smile. "Sounds delicious."

A few hours and several tankards of barley wine later, we headed back home, our bellies full of Lafo's unique culinary efforts. Hexe was right—the cake had indeed been delicious, although I drew the line at the candied sea horses and the deep-fried starfish.

Hexe and I strolled side by side while Lukas walked ahead of us, surreptitiously sniffing the utility poles and trash cans along the street. Part of me longed to reach out and take his hand, but I told myself that we'd both been drinking, and I didn't want either my action, or his reaction, to be the result of too much barley wine and not enough thought. It was a lie, but one I could almost believe.

Lukas, on the other hand, had spent the evening engrossed with Meikei, and he was happier than I'd ever seen him. The chemistry between the teenagers was obvious, which made the course of their romance far easier to chart. Despite his harrowing ordeal in the pits, the young bastet's heart was unafraid of surrendering itself. I envied the bravery his naïveté allowed him.

Despite the warm feeling in my belly and the lightness in my heart, my mind kept going back to what Esau had said about me. After a lifetime of being viewed as a freak, it felt odd to be denounced for not being weird. Even odder was the feeling that came with being condemned as the harbinger of cultural devastation. Although I instinctively disliked him, the necromancer had a point.

All I wanted was to be somewhere I loved living in, shop locally, try to get to know my neighbors, and go about my business as an artist. But I knew that if enough white twentysomething fellow artists joined me, eventually the culture and commodity such a community created would draw those farther up the gentrification chain, triggering the inevitable real estate feeding frenzy and the erasure of everything I loved about Golgotham.

As we walked down the narrow, canyonlike street back to the boardinghouse, I stared up at the lights burning in the high windows of the buildings that surrounded us, and I wondered who—or what—might live there and if they viewed my arrival in their neighborhood the same way as Uncle Esau.

For the most part, everyone I had met in Golgotham had proved to be extremely welcoming. But now I found myself wondering how much of that was not out of genuine friendliness, but because I was under Hexe's royal protection.

Chapter 15

Canal Art Supplies, a second home to the Big Apple's students, artists, and artsy-craftsy set since the Great Depression, is located on Canal Street, on the border between Chinatown and Tribeca. Sandwiched between fly-by-night stalls selling knockoff designer handbags, the store's dingy exterior does little to hint that all six floors house everything from handmade paper to airbrush respirators. Compared to the big arts-and-crafts chains out in the suburbs, it's definitely disheveled, and more than a little rough around the edges. But with its dark wood floors and pressed-tin ceilings, Canal Art Supplies has always offered a classic New York shopping experience.

As I entered, I was greeted by the faint but familiar smell of good oils and turpentine. I ignored the ancient elevator at the back of the store, which was not only excruciatingly slow, but also bobbed up and down like a yo-yo whenever someone set foot inside the car. Instead, I climbed the creaky stairs to the fourth floor, where the sculpting and pottery supplies were kept.

As I poked about the shelves, trying to decide on

which color of plastilina to buy, I was vaguely aware of a half-dozen other fellow shoppers wandering the tightly packed aisles. Then someone tapped me on the shoulder. I turned to find myself staring at a young woman with a shock of copper-colored hair, harlequin-style glasses that framed a pair of emerald green eyes, and a tiny scar on her chin from that time I opened the door to our dorm room without realizing she was standing on the other side.

"Nessie!" I exclaimed as we both squealed in school-girlish delight and embraced each other. "How have you been?"

Vanessa Sullivan and I met our freshman year at Wellesley and became fast friends during Introduction to Sculpture. Our sophomore year we arranged to share a room at Tower Court, and we pretty much lived in each other's back pockets until we graduated. She's the closest thing to a sister I've ever known. We gave each other nicknames—I called her Nessie, and she called me Tate, which I adopted as my nom d'acetylene torch.

"I'm doing okay. I've been throwing art pots for this pet cremation service out on Long Island to pay the bills. You would not believe the cash people will put down for an urn to store Rover's ashes! What's new with you?"

"I've got a show coming up at Templeton Gallery."

"Chelsea? Sweet! You deserve the exposure."

"What about you—you up to anything nowadays?"

"I just joined this new arts collective near where I live in Tribeca. We're looking to do a group show in a couple of months. We're called the Art Farm," Nessie replied with a grimace. "'Art Form,' right? The guy who started it has a thing for puns—God help me. I'll drop off some invites once the dates are set. You still live over on Crosby Street?"

"I moved out of there a few weeks back. I'm living in Golgotham now."

Nessie's jaw dropped as if I'd told her I'd bought a condo on the moon. "No way!"

"It's true. I found this great place over on Golden Hill Street, in the heart of the neighborhood, not the touristy section. Plenty of space. Great light. It's cheap. And, best of all, the neighbors don't care how much noise I make. . . ."

"Wow! What's it like?" Nessie asked, her eyes gleaming. "I mean, I've been to Perdition and Duivel streets—but everyone's been there."

"It's—*different*," I replied, "and it takes a little getting used to, at first, but I love it. You really ought to come over and check out my studio. . . ."

Nessie glanced at her cell phone. "I've got a couple hours before I have to be anywhere. Why not?"

We decided it would be best if we took the Number Six train to City Hall and caught a hack into Golgotham. I was keen to catch up with my old friend, since it was nearly a year since we'd last seen each other. That was due largely to my ex, thank you very much. As we took our seats on the subway, Nessie turned and gave me what I knew was her "Please don't disappoint me" look.

"So—Are you still seeing Dickweed?"

"You mean Roger?"

"Of *course* Roger. What other Dickweed have you been dating? Recently, that is."

"I broke up with Roger a couple of months ago."

"Good. I always hated that jerk. He acted like he was God's gift to women. And to some dudes."

"Tell me about it." I smiled sourly. "I walked in on him 'gifting' himself to some bimbo he picked up at a bar."

"Awk-ward!"

"And he was in *my* loft! I was out of town and the bastard didn't want to take her back to his place, but he was also too cheap to spring for a motel room. Since he hadn't bothered to check the voice mail I'd left him, he didn't realize I was coming back earlier than expected."

Vanessa rolled her eyes in disgust. "Ugh! Now *that's* just tacky. What a he-ho. I hope you burned the sheets."

"I dumped them down the incinerator chute."

"Close enough. Personally, I could never understand what you saw in that guy. . . ."

"Well, the sex *was* good," I conceded grudgingly. "And he laughed at my jokes."

"Good in bed and a sense of humor—the smart woman's Achilles' heel!"

"Sadly, smart women can't live on orgasms alone." I sighed.

"Although, you gotta admit, it's fun *trying*." Nessie grinned.

We collapsed into a giggling fit, just like we used to do back in our dorm room. By the time the train reached City Hall, we had finally regained enough composure to look relatively sane, if not particularly respectable. We exited the car and headed toward the street, hurrying through the Guastavino tile arches of the platform and mezzanine, past the colored glass tile work and antique brass chandeliers that are a hallmark of the station.

Upon reaching street level, we cut across the plaza toward Broadway, where a mixture of yellow taxis and centaur-drawn hansoms lined the cab stand. I looked for Kidron's top hat or Wildfire's garland, but I did not spot them.

Suddenly a man's voice spoke from behind us. "Excuse me, ladies—are you going to Golgotham?"

We turned to find a satyr standing behind us. Due to his crooked hind legs, he appeared slightly shorter in stature than an average man. His upper body was identical to a human male's save for his long, flat ears and horns of a goat. The only item of clothing he had on was a Mets jacket.

"I can take you anywhere you want—cheaper than any centaur," he said, pointing to his rickshaw, which sat nose down next to the curb, awaiting the next customer.

"No, thank you," I said, recalling Kidron's advice about taking rides from satyrs.

"Oh, come on, Tate!" Vanessa grinned. "I've always wanted to ride in one of these."

"I don't know. . . ." I eyed the satyr, who was politely waiting for us to come to a decision. It suddenly occurred to me that I was being unfair to the man-goat. Perhaps Kidron's warning me away from the rickshaw drivers had more to do with the satyrs cutting into his livelihood. No doubt they, too, suffered the same bigotry and prejudice as the Kymerans and the various shape-shifting races endured, with people projecting dark motives onto them simply because they were different. Besides, there were two of us. Safety in numbers, right?

"*C'mon,*" my friend teased. "Where's your sense of adventure?"

"Okay, we'll hire you," I agreed.

"Right this way, lovely ladies." The satyr grinned. The rickshaw he ushered us into was, like most of those found in Golgotham, large enough to accommodate two adults. It was painted bright red, with a canvas canopy that could be folded forward or back, depending on the weather.

I gave the satyr the address, and after we made ourselves comfortable, he stepped between the running posts of the rickshaw. Within seconds we found ourselves rattling down Broadway toward Golgotham. The satyr dodged in and out of the motorized traffic with surprising speed and agility, his hooves clattering loudly against the pavement.

"So, are you still seeing Adrian?" I asked, finally returning to our previous conversation.

"We're still with each other." She sighed. "But I'm afraid we've reached that stage where we need to either get married or break up. I'm not sure which it's going to be, just yet. In fact, he proposed to me a couple of days ago. I told him I had to think about it."

"Adrian's a nice guy, Nessie."

"I know that—but I'm not sure I'm ready to settle down. What if I decide I want to take a lesbian lover?"

"*Do* you?"

"No, not really," she admitted. "But what if I wake up one morning and regret never doing so because I married Adrian and had a bunch of kids?"

"That's what the Internet's for," I laughed. "But all joking aside, it sounds to me you're just trying to find reasons not to make a decision about something you know will change your life forever—whether for good or for bad."

"How about you—?" she asked. "Are you seeing anyone now that Roger's out of the picture?"

"Well, there *is* someone I'm interested in . . ." I admitted, blushing as I spoke.

"Is it anyone I know?" she asked excitedly. "Ooh! I bet it's the bartender at Max Fish! I saw how you were eyeing him the last time we went there. . . ."

"No, I seriously doubt you know him," I laughed. "He's, uh, not from our scene."

"Oh, God—he's not a stockbroker, is he?"

"Of course not," I replied, aghast at the very suggestion. "He's a Kymeran."

"Holy crap, Tate!" Vanessa gasped, genuinely surprised. "Talk about getting some strange! Does Mrs. E know about this?"

"No, she doesn't. Besides, there's nothing for her to know. I haven't even kissed this guy yet."

"Okay—I believe you. But have you fucked?"

"Nessie!"

"I'm just kidding, Tate. But, really, you can tell me—have you?"

"No!"

"Do you wanna?"

"God, yes," I groaned. "Wait until you meet him. He's handsome, kind, intelligent, generous, and he actually thinks about something other than himself."

"He sounds perfect—except for being a warlock."

"He's not that kind of wizard," I insisted. "He doesn't curse people—he's a healer." As I glanced up from our conversation, I suddenly realized we were no longer headed in the direction of my house. "Hey—wait a minute!" I yelled at the rickshaw puller. "This isn't how you get to Golden Hill Street. Where do you think you're going?"

In response, the satyr lowered his head and started running, causing the rickshaw to jounce across the cobblestoned street. I was so mad at myself, I didn't have time to be afraid. I had been so eager to show my old friend around Golgotham to prove to her that it was "safe," I went against my better judgment and ended up played for a nump.

"What's going on?" Nessie yelped.

"We're being kidnapped," I shouted, fighting down the panic that was finally starting to rise in my gut. I didn't know where the man-goat was taking us, but I knew we didn't want to find out. *"Jump!"*

"But we're going so fast—!"

"Don't argue with me, Nessie—just grab your purse and jump!"

Marshaling my courage, I leaped over the side of the wildly bouncing vehicle, rolling as best I could upon landing on the street. Sitting up, I saw the rickshaw disappear around a corner, the satyr still cantering along.

Vanessa was on the other side of the narrow street from me, grimacing as she clutched her left ankle. The locals barely glanced in our direction as they went about their business, as if the sight of women jumping out of runaway rickshaws was a common, everyday occurrence in that neighborhood.

"Are you okay?" I asked as I hurried to her side.

"I think I sprained my ankle."

"Oh, God, Nessie—I'm so sorry about this!" I exclaimed as I helped her up.

"There's no need to apologize," she grunted. "I'm the one who insisted on riding in the rickshaw, even after you said no. Where are we?"

I looked around, trying to get my bearings. "I think we're on Ferry Street. We're not that far from where I live. I need to get you off the street, in case goat-boy comes back." I pointed to a nearby bar, the sign for which read BLARNEY'S. "That looks like a good place for you to get off that ankle."

"You're not going to leave me there alone, are you?" Nessie asked fearfully.

"Of course not," I said reassuringly. "I've got my phone on me. I'll call this cabbie I know to come pick us up. . . ." As I opened the door of the pub, the sound of Flogging Molly played at near-deafening volume greeted us.

"Is this an Irish pub?" Vanessa asked.

"You could say that," I replied as I stared at the child-sized, green-clad men lining the bar.

"Oi! What are you lot doing here?" the bartender snapped. Like the other leprechauns, he was dressed in green and had bright red hair. "Clear off! We don't serve numps!"

"My friend's been hurt," I explained. "She needs to sit down while I call a cab. We won't be any bother, I promise."

Upon catching sight of Vanessa's coppery locks, the bartender's demeanor softened slightly. "You there, the ginger—what's your last name?"

"Sullivan," she replied.

"Very well, you can stay," the bartender said grudgingly. "Just keep your distance from me reg'lars."

"Thank you, sir," I said as I seated Vanessa on a stool better suited for a day-care center than a pub.

The bartender merely grunted and returned to his customers, all of whom glared at us while muttering darkly among themselves. I noticed that those leprechauns not carrying shillelaghs clutched fistfuls of darts, and all of them had a drink in their free hands. Fifteen tense, Celtic-rock-infused minutes later, I received a text informing me our ride was waiting for us outside. I wasted no time in getting Vanessa back on her feet, allowing her to use me as a human crutch as she limped out the door.

Kidron was standing patiently at the curb, awaiting our arrival. "Good afternoon, ladies," the cabbie said politely, tipping his hat in greeting.

Vanessa balked at the sight of the centaur. I suppose it was only natural for her to be hesitant after her narrow escape from the satyr, but I could not help feeling a little embarrassed by her reaction to Kidron.

"It's okay, Nessie," I assured her. "He's straight up."

"Tate informed me of your predicament, Miss Sullivan," Kidron said solemnly. "I hope it will not taint your view of Golgotham and of those of us who live here. Not all half-beasts are as untrustworthy as satyrs."

"I sent Hexe a quick text, to make sure he was home," I said as I gave Vanessa a boost into the hansom. "He'll get you fixed up right away."

"Who's Hexe?"

"He's that Kymeran healer I told you about," I explained. "He's also my landlord and one of my housemates."

"Who are the others?"

"A geriatric soothsayer, a were-cougar, and a demonic familiar."

"You know, my ankle doesn't really hurt *that* bad...."

"C'mon, Nessie." I grinned. "Where's your sense of adventure?"

Hexe was standing on the front stoop as we arrived, a concerned look on his handsome face. Vanessa grabbed my arm. "Is that him?" she whispered.

"Uh-huh." I nodded.

"He is *dreamy*!"

Before the cab could come to a halt, Hexe hurried down the stairs to meet us, his golden eyes intent on me. "Are you all right?" he asked. "Your text said something about an accident—"

"I'm okay," I replied. "It's my friend here who's hurt.

Vanessa, I'd like you to meet Hexe. Hexe, this is my old college roomie, Vanessa."

"*You* can call me Nessie." She smiled.

"Pleased to meet you, Nessie," he replied, helping her out of the cab. "What seems to be wrong?"

"I sprained my ankle." She abruptly grimaced in pain as her left foot touched the sidewalk.

Hexe produced a thumb-sized, tea bag–like pouch from his pocket. "Stick this under your top lip, against your gum, and let it sit there. It'll help with the pain. So how did you come to injure yourself, Nessie?"

"It happened when we jumped out of the rickshaw," she replied. The pouch under her lip made it sound as if she were talking around a chaw of tobacco.

"Rickshaw?" Hexe turned to look at me, his previous concern replaced by alarm. "What in seven hells were you doing riding in one of those?"

"I thought it would be safe if there were two of us," I explained. "I was wrong. The satyr pulling the rickshaw tried to kidnap us, no pun intended."

"Satyrs can be extremely dangerous," Hexe said grimly. "You and Nessie could have ended up in a lot of trouble."

"Oh, I get it," Vanessa giggled, her pupils the size of dinner plates as Hexe and I helped her up the front stairs. "*Kid*nap, because he's part goat. Ha!"

"What exactly did you give her?" I asked. The last time I'd seen her that loopy was after a couple magnums of bubbly at her kid sister's wedding.

"Just some smokeless cannabis, mixed with a couple of special herbs from the garden," he replied. "Don't worry, she'll be fine."

"*Ooooh* look, a kitty!" Vanessa exclaimed as we entered the parlor, pointing at Scratch, who sat perched atop the horn of the antique Victrola.

"Great. Another nump," the familiar said sourly. "Allow me to befoul myself with delight."

Hexe and I carried Vanessa to his office, where he carefully examined her ankle to make sure it wasn't broken.

"Has anyone told you that you have a *marvelous* touch?" Vanessa said with a blissful smile on her face.

"It's merely a sprain," Hexe announced. "I'll boil up some fenugreek leaves and wrap them around her ankle with some elastic bandages. She'll be good as new in no time. Do you want to help me make up the poultice—?"

"I think I'd better stay here with her—in case Scratch decides to taunt her some more."

The moment Hexe left the room Vanessa turned around to look at me, her mouth hanging open in exaggerated disbelief. "He is sooo hot!" she whispered.

"I *know*," I groaned.

"And you're telling me you haven't even kissed? Girl, what are you *waiting* on?"

"It's complicated, Nessie. I'm still getting over Roger. . . ."

"Bullshit! You're just scared of taking a chance and putting your heart on the line—just as I am with Adrian." She blinked, a look of surprise on her face. "Whoa. Did I say that? What just happened?"

"It's called an epiphany," I said, patting her shoulder. "You're also as high as a kite."

We fell silent as Hexe reentered the room, carrying a small bowl of steaming fenugreek leaves in one hand and a roll of Ace bandages in the other.

"This should bring the swelling down right away," he explained as he began applying the warm poultice, massaging it into her wounded ankle. "However, I don't want you walking on it too much for the next day or so.

Try and keep it elevated when you go to bed tonight, as well."

"Are you sure this stuff will work, Doctor?"

"Please, don't call me that," Hexe said as he wound the length of bandage about her foot. "I'm not a man of medicine. I'm a hedgewitch, an herbal healer, if you will. But as to the efficacy of this cure, you can ask Kidron if it works or not. I brew up poultices like this all the time for him and the other centaurs who work for the cab company. Their fetlocks become swollen from walking on pavement all the time."

"Too bad you're not a doctor," Vanessa said, batting her eyes as he pinned the bandage into place. "I'd *love* to check out your bedside manner."

Hexe glanced up at me, his cheeks flushing bright pink. "Yes, well . . ."

"I think it's time I escorted you back home, Nessie," I said firmly. "I'm sure Adrian is worried *sick* about you."

"How much do I owe you for the, uh, hedgewitchery, then?" Vanessa asked, reaching for her purse.

"On the house." Hexe smiled, wiping his hands on his shirttail. "Any friend of Tate's is a friend of mine. Now, if you'll please excuse me, I really have to get back to work. I have a cyclopean client with a bad case of pink eye."

A couple minutes later, as we were climbing back into Kidron's cab, I delivered a quick punch to Vanessa's shoulder. "Ow!" she yelped, in surprise. "What was that for?"

"'I'd *love* to check out your bedside manner,'" I said, mimicking her voice. "What the hell, Nessie?"

"*Oooh!* You *are* serious about him, aren't you?" she giggled. "Sorry about that—don't mind me. I'm hopped up on goofballs, or something."

"So—what do you think of Hexe?" I knew that Vanessa's initial assessments of my boyfriends were always correct. I might not always follow her advice, but at least I was certain she would never steer me in the wrong direction.

"I think he's absolutely incredible. And I'm not just saying that because he isn't human. I've *never* seen any of your exes look at you the way he does."

"How does he look at me?" I asked. It was as if we were back in our old dorm room, eating cookie dough ice cream while talking about boys.

Vanessa paused for a second as she tried to find an analogy. "He looks at you—the same way Adrian looks at *me*. But, if you decide you're not gonna hit that, let me know"—she winked—"just in case things on my end don't pan out. . . ."

Chapter 16

And so it came to pass, after what seemed like an eternity of hard work, that the gallery opening was finally at hand. A week before the show, I received a call from Derrick Templeton, owner of Templeton Gallery. I had not seen him since the day he agreed to book the show, and I had spoken to him on the phone only once, as most of our correspondence since then had taken place online.

"How's my favorite sculptress? Is everything ready?" he asked, somehow managing to sound both laid back and anxious at the same time.

I automatically glanced at the gleaming *Cyber-Panther*, which I had finished only the night before. It took sixty hours to complete, once I had all the parts I needed. It measured two feet high and was five feet long from nose to tail, weighing in at just under a hundred pounds.

"Yes, everything's ready, Derrick. There are six pieces."

"How much do they weigh, total?"

"Around six hundred pounds."

"Very good," he muttered. I could hear him scribbling something on a piece of paper. "I'll send a van around to collect everything. Give me your address again. . . ."

"Yeah, about that . . . I've moved since we last spoke. I'm living in Golgotham now. Is that going to be a problem?"

"The company I use isn't licensed for cartage in that part of town," he said flatly. "You're going to have to arrange transportation to the Relay Station on South Street. My guys can do pickup from there."

"That's what I thought." I sighed. I'd run into problems moving my stuff into Golgotham; now it looked like I would face stumbling blocks getting things *out* as well.

"Is that going to be a problem for you?" Derrick's laid-back tone was completely gone, leaving only anxiousness. The last thing I needed was for him to decide to get cold feet about the show.

"I've got it under control," I assured him. "I know a guy."

After I finished talking to Derrick, I dug around in my purse until I found the business card I needed. After a couple of rings, the receiver on the other end picked up.

"Faro Moving!"

"Hey, Faro, this is Tate. . . ."

"Sorry, but I'm not in the office right now! I'm in Greece on my honeymoon! I'll be back in two weeks! Please leave a message after the beep."

"Damn it!" I slapped my cell phone shut in disgust. "I *knew* that was too easy!"

I headed downstairs to find Hexe. He was sitting at

his desk in his office, polishing his scrying crystals. He motioned for me to take a seat.

"What's new?" he asked without looking up from his work.

"Did you know Faro got married?" I queried, swiveling so that my legs were draped over the arms of the easy chair.

"Yeah, I just heard about it last night. Turns out he and Chorea hooked up at my birthday party, and now they're honeymooning on the Aegean. A real whirlwind romance, apparently. Lafo's pissed because she left without giving any notice, so now he's short-staffed at the Calf."

"Chorea? The maenad?" I grimaced involuntarily. "Isn't that sorta dangerous?"

"Yeah, well," Hexe replied with a shrug, "Faro likes living on the edge."

"I should get them a wedding present," I said, eyeing the paperweight made from a monkey's skull.

"I'd wait to see if the groom survives the honeymoon, first."

"I'm happy for them, I guess." I sighed, "But this honeymoon of theirs really puts me in a bind. I hate to keep bothering you for favors, but do you know anyone else in Golgotham with Faro's teleportation talent?"

"There are a couple, but they're nowhere as good. Teleportation is a tricky business. Faro makes it look simple, but it's *real* easy to make mistakes. One little mix-up and poof! Your stuff is at the bottom of the Mariana Trench or orbiting one of Saturn's moons."

"Crap. I was afraid you were going to say something like that." I scowled.

"What do you need moved?"

"I've got to get my sculptures to the Relay Station, so Derrick's guys can pick them up and take them to the gallery."

Hexe looked up from his work. "Who's Derrick?"

"Derrick Templeton. He owns the gallery I'm showing at."

"Oh." He nodded to himself and returned to his polishing. "Why don't you give Kidron a ring? His brother is a Teamster. They run the Relay Station. I'm sure he can arrange a pickup for you."

"Thanks, Hexe. I appreciate your helping me with this. You must really be sick of me asking you for help all the time. . . ."

"It's not a problem." He smiled. "Besides, I like helping you."

"What exactly *is* the Relay Station?" I asked.

"It's this huge distribution hub over on South Street, near the Brooklyn Bridge, where goods going into and out of Golgotham are switched from trucks to Teamster wagons, and vice versa. Pretty much everything from the outside has to come into the neighborhood through the Relay Station."

"Sounds like a real pain in the ass."

"It *is* a pain in the ass," he conceded. "But it's also what keeps Golgotham the way it is. The Golgotham Business Owners' Organization made sure the city charter outlawed automobiles in the neighborhood shortly after they were invented—otherwise they'd have widened the streets and put in subway tunnels a long time ago. It also keeps the centaur population gainfully employed."

I swung my legs back around and stood up. "I think I'll go call Kidron and see what I can work out with his brother. Once again, thanks for everything."

"You're welcome," he replied, returning his attention to the crystals. "This Derrick guy—how old is he?" He was pretending not to look at me as he turned the larger of the scrying eggs over in his hands, studying it for flaws.

"I dunno." I shrugged. "Thirty-five. Forty, maybe."

"Is he married?"

"What does that have to do with anything?" I frowned.

"Nothing at all," Hexe replied hurriedly, his cheeks suddenly pink. "Just curious, that's all."

As I closed the door to the office behind me, I allowed myself a little smile.

Just curious? Yeah, right.

Later that same evening I spoke on the phone to Kidron, who agreed to talk to his brother for me. An hour later he called back to inform me the pickup was scheduled for the day after next and would run me two hundred bucks, cash on the barrelhead.

The next day I dragged out the two wooden crates I had used during my recent move to transport my sculptures and placed them in the front parlor. Then I went and arranged for the delivery of a "slightly used" plywood import box from a waterfront warehouse for the ones I had recently finished. Later that same afternoon, a wagon pulled by a sorrel centauride dropped off my purchase, and by that evening the front parlor was almost as impassable as Mr. Manto's apartment.

"What's going on?" Hexe asked as he squeezed through the front door. He kicked at a tumbleweed of snarled excelsior at his feet. "It looks like a roc's nest in here!"

"Kidron's brother is picking up the sculptures tomorrow," I explained as I distributed wood shavings between the containers. "I have to get them ready."

"That's great!" He smiled. "You must be very excited—this is your first show, isn't it?"

"I've displayed my work at group shows at university, and I was involved in a couple of art installations in Williamsburg, but this is the first time my stuff will be in a real gallery. Templeton isn't exactly Gagosian, but it's a good start. So, yeah, I'm pretty excited."

"You know, I've never really seen your work—"

"What are you talking about?" I snorted. "You've seen me in a welding helmet more than you have a dress!"

"That's the thing—I've seen you *at* work, but not the finished pieces themselves."

"Would you like to take a look at them before they're packed up?" I asked.

"I should, in case you sell them all."

"I hope so!" I smiled as we headed upstairs. "But this won't be your last chance to see them. You *are* coming to the opening, aren't you?"

"Of course. I wouldn't dream of missing it."

"Good, because I'm totally counting on you and Lukas to be there. I need all the moral support I can get."

"What about your parents? Aren't they going to be there?"

My smile dimmed. "I haven't told them about it yet." I opened the door and ushered him into the room before he could ask any more questions—only to cringe at the sight of the tools strewed across my workbench, my unmade bed, and several days' worth of dirty clothes scattered about the floor.

Oh, yeah. I forgot my place looks like a disaster area right now.

"Please forgive the mess," I said as I hastily gathered wadded-up socks and panties and tossed them in the full-to-overflowing laundry hamper behind the door "Things have been hectic lately, and I kind of let things slide...."

If Hexe heard my feeble excuses for why I lived like a pig, he showed no sign of it. He pointed at the collection of sculptures in the far corner of the room. "Is that them?"

The Dying Gaul lay on the floor, atop his fallen shield, staring with repurposed taillight eyes at his dropped sword, a torque fashioned of recycled copper wire about his pipelike neck. With his exposed machine-made joints and ligaments, he looked more like a chrome-plated skeleton than an ancient gladiator.

The Thinker sat opposite him on a folding chair, metal chin resting on a fist made from old typewriter parts, lost in cold steel thought. I wasn't sure if he was pondering the *Dying Gaul*'s fate or trying to ignore the *Lovers* beside him, wrapped in their eternal kiss.

Lover Number One twiddled the hollow nipple of *Lover Number Two*'s aluminum funnel-breast with typewriter-key fingers, while she wrapped hers about the piston jutting from his galvanized thighs.

Next to them was the regal *Ariadne*, her face fashioned from a silvered Venetian carnival mask. She reclined upon the metallic panther as if it were a chaise lounge, her clock-spring tresses held in place by a hair band made of baling wire. A length of silver lamé cloth hung from one shoulder, exposing breasts made from vintage Bugatti headlights. The *Cyber-Panther* bore his mistress's weight without complaint, green plastic LED eyes glowing in their metal orbits, his head turned toward hers in snarling adoration.

"Heavens and hells, Tate," Hexe said, shaking his head in wonder. "These are absolutely incredible!"

"Yeah," I replied drily. "But all I can think about right now is that it's going to be a real bitch hauling these things downstairs."

"I think I can help you out with that," he said, a gleam in his eye. "I'll be right back." He hurried out of the room and ran downstairs, only to return a few moments later carrying a small chafing dish and a Grecian urn decorated with satyrs and nymphs. He placed the chafing dish on my workbench and, after removing the lid, poured out a light green oil that smelled strongly of frankincense. He then dipped his extra ring finger, what the Kymerans called their "magic" digit, of his right hand in the scented oil and pressed it against the *Dying Gaul*'s polished brow, muttering an incantation in Kymeran under his breath. He then did the exact same thing with the other statues. Once finished, he produced a cigarette lighter and set fire to the oil in the chafing dish.

Before I realized what was happening, Hexe dipped his right hand into the blaze. I cried out in alarm and moved to stop him, but it was too late; he was already wrist deep in the flames. To my surprise, he showed no sign of either pain or concern. When he withdrew his hand a few moments later, licks of flame danced on the end of each digit.

As I watched, transfixed, upon the air he traced, with fingers tipped in fire, a word never spoken. It shimmered for a heartbeat in midair before returning to the unknown. Hexe then picked up the lid and quickly smothered the flame in the chafing dish.

"There you go." He smiled. "This should make getting these things downstairs a little easier for you."

I scratched my head, baffled as to how any of what I had just witnessed could make carrying several heavy statues down two flights of stairs any less cumbersome. I was startled by a loud rattling sound, like that of hailstones striking a tin roof. The cacophony was so thunderous, I covered my ears. As I looked around for the source of the racket, I realized that the noise was coming from the statues, which were vibrating in place like tuning forks. Just as I thought all my hard work was going to collapse in a pile of loosened bolts and torn welds, the noise stopped.

To my amazement, the Dying Gaul picked up his shield in one hand and his sword in the other and levered himself upright. The Thinker rose from his chair, standing shoulder to shoulder with his fellow creation. The Lovers freed themselves from their embrace, their fingers flexing and clicking like the legs of metal spiders. Ariadne abandoned her repose, gathering the silver lamé about her so as to hide her nakedness, while the Cyber-Panther ghosted forward on his paws. Together they turned to stare at me, like troops awaiting an order, their eyes aglow in their empty faces.

I felt a swell of true pride as I watched my creations move. While I had designed them to be poseable, it had never occurred to me that they could truly be capable of walking. It was both exhilarating and disturbing to see my handiwork moving about under its own steam. With their metal skin, exposed hip and shoulder joints, and polished steel bones, they looked like chrome-plated cadavers brought to life. I wasn't sure if I was supposed to be playing the part of Pygmalion or Dr. Frankenstein.

"Why are they looking at me?" I whispered nervously.

"Because you are their maker," Hexe explained. "They're waiting for you to tell them what to do."

"But *you're* the one who brought them to life—shouldn't they be paying attention to you?"

"I merely provided the spark that animates them. It is your hands and will that fashioned them. That makes them an extension of your spirit."

"Are they—alive?"

"Not as you mean the word, no. They are animate. They have the power to move, but not the will. They must be told what to do, like golems. Go ahead, give them a command."

I cleared my throat, uncertain how loud I should speak, since the only one that had ears was the Cyber-Panther. I decided I would utilize the same basic volume I used whenever I talked to my grandparents—something just this side of shouting.

"Go downstairs and get inside your crates."

The Dying Gaul brought his sword hand up to his chest in a centurion's salute and dutifully clanked his way toward the door, the others falling in line behind him. Last in the parade were Ariadne and the Cyber-Panther. The mechanical princess walked with her head held high, as befitting the wife of a god, while her feline companion switched its segmented metal tail like a mouser on the prowl.

I followed them downstairs and watched as they placed themselves inside their respective crates, pairing up without being told to do so. The Lovers crawled inside their crate together, pulling the excelsior down around them like children preparing for bed. Ariadne carefully lowered herself into her plywood container, and then motioned for the Cyber-Panther to join her. The great metal cat hopped in after its mistress, curling up beside her like an overgrown tabby. The Thinker stepped inside his box, followed by the Dying Gaul, who placed his sword and shield upon his chest as he lay down, like a sleeping warrior awaiting reveille.

I was downstairs in the kitchen when I heard the knock on the door. I threaded my way through the crowded parlor, trying my best not to bruise myself on one of the wooden crates awaiting pickup.

Upon opening the door, I was taken aback to find myself staring at a fat, bald man with a squat nose, thick lips, and horse's ears. From the waist down he was built like a satyr, but instead of goat's legs, he sported a pair of horse's legs, as well as a tail to match. He wore a T-shirt emblazoned with the Teamster logo—a wagon wheel with the profile of a horse's head on one side and a centaur's on the other—and seemed just as nonplussed to see me as I was to see him. He frowned and double-checked the clipboard in his hands, then frowned even harder.

"You Tate?" the horse-legged Teamster growled.

"Yes," I replied, trying to cover my surprise. I held out my hand in greeting. "You must be Rowdy."

The Teamster did not accept my offered handshake, but instead turned to the bay centaur hitched to the draft wagon parked on the curb. "Check it out, Rowdy!" he brayed. "This nump thinks I'm you!"

"You wish, Sylvester!" the centaur-horse laughed.

"I'm sorry. I—I didn't realize—" I stammered, my cheeks bright red.

"Who you apologizing to, lady?" Sylvester snarled as I brushed past. "Me or Rowdy?"

The centaur hitched to the wagon was considerably

larger that Kidron, his lower body resembling that of a Clydesdale. His upper torso was correspondingly stocky, with muscular shoulders and bulging forearms. His hand engulfed my own as I introduced myself.

"I'm Tate. *You* must be Kidron's brother, right?"

"Three-quarters, actually," Rowdy replied. "We got the same mom, but our dads are half brothers. It's kinda complicated, but that's how it is in the herd."

"I'm awfully sorry for the mix-up," I apologized.

"That's okay," Rowdy said, taking off his Teamster cap so he could shake out his mane. "I realize there ain't much of a family resemblance. First time I've been mistook for an ipotane, though."

I frowned. "An ipo-what?"

"Like my buddy over there," Rowdy explained, nodding in Sylvester's direction.

"Is that what he is?" I replied in surprise. "I thought he was some kind of satyr or something. . . ."

Sylvester hurled down his clipboard, stamping his hooves in anger. "A *satyr*?" He spat on the sidewalk. "We all look alike to you damned numps, don't we? Chuffin' human can't tell a hard-workin', gods-fearin' ipotane from a worthless, lolly-gaggin' satyr! I bet you couldn't tell a basilisk from a cockatrice, neither!"

"Syl, calm down," Rowdy said evenly. "She didn't mean nothing by it."

I glanced about uneasily, hoping the ipotane's outburst might go unnoticed, but no such luck. A passing Kymeran with maroon hair slowed down to stare, while a trio of leprechauns watching from across the street sniggered among themselves.

"I'm sorry I offended you, Mr., uh, uh—Sylvester," I said, trying to figure out some way of mollifying the half-horse. "I really don't want to cause any trouble. . . ."

Sylvester barked a humorless laugh. "Ha! If you ain't lookin' for trouble, lady, then what in seven hells are *you* doin' in Golgotham?"

"You tell 'er, boyo!" one of the leprechauns shouted from across the street as he recorded the event for posterity with his cell phone camera.

I froze, unable to think of anything I could say that would not make matters worse than they were already. A crowd was starting to gather, as everyone on the street stopped what they were doing to stare at me. I was alarmed by the open dislike I saw in the eyes of some of my neighbors, and for the first time since moving to Golgotham, the realization I was the only human on the street was actually frightening.

Without warning, a beer bottle came flying toward my head. Unable to dodge the missile, I instinctively raised my hands to protect my face. Just before it was about to hit me, the bottle stopped as if caught by a phantom hand. It was so close I could clearly read the label, BLARNEY'S ALE.

The bottle hung suspended in midair for a split second before flying back the way it came, smashing to the pavement next to the trio of leprechauns across the street. The one with the cell phone nimbly jumped aside to avoid the flying shards of glass.

"Oi!" he shouted, shaking his fist in my direction.

"Is there a *problem*?"

I turned to see my knight in shining armor—or, in this case, My Chemical Romance T-shirt—standing framed in the doorway of the house, his right hand held up, palm outward, in a warding gesture, all six fingers bent in strange angles. The look on Hexe's face was the most serious I had seen since the meeting with Boss Marz.

Sylvester gulped audibly. "No. No problem at all, Serenity." The ipotane bent and picked up his clipboard, signaling the end of the confrontation. The various on-lookers quickly turned away and went back to their business.

Sylvester coughed nervously into his fist and glanced back at Hexe, who had yet to leave the doorway. "You got your cartage fee, ma'am?" he asked, suddenly the soul of courtesy.

"Yes, I do," I said, reaching into my pocket.

Sylvester quickly counted the cash I handed him and tucked it into a fanny pack zippered about his equine waist. He removed a hand truck from the back of the wagon and dragged it up the stairs into the house. Hexe stepped out of the way to allow him to enter, but not before fixing Sylvester with a glare sharp enough to cut glass.

"Sorry about my friend there," Rowdy said, a look of genuine embarrassment on his face. "Sylvester's already got a horse's ass, but that don't give him the right to act like one. If any of this got back to our boss . . ."

"It's okay," I said, eager to put the whole unpleasant episode behind me. "It was just a misunderstanding. Nobody got hurt."

"That's pretty decent of you," the centaur said gratefully. "Kidron said you were straight up for a, uh, I mean—"

"Nump?" I suggested wryly.

"I *was* gonna say 'human.'" The Teamster smiled. "Anyway, my brother's a good judge of character, and if he says you're okay with him, then you're okay with me."

"Thank you, Rowdy. I appreciate that."

Despite his paunch, Sylvester proved as strong as his lower half, and managed to load the three large crates into the back of the wagon in just a matter of minutes. After getting my signature (in triplicate) on some forms, he climbed back into the wagon.

As he and Rowdy rumbled off down the street, the ipotane cast a final, worried look over his shoulder at Hexe, who still stood watching on the front stoop.

"You don't have to stand guard," I told him as I reentered the house. "Everything's okay now."

"I'm sorry that happened," he said grimly. "If I'd been there from the start, none of this would have happened. . . ."

"Don't worry about it. I knew when I first moved here that I might run into some antihuman resentment." I smiled and placed my right hand atop his. "I'm beginning to understand how much my being your friend has shielded me. But you can't protect me *all* the time."

"I can try," he said, giving my hand a gentle squeeze.

A peculiar feeling stole across me, and the world seemed to curve gently around me, as if I were standing inside a giant soap bubble. I had the strangest feeling that not only did I know the man standing before me, but that I had always known him. I looked into his eyes and found myself there, just as he saw himself in mine. I could sense his presence in my heart, filling my soul with every breath I took.

I was being drawn toward him, his handsome face filling my view, as if I were a compass and he were true north. His smell was intoxicating, and his breath was warm and sweet against my cheek. And I knew that all I wanted right there, in that moment, was to have his arms around me and feel his lips against my own.

Suddenly my coat pocket began to play the chorus from They Might Be Giants' "Instanbul (Not Constantinople)."

The magic bubble that seemed to surround us disappeared, shattered like a hammer tossed through a stained glass window. Despite myself, I let go of his hand and reached for my phone.

"I'm sorry. I've *got* to take this," I explained apologetically as I turned my back. "It's Derrick calling to find out about the delivery...."

My conversation was brief—no more than a minute—but when I turned back around, Hexe was gone, like moonlight come the dawn.

Chapter 17

"**W**hy are you taking an overnight bag?" Lukas asked. He was sitting on the edge of my bed, watching me pack. "Is Chelsea that far away?"

I had spent the last few days shuttling between the house and the gallery, making sure the sculptures were unpacked and posed properly, and arranging the lighting for each piece. The time for preparations was finally over. Tonight was the big night.

"No, it's not. But I'm not going to wear my good clothes on the subway," I explained. "I'm taking a bag with me so I can change when I get to the gallery."

"You must be so excited, Tate," Lukas enthused. "This is an important night for you!"

Lukas was right. It *was* an important night, as it marked a decisive victory. After years of struggling against the expectations of my parents and my childhood peers, I was finally having my first show, in a moderately important gallery, and it was due entirely to the strength of my art, not the family name.

"It's an important night for you, too," I pointed out.

"You were the model for the *Cyber-Panther*, which Derrick went absolutely gaga over, by the way."

"Is that good?"

"It's *excellent*!" I grinned, handing him one of the postcard-sized invitations.

Lukas stared at the black-and-white photograph of *The Dying Gaul* that graced the invitation. "Why does it say 'Action Figures' at the bottom?"

"That's the name of the show," I explained. "It's what I call my sculptures, because they're movable like a G.I. Joe doll, excuse me, *action figure*."

"It's really wonderful, Tate," he said wistfully as he handed the card back to me. "I'm happy for you."

"You'd better keep that on you," I said. "You'll need it to get into the opening."

Lukas's eyes widened in surprise. "You mean, I can finally go somewhere?"

"You didn't think I'd have an art show and not invite my model, did you?" I grinned. "Hexe and I discussed it the other night. He and Dr. Mao decided you are ninety-nine percent recovered. Plus, Chelsea is way outside the Malandanti's stomping grounds. The chance of your being seen and recognized is almost zero once you're out of Golgotham. Hexe has arranged for Kidron to drop the two of you off as close to the subway as possible. From there it should be easy to make your way uptown."

"Thank you, Tate!" Lukas said, throwing his arms around me. He was so happy, he was purring.

I emerged from the subway at Eighth Avenue and West Twenty-third. After spending the last two months in Golgotham, I was having difficulty transitioning back to the New York I once knew. As I made my way to Derrick's gallery on Twenty-fourth, people hurried past me in all directions.

I found myself unconsciously searching the crowd for those characteristics I had come to view as "typical," such as cat-eye pupils and pointed ears, even the occasional set of horns, and was saddened to find them missing. Despite the recent confrontation, I still felt far more comfortable traveling the streets of Golgotham than anywhere else.

Like the rest of the city, the gritty, industrial romance of West Chelsea was rapidly succumbing to the onslaught of towering condos that threatened to turn Manhattan into a featureless mass of glass and steel. As I neared Tenth Avenue, I spotted the refurbished High Line, looking like a cross between a cast-iron window box and an elevated terrarium. I reflected sourly on how the only things left from the old neighborhood would soon be the Chelsea Hotel and the Empire Diner, and even then they would probably only be spared because they were tourist attractions.

A delivery van honked loud and long as I stepped off the curb, forcing me to jump back. I shook my head in wonderment. Although I had grown up in this city, I suddenly found myself unaccustomed to its traffic. The streets of Golgotham might be crowded, but they at least were free of automobiles and trucks. It seemed strange to me now to look around and see only yellow taxis instead of centaurs and their hansom cabs.

If I was feeling this out of step, I could only hope the culture shock would not prove overwhelming for Lukas and Hexe.

*   *   *

Templeton Gallery was in the heart of West Chelsea's thriving arts district, situated on the second floor of a converted commercial building and accessible only from the street via a narrow staircase. On the street-level door was a poster-sized version of the postcard invitation. I paused to stare at my name and then headed upstairs.

The moment I set foot inside the gallery, Derrick, hurried forward to greet me. He was a moderately handsome man in his early forties, with collar-length gingerish hair.

"There you are! The phone's been ringing off the hook," he exclaimed breathlessly. "I have critics from the *Village Voice* and the *New York Press* confirmed for tonight, as well as the critic for the *Times*. There are also a couple of very wealthy collectors showing interest, especially after I described the *Cyber-Panther* to them over the phone. . . ."

The gallery was divided into two sections, the first of which was the reception/sales area, where the unsold remnants of previous shows hung on the walls, hoping to entice a buyer. The front of the gallery also had a floor-to-ceiling glass window that looked out onto the street with a neon sign that said in huge block letters, TEMPLETON. The second, larger section of the gallery was reserved for the current show, and it was there I found my "action figures," posed atop white wooden boxes. The carefully angled track lights made their metallic skin glisten like the jeweled carapaces of scarab beetles. Presented in such a manner, they seemed more like idols dedicated to some strange, future faith than works of art.

"So, what do you think?" Derrick asked.

"They look amazing, Derrick," I said, nodding my head in approval. "You've done a wonderful job."

"I'm only as good as my artists." He smiled, brushing up against my right arm. The contact was brief, but far from coincidental. While setting up the show, I had discovered Derrick was what you might call "touchy-feely." He wasn't a gropey bastard, like the life-modeling teacher I had to punch in the balls my sophomore year of art school, but it was still a little disconcerting.

I continued to smile as I stepped away, pretending to pay attention to another of my sculptures. I didn't want to get on Derrick's bad side by punching him in the nuts, but I didn't want him to get the wrong idea, either.

"I see you brought a change of clothes." He smiled, motioning to my overnight bag. "You're perfectly welcome to use my apartment upstairs as your dressing room."

"You actually live over your own gallery?" I glanced up at the ceiling in surprise.

"Not really," he admitted. "It's where I stay when I'm in town. My actual home is in Connecticut, with my family."

"I see," I said, stealing a glance at his hands. Although there was no wedding ring in sight, I doubted the "family" he referred to meant his mom and dad. "I appreciate the offer, Derrick, but I already have a place to go change."

A flicker of disappointment crossed the gallery owner's face. "Oh. Very good." He frowned at the expensive watch on his wrist. "The opening isn't until seven, but I need you back by six thirty. That's when the photographer from the *Village Voice* is supposed to show up to snap a few pictures. I definitely need you here for that."

After assuring Derrick I'd return in plenty of time, I left the gallery and made my way back to Tenth, where I flagged down one of the numerous taxis crowding the wide avenue.

The cabbie didn't blink twice at my tattoos and eyebrow piercing. "Where ya headed, lady? West Village? Hell's Kitchen?"

"Eighty-third and Fifth," I replied as I slid across the backseat.

Now *that* made him blink.

Chapter 18

I hadn't lived under the same roof as my parents since I left for college, nearly seven years ago. I had been back to their apartment numerous times since then, but only as a guest. As I stepped out of the elevator, I was greeted by the life-sized portrait of my ancestor, the original Timothy Alden Talmadge Eresby, which had hung in the marble-clad lobby of the penthouse for as long as I could remember.

Back in the day, he'd owned railroads and newspapers and factories that made everything from burlap bags to steam whistles. Not bad for a guy who came to this country on an English cattle boat to escape debtor's prison.

I reached behind the portrait and retrieved the house key tucked between the frame and the canvas and unlocked the front door. My father's family had lived in the six-bedroom, seven-bath penthouse for more than eighty years, passing it down from one generation to the next. I smiled as I stepped into the grand foyer, with its familiar crystal chandelier and antique furnishings.

"Home again, home again, jiggity-jig," I said aloud to myself. I ambled down the main hallway, looking for signs of life. I peeked into the library, which my grandfather Timothy Alden Talmadge Eresby III had transplanted in toto from an eighteenth-century French villa, but I saw only shelves of leather-bound books. I then looked into the dining room and found the family butler, Clarence, sitting at the end of the eight-foot-long table, stolidly polishing the silver while staring out the window at Central Park.

"I see my mother is putting you to good use," I said wryly.

Clarence blinked as if started from a daydream, his eyebrows lifting in surprise. "Miss Timmy! I didn't hear you come in! It's so good to see you!"

"It's good to see you, too, Clarence," I replied, moving to embrace the elderly servant. "You're the only person alive who can still call me 'Timmy' without getting a knuckle sandwich, you know."

Like the portrait of my great-great grandfather, Clarence had been around since before I could remember. To my shame, I wasn't sure if Clarence was his first or last name. Not that it mattered. He was Clarence, just as the sun is the sun and the moon is the moon.

"Are my parents home?" I asked.

"Not at the moment," he replied. "Your mother is taking tea with Mrs. Petrie, and your father flew to Chicago on business. He's expected back later this evening."

"Just as well." I sighed. "I only stopped by to freshen up and change my clothes. I have an event in Chelsea tonight." I handed him one of the postcard invitations. "You're more than welcome to attend."

Clarence smiled as he studied the photo of *The Dying Gaul*. "You were always quite talented at creating things, even as a child. I still have the ashtray you made for me when you were in second grade."

"Even though you don't smoke," I laughed.

"True. But I did contemplate taking it up after you presented it to me. It is a *very* nice ashtray."

I went upstairs to my old bedroom, which had been converted to yet another guest room. I laid out my change of clothes across the queen-sized bed and headed into the en suite bathroom. After months of sharing a bathroom with my housemates, I allowed myself the luxury of soaking in a bath of warm bubbles. Once I was finished, I toweled off and put on a particularly alluring little black dress I had bought for the occasion, one that would show off both my tattoos and my figure to their best advantage, and a pair of matching strappy high heels. As I applied my makeup, I mulled over how I should wear my hair, which I kept fairly short because of the welding helmet, and black because, well, because that's what I was born with. Should I go punk or pixie? In the end I decided to split the difference.

As I got ready, I kept telling myself that I was dressing up for my "public." People have expectations of what artists look like, especially those who work in metal, and I wanted to both play to and subvert my audience's preconceptions. But that's not why I was humming a little song while I applied my lipstick and mascara. Critics and collectors be damned, I was dressing up for Hexe.

Since the day we first met, Hexe had graciously included me in his world, showing me about Golgotham and educating me as to its mysteries and mundanities. Now it was my turn to return the favor and bring him into *my* world. It might not be supernatural in origin, but it was easily as strange and exotic in its own right. Besides, what good is an opening night—or any night, really—without someone to share it with?

As I was applying the finishing touches to my toilette, there was a rap on the bedroom door. I opened it to find Clarence standing in the hallway, looking apologetic.

"I'm sorry to interrupt you, Miss Timmy, but madam has returned from her afternoon tea. She requests your presence in the Grand Salon."

"Tell her I'll be down shortly."

"Very good, Miss Timmy."

"Oh, and Clarence? Please call me 'Tate' from now on, won't you?"

"I'll do my best to remember that, Miss Timmy."

Over the years I have developed pretending to talk to my mother into a fine art. I long ago learned how to appear to be attentive, utilizing both physical and verbal signatures triggered by shifts in her tone of voice that do not actually require me to listen to her conversation. To tell the truth, "conversation" is something of a misnomer. My mother has never engaged in discourse, only monologues. As long as I made the proper number of "ah's," "uh-huh's," and "Is that so?'s" during the appropriate lulls and breath stops, my mother seemed satisfied that I was paying attention to her.

Still, there was always the danger of the occasional pitfall, since she occasionally expected me to respond in something other than monosyllabic grunts or shrugs. I dreaded those prickly occasions, as it required me to actually listen to what she was saying, which meant I was probably going to lose my temper.

These verbal sorties were usually presaged by a rhetorical question, spoken with more than the usual dollop of disdain, thereby guaranteeing a response on my part. I had come to recognize these lead-ins as a sign of danger, like the fin of a shark briefly cutting the surface of an otherwise glassy sea.

The Grand Salon was indeed that. Forty feet long, with a coffered ceiling taken from a seventeenth-century Venetian palace, it was a sunken room, five feet below the main hallway, and only accessible via a pristine marble staircase said to have originated from the same quarry as Michelangelo's *David*.

Across the room, huge windows started below the level of the top stair, creating a vertiginous effect as I looked down onto MoMA's roof. I remembered riding my Big Wheel across the room's polished stone floor as a child, weaving in and out between the priceless Italian Renaissance statuary my great-grandfather brought back from Europe. And my parents were at a loss to understand why I would take up the arts?

My mother was seated in front of the wood-burning fireplace, still dressed in what I recognized as her "lunching" ensemble. She was holding the invitation I had given to Clarence earlier.

Once, long before I arrived on the scene, my mother was a stunningly beautiful woman. Over the years she had worked very hard at maintaining her face and figure, all too aware of how easy it would be to wake up one day and find herself replaced in her husband's affections—not to mention his last will and testament—by a piece of giggling arm candy. That was why she limited herself to one, and only one, pregnancy. Much to her chagrin, I did not prove to be a son. Oh, well. My father would simply have to make due with an heiress instead of an heir, because she certainly wasn't putting herself through *that* again.

It was also why she had surrendered the nursing, toilet training, and upbringing of her only child to a brace of qualified professionals. It was too easy to lose track of one's husband if one paid too much attention to one's children. Although I could tell by the way she eyed the tattoos on my arms and the surgical steel ring adorning my brow ridge, she now wished she had double-checked the references on a few of the nannies.

"Hello, Mom," I said as I sat down in the chair across from her. "You're looking well."

"*What* is the meaning of this, young lady?" she demanded, thrusting the invitation at me as if it were a bad report card.

"I would think it's self-evident." I sighed. "It's an invitation to my gallery showing. The opening is tonight."

"How can that be?" she sniffed. "Your name isn't mentioned anywhere on this postcard."

"Don't be obtuse, Mother. You know better than that."

"Well, what kind of name is 'Tate' for a woman, anyway? Honestly!"

There it was. The question that did not require my answer, yet one she knew I could not ignore. Although I fully realized she was leading me into a discussion I did not want to have, I could not keep from responding. Was this how the bulls felt when they saw the red cape before them, barely concealing the flash of the matador's sword?

"It's the name *you* gave me." My reply sounded sullen and childish in my ears, as it always did when I stooped to her level.

"Your name is Timothea Alda Talmadge Eresby," she shot back haughtily.

"The Fifth. Don't forget my numerical sequence," I

sneered, sliding back into adolescent habits. "After all, only royalty, popes, and manufacturers put numbers behind their names."

"And what is *wrong* with that? You certainly don't have problems cashing the checks signed to your *real* name!"

"You're the one who was afraid I'd besmirch the good name of Eresby Industries with my art in the first place!" I exclaimed, rolling my eyes in disgust. "I'm just saving you some worry, that's all."

My mother shot me a venomous look as she removed the stopper from the cut crystal decanter beside her chair. For as long as I could remember, her personal scent had been a mixture of Chanel No.5, Benson & Hedges, and twenty-three-year-old Evan Williams. It was not an aroma that triggered pleasant childhood memories.

"Don't you dare pretend you're thinking of anyone but yourself!"

I lifted a hand to my mouth, but not before she noticed my smirk.

"What's so funny?"

"Nothing." Which was true enough. My mother's gross self-involvement was many things, but amusing wasn't one of them.

She gave me a lengthy glare, as if dimly aware that something, somewhere, was occurring at her expense, and then resumed filling her glass.

"I don't like your tone of voice," she said petulantly. "I am your mother, after all. I believe I would never see or hear from you at all if it weren't for your quarterly trust fund payments."

"I'm here now, aren't I? And it's at least another month before my next check."

"That's true," she admitted. "So why *are* you here?"

"I stopped by to change my clothes, and"—I paused and took a deep breath—"I came to invite you and Dad to the opening."

It was then the matador's sword came out from hiding and plunged itself deep into my heart.

"You father and I couldn't possibly attend on such short notice," she said dismissively. "Besides, all it would do is encourage you even further with this foolishness."

I felt the old resentments swelling up inside me, but I tried to tamp them down. Getting visibly angry would only prove that she still had the power to hurt me.

She opened the enameled box next to the decanter and took out a cigarette. Despite the trend toward nonsmoking in fashionable society, she had yet to drop the habit for fear of gaining weight. As she saw it, the risk of cancer was a reasonable trade-off for remaining a size two. She eyed my outfit as she lit up yet another Benson & Hedges.

"Is that what you're wearing tonight? Well, at least you're not going dressed in overalls and a welder's helmet." I knew from past experience that was the closest I was going to get to her approving of how I was dressed. "So where have you been keeping yourself, lately?" she asked, knocking her ash into a silver Cartier tray. "I've been told you moved out of SoHo. Felicity Arbogast's nephew lives in the same building, and he told her he saw movers carrying furniture out of your apartment."

"I needed a bigger place, where I could live and work in the same space. . . ."

"You didn't move to Jersey, did you?" she asked, a touch of alarm in her voice.

"Nooo . . ."

"Thank goodness!"

"I'm living in Golgotham now."

"You're doing *what*?!?" She came out of her seat as if someone had stuck a joy buzzer under her ass.

"You heard me," I said, taking far more pleasure in my mother's distress than someone my age probably should. "I'm living in a boardinghouse in the heart of Golgotham, between Beekman and Perdition streets. It's a great old house, the rent is crazy cheap, and my landlord is a really cool guy. . . ."

"Is he a warlock?" she asked suspiciously.

"He's a Kymeran, if that's what you mean," I replied.

She grabbed my arm, squeezing it so hard I yelped. "Whatever you do, Timmy, *never* eat or drink anything he offers to you, you understand? Everybody knows they slip you aphrodisiacs when you're not looking!"

There was a frightened, almost frantic look in her eye, which unnerved me. This was the first time in ages I could remember my mother showing concern for someone besides herself. Because of that, I tried to calm her fears by explaining the situation to her.

"It's not like that, Mother. Hexe isn't some creepy date rapist. Kymerans might make come-hithers and love potions, but they don't use them. Numps—I mean, humans—do. Besides, you don't have anything to worry about, because Hexe doesn't practice Left Hand magic, the kind that harms people."

"Don't let him fool you, Timmy," she sniffed. "They all know how to curse people, every last one of them. Never forget that. And *never* trust a kymie."

"Don't call him that!" I shouted.

My mother looked genuinely startled, at least as much as the Botox would allow. Her eyes widened and her mouth fell open and, for once, she was at a loss for words. People didn't raise their voices in our family. And they certainly didn't raise their voices to *her*.

I got to my feet, thrusting a trembling finger in her face as anger spread through my veins like poison. "You're never to talk about him like that to me again, you hear me?"

The door opened slightly and Clarence stuck his head inside the Grand Salon. "Madam? Is there something wrong?"

"There's a *hell* of a lot wrong, Clarence!" I snapped. "But I'm leaving now, so it doesn't concern you!"

"Very well, Miss Timmy," Clarence replied evenly as he withdrew from the room.

"Here," I said to my mother, as I hurled the pair of invitations I had set aside for my father and her into a nearby wastebasket. "Let me save you the trouble!"

I stormed out of the room without looking back. I had suffered my mother's thoughtless cruelty for years without once yelling at her. Instead, I would laugh and shrug and tell myself it didn't matter, because the alternative was to cry like a heartbroken child. But to hear her talk about Hexe in such a way, as if he were some kind of subhuman beast, made my blood boil. I would never dare speak up for myself, but I had no problem shouting my mother down in his defense.

Upon entering the Grand Foyer, I found Clarence waiting to see me out. "May I inquire as to where you are living nowadays?" he asked as he helped me into my coat. "Chelsea? The East Village? Tribeca, perhaps?"

"Golgotham," I replied flatly.

A flicker of alarm crossed Clarence's stone face, only to be quashed by decades of training. "Very good, Miss Timmy."

Chapter 19

Family drama aside, I was able to get back in time to have my picture taken by the *Village Voice*'s photographer. Not long after she finished snapping the last shot, the first of the evening's visitors started showing up at the gallery.

A bar was set up in the corner, dispensing white wine to those looking to get their drink on, as well as mineral water for the Twelve Steppers in attendance, while a couple of waiters carried trays of hors d'oeuvres about the room. It wasn't long before the main gallery was full of well-dressed young urban professionals, scruffy hipsters, and art world scenesters, sipping at their drinks and nibbling cubes of cheese as they milled about, talking among themselves as they stared at my sculptures.

As I stood on display beside my handiwork, I scanned the slowly shuffling crowd for a sign of the arrival of Hexe and Lukas, but my efforts went unrewarded. I checked my watch. It was going on seven thirty. Where could they possibly be? I glanced up at the Thinker, as if he might have an answer. He sat there frozen, silent, yet somehow more alive than the scores of art fanciers who crowded the gallery. I searched the room yet again, and this time I was rewarded by the sight of familiar faces, although not the ones I had been looking for.

"Templeton really made sure you got a nice turnout," Vanessa said by way of greeting. "These sculptures are awesome! They're your best work to date." She was accompanied by her boyfriend, Adrian Klein, who taught art history at NYU. Where Vanessa was outspoken and something of a firecracker, Adrian was understated and laid back, but with a mordant sense of humor.

"Thanks for coming, Nessie," I said, giving her a hug. "It's good to see you again, Adrian."

"Same here, Tate. Nessie told me all about your wild ride together," he laughed. "I'm looking forward to meeting this 'magic man' of yours, Tate. It seems I owe him a favor."

"How so?" I frowned.

"After Nessie came back from visiting you in Golgotham, she accepted my proposal. She claims the reason she agreed to marry me is because your warlock friend got her stoned and opened up her third eye, or something like that."

I gasped and turned to look at Vanessa in disbelief. "You said *yes*?"

"Afraid so." Vanessa grinned, displaying the diamond engagement ring that now decorated her left hand.

"Oh, my God!" I exclaimed, throwing my arms about the two of them. "I'm so happy for you. You are *perfect* for each other."

"Where's Hexe?" Vanessa asked. "I can't wait to introduce him to Adrian."

"I'm writing a paper on Goya, the Kymeran painter," he explained. "And I thought it might be interesting to find out how accurate his portrayals of Kymeran life and culture at the time really were. I'd love to talk to your, um, landlord, and get his take on the whole thing."

"He's not here yet," I explained. "But he should be arriving any minute now. Why don't you two get yourselves something to drink? I'll be sure to introduce you once he arrives."

"Don't mind if we do," Vanessa said, pulling her new fiancé along behind her.

There was a sudden tap on my shoulder, and I turned to find Derrick at my elbow.

"I'd like you to meet another of my artistic 'discoveries,'" the gallery owner said, indicating the dark-haired young man standing next to him. "This is Greer Bartholomew. He goes by the name of Bartho."

"Oh, yeah, the photographer," I said as I shook his hand. "You had the show before mine. I saw what was left of it in the foyer. You take some mean pictures."

"Derrick tells me you've recently moved to Golgotham," Bartho said, a gleam of excitement in his eyes. "How do you like it there?"

"It's as though I've moved to a completely different world without having to leave the city," I replied. "Every time I set foot out of my door I can honestly say I see something I've never seen before in my life. It's proved an immense inspiration, both artistically and personally."

"I've been fascinated by that part of the city all my life," Bartho confessed. "I think it's wonderful that you found the courage to actually move there." He leaned forward and whispered, "But aren't you frightened? I mean, you *are* surrounded by witches and monsters."

"I assure you, Golgotham is a lot safer than the Bronx or Bed-Stuy," I laughed, warming to the subject. This was the first time anyone had reacted to the news of where I lived with something besides open horror. "Knowing your neighbor is a witch or a warlock isn't any different than knowing they're a stockbroker or a civics teacher. It's just what they do for a living, not who they are. I'll admit I've had a couple of brushes with antihuman bias, but for the most part my neighbors treat me just like any other New Yorker would. The worst I can say about Golgotham is that it can be a little inconvenient at times, because they do things so differently, but that's also part of its charm. There's a real sense of community there, and I've made some very good friends since I've moved to the neighborhood. I can honestly say I'm happier there than I ever was living in SoHo."

"I really like your sculptures, Tate, especially the *Cyber-Panther*," Bartho said, handing me one of his cards. "I'd *love* to use it and a couple of your other pieces in a photo shoot. Maybe we can work something out?"

"Yeah, that sounds cool," I agreed. "It kind of depends on Derrick, though. The pieces are supposed to be on display for six weeks. . . . " I glanced over at the gallery owner, who nodded his head.

"I think we can work something out." He smiled.

Just then the girl who handled the sales in the front of the gallery popped in, looking extremely nervous. "Excuse me, Mr. Templeton . . ."

"Yes, what is it, Gretchen?" Derrick replied.

"There's an 'issue' up front, sir."

"Very well." Derrick sighed. "I'll be right there."

Although I was somewhat perturbed that Hexe and Lukas had yet to make it to the gallery, it was still necessary for me to socialize with the prospective buyers and casual well-wishers floating through the gallery. But while I was talking to one of Derrick's wealthier collectors, a familiar voice cut through the babble of the crowd.

"Why won't you answer my messages and e-mails, Tate? I thought we were still friends? Oh, and thanks for not inviting me to your opening."

I turned to find Roger standing behind me. From the way he had his arms folded across his chest and from how he was scowling at me, I knew he thought he looked like a brooding, romantic hero, like Heathcliff or Mr. Rochester. Instead, he came across like a spoiled, sulky child trying to guilt me into being nice to him, for fear of his causing a scene.

"For crying out loud, Roger, can't you take a chuffing hint?" I retorted. "Just because I restrained myself from kicking you in the balls the last time we spoke doesn't mean I want you in my life."

"But I *apologized*," he said, still pouting. "That means you're supposed to forgive me."

"Really?" I snorted. "Is *that* how you think it works?"

Just then I spotted a flash of purple-and-blue hair over Roger's shoulder. I pushed him aside and hurried to the front of the gallery. There I saw Hexe and Lukas locked in an animated discussion with Derrick. Hexe was wearing a shiny gold vintage jacket and black pegged, Elvis-style trousers, while Lukas was dressed like a skate punk, complete with hoodie and NOFX T-shirt. The teenaged were-cat was holding out the invitation I'd given him earlier.

"You don't understand," Lukas protested. "We have invitations, see? We're her guests. We were *invited*."

"These things aren't engraved invitations," Derrick said, folding his arms across his chest. "You could have gotten them anywhere. My PR girl drops off stacks of these things at every hipster joint on the Lower East Side and Williamsburg. . . ."

Lukas broke into a relieved grin upon seeing me approach. "Hexe, look! There she is. Tate! Over here!"

"I see you, Lukas. You don't have to wave." I turned to frown at Derrick. "What's the problem here?"

"Do you *know* these . . . people?" Derrick asked, looking genuinely aghast.

"These are the friends I was telling you about," I explained. "This is my landlord, Hexe, and that is my model, Lukas."

"Your model?" The consternation drained from Derrick's voice. He smiled as he shook Lukas's hand. "Ah! So you're the young man who posed for *The Dying Gaul* and the other male statues?"

Lukas shook his head. "I posed for the *Cyber-Panther*."

Derrick dropped Lukas's hand as if it were attached to a leper. He grabbed my elbow and steered me away from my friends.

"Did I hear him right?" Derrick whispered, shooting a worried glance at Lukas, who smiled and waved hello at him.

"Afraid so." I sighed.

"I can't have a were-cat running around loose in my gallery," he hissed. "*Especially* one that turns into a tiger!"

"Cougar, actually. And he's harmless, I assure you."

"I don't care if he turns into Snagglepuss!" Derrick snapped. "My insurance *doesn't* cover shit like this! Damn it, I wish you'd discussed this with me beforehand."

"I *told* you I was inviting some friends," I reminded him.

"Yes, but I thought you meant *human* ones!" He paused to take a deep breath to steady himself. "Look, I'm not prejudiced. In fact, one of my best clients is Kymeran. But, that said, openly consorting with a warlock at your show looks bad. People will talk. They'll say your success isn't natural. They'll say you charmed your way into the art world...."

I shot the gallery owner a withering look. "I don't care what 'they' think! And you shouldn't, either, if you truly believe in my art. Hexe and Lukas are my friends. I invited them here because I wanted them to share this evening with me, not to be insulted!"

"I'm sorry, Tate," Derrick said sincerely. "I wish things were different, but the truth of the matter is that you can't afford being seen with a Kymeran at this stage of your career. If people think your artwork is charmed, they won't buy it for fear the spell will break when you die and they'll be stuck with a piece of worthless junk. Remember what happened to Bouguereau? He was the most popular painter in France during the late nineteenth century. His paintings sold for astronomical sums during his lifetime. Now you can't *give* his canvasses away."

Hexe stepped forward, gently touching my arm. "Mr. Templeton's right. Lukas and I should go."

"You don't have to leave!" I protested. "This is twenty-first-century America, damn it! You have as much right to be here as anybody else!"

"I know that," Hexe replied. "Believe me, I *really* want to be with you for this. But it's more important that your work get the proper recognition it deserves, without people getting the wrong idea. You've worked long and hard for this night, Tate. I'm not going to be the one who ruins it for you." He turned and motioned to Lukas. "Come along, kiddo. Time to leave."

"Awww ..."

"You heard me, Lukas," Hexe said firmly. As they headed back down the stairs, he flashed me an encouraging smile. "Good luck with the opening, Tate. We'll see you back at the house. Nice meeting you, Mr. Templeton."

"Same here," Derrick replied.

As I watched him leave, I felt a painful ache of longing that was as maddening as it was exhilarating. "This really blows," I grumbled.

"Your friend made the right decision," Derrick assured me. "And he was quite the gentleman about it."

"Yeah," I agreed. "He's a real prince."

"I can't believe they made Hexe leave," Adrian exclaimed between sips of chardonnay. "Doesn't Templeton know the Unholy Wars are over?"

"Derrick didn't *make* them leave—Hexe left of his own accord," I explained. "He said he didn't want to screw things up for me by being here."

"That's more than your ex is willing to do," Vanessa commented acidly. "Roger's been tossing back glasses of wine like they're shots of tequila. Why couldn't Templeton tell *him* to leave?"

As if summoned by the mere mention of his name, Roger suddenly barged into the conversation. "Hey, Nessie! Adrian! Long time no see!"

"Hi, Roger," Adrian replied stoically.

If Roger noticed Vanessa's and Adrian's coolness, he didn't show it. "It's been months! What have you been up to? You still teaching at NYU?"

I groaned inwardly. Where did this idiot think he was? Facebook?

"Yes," Adrian answered.

Finally realizing that Adrian wasn't going to provide anything more than monosyllabic responses, Roger turned his attention back to me. "So—are your parents coming tonight?"

"No," I replied, shooting him a poisonous glare. The son of a bitch *knew* how things were between my parents and me. Having failed to guilt me into doing what he wanted, he had switched over to trying to push my buttons.

Before I had the chance to lose my temper, there was a loud commotion at the front of the gallery. I looked up to see Hexe pushing through the crowded room, his jacket muddied and his face bruised.

"Let me in!" he shouted. "I need to see Tate!"

Roger stepped forward, blocking Hexe's path. "What do you want with her, witch-boy?" he sneered.

"Please . . . It's *important* I speak to her!"

"Leave him be, Rog!" I snapped.

Roger's eyes narrowed. "You're him, aren't you? You're the one who lured her away from me."

Hexe raised an eyebrow in recognition. "Ah! So you're Roger? For your information, I didn't 'lure' anyone. And from what I've heard, she wasn't *yours* to begin with."

"Don't give me that bullshit!" Roger spat. "Everyone knows how it is with you kymies. You slipped her something, didn't you? You put a love potion in her food. Or maybe you've got a poppet with a lock of her hair wrapped around it hidden somewhere? Is that it?"

"Roger, shut up! You're embarrassing me." I grabbed his sleeve, trying to pull him away from Hexe, but he yanked his arm free. The gallery had fallen deadly silent as everyone turned their attention to the confrontation between the two men.

"I'll handle this, Tate," Roger said, from over his shoulder. "Can't you see? You're under this creep's spell." He then turned and stiff-armed Hexe, sending him staggering backward. "Are you going to get lost, or am I gonna have to kick your kymie ass?"

"I'm not leaving until I speak to her," Hexe insisted.

Roger advanced, fists raised in anticipation of the promised ass-kicking. Hexe straightened his lapels, smoothed back his tousled hair, and pointed the extra ring finger of his right hand. Roger froze in midstep, as if someone had hit the PAUSE button on a DVD. Gretchen, Derrick's assistant, squealed in terror and darted off in search of her boss.

"What did you do?" I gasped, peering into Roger's face for some sign of life. He was still staring straight ahead at Hexe, but his eyes did not seem to register any awareness of his situation.

"Is he dead?" Adrian asked. He tentatively pushed his finger against Roger's chest, causing him to slightly rock in place like a statue.

"Don't worry about him," Hexe said with a dismissive shrug of his shoulders. "He's very much alive. He'll snap out of it in a few minutes."

"Too bad," Vanessa snorted. "I like him better this way. Oh, where are my manners? Hexe, this is my fiancé, Adrian."

"Nessie told me about you," Adrian said, staring at Hexe in open awe. "Apparently it was all true."

For the first time since he reappeared in the gallery, I realized Hexe was alone. "Where's Lukas?" I asked, looking around for some sign of the young were-cat.

"Boss Marz has him," Hexe said grimly. He reached into his pocket and withdrew the smaller of the scrying eggs. He quickly breathed upon it and held it up so Vanessa, Adrian, and I could see the grainy black-and-white images that flickered inside the crystal's depths.

Hexe and Lukas were walking back toward the subway, talking to each other. Suddenly, an unmarked black panel van swerved out of traffic and onto the sidewalk, heading right at them. Hexe jumped out of the way, landing in the street. Lukas, however, was struck head-on. I gasped in horror as the young were-cat's body was sent flying through the air, only to land as a tangled mass of broken limbs on the pavement.

Two figures jumped out of the van. I recognized them immediately as the werewolf Phelan and the Malandanti called Nach. The two men snatched up the unconscious were-cat and threw him into the vehicle, pausing only long enough for the Malandanti to kick Hexe in the face as he struggled to his feet. The vision inside the scrying egg ended as Hexe staggered back toward the gallery.

I touched his bruised face. "Are you okay?"

"I'm banged up, but nothing's broken," he replied, giving my hand a gentle squeeze. "But if we don't move fast, Marz is going to turn Lukas into a fur coat. And we're going to need an army to get past his croggies."

No sooner had Hexe said those words than I heard Mr. Manto's prophecy inside my head, echoing as if the oracle were speaking to me from the bottom of a well.

"'Rise shall a fire-born army forged of woman to the bestiarii free.'"

"Huh?" Vanessa, Adrian, and Hexe exchanged confused looks.

"It's something I just remembered," I explained. "Something Mr. Manto told me."

"Aloysius read your fortune?" Hexe asked in surprise.

"Yes. At the time I didn't understand. But now I think I do." I turned and looked into the main gallery.

The art patrons were watching us apprehensively, muttering among themselves, unsure if what was going on was part of the opening or not. "The statues—are they still enchanted?"

"Yes." He nodded. "All they need is for you to command them."

"We have our army, then."

Thrusting my thumb and index finger into my mouth, I whistled as hard as I could. The chatter filling the gallery fell silent. Stepping forward, I threw out my chest and bellowed in my best *Full Metal Jacket* imitation. *"Atten-shun!"*

The art critic from the *Village Voice* uttered a piercing scream as the Thinker stood up. This was followed by an alarmed yelp from the *New York Press* critic as the Lovers belonging to *The Kiss* unwrapped themselves from their embrace, and Ariadne abandoned her feline couch.

Everyone else started to scream as the Dying Gaul got to his feet, brandishing his sword and shield, and the Cyber-Panther, arching his metal-clad back, turned his head in my direction.

"Fall in!"

As the statues descended from their pedestals, the gallery visitors shrieked and began falling over one another in a desperate attempt to get out of the way. Hexe hurried forward, motioning for the panicked art fanciers to stay calm.

"There's nothing to fear! These things mean you no harm!"

The Dying Gaul stepped forward and stood before me, bringing his sword to his chest in the time-honored salute of the gladiator. At that moment I could not have been prouder of him if he were my own son.

"*March!*" I yelled.

My army of animated statues moved forward, like ducklings following their mother, with the Dying Gaul leading the way. As the Cyber-Panther stalked past, Bartho reached out to stroke the figure's steel hide, only to have the metal beast flash his glowing eyes at him and make a screeching noise that sounded like a band saw cutting through sheet metal. I saw Gretchen pressed up against the wall, looking as if she were about to piss her panties. I wanted to feel bad about that, but really didn't have the time to bother.

"What the *hell* do you think you're doing?" Derrick shouted as he pushed his way through the group of frightened gallery patrons.

"My friend's in danger, Derrick," I explained as I led my handiwork toward the exit, "I have to save him."

"But what about the show?" he implored, grabbing my arm.

"I don't have time to think about that now," I said, shaking myself free.

"Well, you'd better think about it," Derrick snarled, dropping all pretense of affability. "Because if you take those . . . *things* out of my gallery, I'll see to it that you'll never get another show in this city again!"

Derrick was literally trembling with rage, the veins on his forehead throbbing in time with his pulse. The last person I had seen that furious had been Hexe's uncle. I glanced over my shoulder at my sculptures, waiting patiently for my next order, and then back at Derrick. I shook my head and shrugged.

"Then that's how it's going to be," I said, my voice steadfast. "I'm not going to let my friend die just to save my career."

As I started to move again, Derrick jumped in front

of me, arms spread wide, in a desperate attempt to block my path. "No! I won't let you do this!"

"Get out of my way, Derrick."

"But I've already sold two of those pieces!"

Hexe sighed as he raised his right hand. "You heard the lady, mister."

Derrick froze in midplea, his arms sticking straight out like those of a scarecrow. I motioned to Lover Number One, who clanked forward and dragged the petrified gallery owner out of the way, placing him alongside my equally frozen ex-boyfriend.

"You've killed him!" Gretchen wailed as she scurried forward to check on her boss.

"He's perfectly fine," Hexe assured her. "He'll come out of it in a few minutes."

"What about us?" Vanessa asked, gesturing to herself and Adrian. "Is there anything we can do to help?"

"No," Hexe said. "I'm afraid not. If I were you, I'd get out of here before the PTU show up and arrest you as accomplices to illicit magic after the fact."

"He's right, Nessie," Adrian said, grabbing his fiancée's hand.

"Call us when it's over!" Vanessa shouted over her shoulder as Adrian dragged her down the stairs and out the door. "Let me know you're okay!"

"We will," I promised. I turned back to look at my homemade army, and saw that half of the gallery attendees were trailing after us at a safe distance. Perhaps they thought all of this was some kind of elaborate experimental theater being performed for their benefit.

However, once we reached the street, the chorus of screams that greeted us as pedestrians found themselves confronted by a group of animated metal sculptures, erased whatever misconceptions the remaining gallery patrons might have had about being part of living theater. Some turned and fled, while others simply stood and stared at the chaos unfolding around them.

Everywhere I looked, people were calling 911 on their cell phones. There was the sound of squealing brakes as a taxi driver, startled by the sight of the Cyber-Panther leaping atop the roof of a nearby parked car, ran up onto the sidewalk, smashing the front window of yet another art gallery. I heard the sound of sirens in the distance headed our way.

"There's no way we can get to Golgotham in time if we stay on the streets," Hexe said matter-of-factly. "The cops are already on their way, and the Paranormal Threat Unit won't be far behind. We have to go underground."

"Take the subway?" I rolled my eyes at the thought. "The transit cops are gonna *love* us."

"No," Hexe said, shaking his head. "Not the subway." He pointed to the manhole cover in the middle of the street.

"Why not?" I shrugged. "Looks like that's where my career's headed, anyway." I turned and gestured to the Thinker. The sculpture walked over and, without hesitation, lifted the manhole cover as easily as I would a paper plate.

As I climbed down the ladder into the hidden underbelly of the city, I looked up to see Hexe, still topside, frantically texting on his BlackBerry.

"This isn't the time to update your Facebook status!"

"I'm putting out the call for reinforcements before I lose my signal," he explained.

"Hurry up—the cops are gonna be here any moment!"

Hexe pocketed his BlackBerry and clambered down the utility ladder to join me. I pointed at the Thinker, who climbed back up and dragged the cast-iron cover back into place.

"You know, I think I could get used to this five-star-general gig," I said drily.

Hexe spoke a few words in Kymeran, and a ball of milky blue witchfire spontaneously combusted in the palm of his right hand, illuminating our immediate surroundings. He then tossed it up in the air, where it hovered over his head like St. Elmo's fire. The flickering light made the faces of the sculptures gathered about us look truly alive.

"Do we even know where we're headed?" I asked.

"I heard one of the bastards mention Ghastly's. It's this hole-in-the-wall on Duivel Street."

The adrenaline was starting to ebb, and my heart sank as I realized that we were still miles away from Golgotham, and on the wrong side of town, to boot. "It's going to take hours to get there—assuming we can get there at all," I said mournfully.

"Don't give up hope," Hexe said, squeezing my hand. "I know a shortcut."

Chapter 20

"Why aren't we in the sewer?" I asked, looking around at the coils of fiber-optic cable, telephone lines, and public utility pipe work that surrounded us on all sides. "Not that I'm complaining, mind you."

"The sewer system for the city is hundreds of feet belowground, past the subways," Hexe explained. "The first thirty feet is mostly Con Ed, telephone lines, steam pipes . . . that kind of stuff. We have to move fast. NYPD might be hesitant about following us under the streets, but the PTU won't have any such reservations since they have Kymerans and other paranormals working for them." He took out his scrying egg and held it between his thumb and forefinger, just above his head. A dim, purplish light sparked within its depths, like a lamp seen through a heavy fog. "This way," he said, ducking down a narrow off-branch from the central tunnel, the witchlight bobbing over his head like a luminous toy balloon.

I hesitated for a moment. I do not like cramped, closed-in spaces that are dark and might electrocute me, blow up, or contain rats—*especially* that last part. I glanced nervously over my shoulder at my self-made army, their LED eyes burning in the gloom like small lamps. I took a deep breath and hurried after Hexe, heartened by the sound of my creations clanking after me. *That'll scare off the rats,* I tried to reassure myself.

"So what's this shortcut of yours?" I asked, trying to push from my head the image of hundreds of filthy, disgusting rodents watching me with their beady little eyes.

"The Sub-Rosa Subway."

"I've never heard of it."

"That's the whole point. Back in the 1870s, there was this inventor Alfred Beach, who designed a pneumatic subway system. . . ."

"You mean like those tubes you use at the drive-up teller?"

"Exactly! Except in this case he planned on moving people back and forth, not bank deposits. Beach wanted to build a demonstration model, only a block long, running under Broadway from Warren Street to Murray Street, to show the public how a full-scale model would work. But when Tammany Hall turned down his permit, he decided to go ahead and build it in secret, anyway, using dwarf laborers from Golgotham. No one knew he was tunneling a hundred feet under the busiest street in the entire city until Beach Pneumatic Transit opened for business in 1870.

"However, he created a lot of enemies at City Hall with that stunt, and they made sure his subway went out of business. Eventually the line was sealed off and forgotten, at least by human society. The dwarvish community, on the other hand, saw the benefit in having a means of commuting underground, as most of them worked as sandhogs, digging water tunnels for the city hundreds of feet below street level. Once the project was abandoned, they moved in and took it over for themselves."

"You mean there has been a secret dwarf-only subway running under this city for more than a hundred years? Are there even enough dwarves to make it worthwhile? I mean, I don't remember seeing a single one the whole time I've been in Golgotham."

"Are you kidding?" Hexe laughed. "Subterranean Manhattan is absolutely *riddled* with dwarf-warrens! They're probably the largest minority community in the triboroughs! Just because you don't see them topside doesn't mean they're not around. They're like rabbits or badgers. The Sub-Rosa strings the various warrens together and allows them to commute to and from work, just like the Long Island Rail Road."

"So how do we get on this secret subway?"

"We have to find a dwarf warren, first," he explained. "I'm using the scrying egg as a form of radar. It should lead us to the nearest one." He glanced over his shoulder at me, a quizzical look on his face. "So . . . when did Mr. Manto tell your fortune?"

"It was a while back—before your birthday party."

"Why didn't you mention it before now?"

"Well, to be honest, I thought it was just a bunch of gibberish," I admitted. "He's a sweet old dude and everything, but he was tripping his face off at the time. And by the next day, I'd pretty much forgotten what he told me. But when you said we'd need an army to save Lukas—it all came rushing back. 'The fire-born army forged of woman'—the fire is my welding equipment, right? And I made these guys out of metal. That's pretty obvious, or at least *now* it is.

"Before I built *The Dying Gaul*, I did a lot of research on the Roman Empire, especially the gladiatorial games.

That's where 'and the *bestiarii* free' comes in. *Bestiarii* is Latin for 'beast fighters.' They were a special type of gladiator who fought only wild animals. But it also referred to slaves who were thrown to the beasts. I'd forgotten all that, as well. But *now* I understand. Lukas is the beast fighter I'm supposed to set free. It's funny, but it's as if Mr. Manto's words had been hiding inside my head, waiting for the right time to come out."

"Did he say anything else?"

"Yeah, but I can't really remember what. Except that the word 'blood' was involved."

"*That's* encouraging," Hexe grunted.

"I don't think it has anything to do with Lukas and Boss Marz, though, or I would be able to remember it," I replied. "I guess I'll just have to wait until the time is right, and then I'll understand what it means."

"Assuming we survive this little adventure," Hexe said solemnly. "I'm not going to lie, Tate. What we're setting out to do is incredibly dangerous. You should go back to the gallery, apologize to Templeton, and try to salvage what's left of your career."

"Maybe I should try and get back with Roger, while I'm at it?" I chided. "C'mon, you know me better than that, Hexe."

"I wouldn't go *that* far," he laughed. "I thought Dori was bad, but that guy is a real asshole."

"Yeah, there's a reason he's an 'ex,'" I snorted. "But if you think you can talk me into going back to the gallery, forget it. I'm not going to stand by and let that kid get hurt again; not if there's something I can possibly do to prevent it."

Hexe stopped and turned around to face me. The space in the tunnel was cramped, pressing us in so that our bodies touched. His face was close to mine, his breath against my ear. Even engulfed by the stifling heat from the steam pipes, I felt a chill of anticipation as he took my hand.

"You're a good friend, Tate—and an amazing woman," he said. "I saw that in you the moment we first met. If we get out of this . . ."

"*When* we get out this," I corrected gently.

"You're right." He smiled. "*When* we get out of this, I wonder if you would do me the great honor of accompanying me on a date?"

"Only if you promise to take me somewhere besides the Two-Headed Calf," I replied.

"It's a deal."

"We're close to a warren," Hexe said, holding up the scrying egg. The faint light had grown in its intensity, until the entire crystal was filled with its unearthly glow.

We had been trudging for several blocks, taking a series of increasingly claustrophobic service tunnels. I had no idea which direction we were headed, or whether or not we were still under the streets of Chelsea.

"There has to be an entrance around here somewhere," he muttered.

"I don't see anything," I said, looking about the cramped passageway.

"You wouldn't," he replied. "The entrances to dwarf warrens are camouflaged using magic." His eyebrows suddenly lifted. "Aha! There it is!" He pointed to the large circuit box opposite us.

"Are you sure about this?" I asked, eyeing the numerous DANGER! HIGH VOLTAGE! signs.

Hexe did not answer, instead holding the scrying egg so I could look through it with my right eye. To my surprise, the circuit box disappeared and was replaced by a thick wooden door with hand-forged iron hinges and a door handle. The frame was carved into an arbor, with faces of gnomes and goblins peeking from the leaves, mischievous smiles on their faces.

"Well, now that we've found it, how do we get in? Do we knock or what?"

Hexe cleared his throat, stepped back, and made a noise that sounded like someone strangling a Dutchman. There was a deep rumbling noise, and the wooden door swung inward, revealing a lighted corridor.

"My grandfather taught me a little of the dwarves' language," Hexe explained. "I took a wild guess at what the password might be. I was right."

"What was it?"

"'I am a dwarf.'"

"Do you think it's safe to enter?" I asked warily.

"There's no reason to worry," Hexe replied confidently. "Dwarves like to keep to themselves, but they're not hostile."

"Okay, I'll take your word for it. But if we end up beaten to death with pickaxes and shovels, I'm never going to talk to you again."

Gathering up my courage, I stepped out of the utility tunnel into a long corridor, the floors and walls of which were paved with polished stone. Instead of guttering braziers, every twenty-five feet there were burnished metal electric wall sconces. The only indication that we hadn't accidentally wandered into the lower levels of a luxury department store was that, despite the twenty-foot-wide hallway, the ceiling was barely a foot above my head. Hexe sighed in relief and drew the witchfire back into his body.

Fifty feet later we reached the end of the corridor

and stepped out onto a walkway that overlooked a huge atrium that plunged twenty stories down into the earth. As I peered below me, I saw numerous levels interconnected by escalators, elevators, and elevated catwalks. I had expected the dwarves' underground city to look like a cross between a coal mine and a catacomb, but with its wide corridors and art deco touches, it bore a closer resemblance to the Concourse at Rockefeller Center.

Everywhere I looked, dwarves of every age and gender were busily going about their day, no differently than any other New Yorker. They were of stocky build, male and female alike, with thick features and strong, hairy-knuckled hands. All the males had beards, but only the older ones wore them long enough to tuck inside their belts. The females tended toward busty and full figured, with a penchant for peasant skirts and Birkenstocks, and wore their hair in coronet braids. Outside of these general similarities, the individual dwarves were as varied in their personal appearance as any other Americans.

Hexe and I were on the highest level of the warren, which was virtually deserted, so we took an escalator to one of the lower levels, where there was far more foot traffic. As we stepped off the moving staircase, the statues trailing behind us like clockwork ducklings, the nearest dwarves stopped to stare at us. When we came to a standstill, the sculptures followed suit, reverting to their "natural" state.

A dwarf mother the size of a nine-year-old grabbed her baby-sized child and hid it behind her skirts, while a young dwarf couple pointed at us and talked behind their hands to each other. I nervously scanned the crowd for pickaxes and shovels.

Hexe stepped forward and addressed himself to an elderly dwarf woman, dressed in a shawl and a babushka, who looked like a doll carved from a withered apple.

"We beg your pardon, Grandmother," Hexe said politely. "Which warren is this?"

The old woman shook her head and said something in the phlegmy language of her people, then scurried off as fast as her stumpy legs could take her.

"What'd she say?" I asked.

"I'm not sure." He frowned. "She either told me to touch my nose to my shoe or she said she has no ears. My dwarvish isn't that good."

A deep bass voice suddenly spoke up from the crowd. "She told you she doesn't understand topsider language."

Hexe and I turned to find an older dwarf standing behind us, his long beard liberally shot with gray. To my alarm, I saw he was carrying a pickax over one shoulder, as were the two younger, shorter-bearded dwarves who flanked him. He also wore a Taser in a holster on his hip and a shiny badge pinned on the breast pocket of his Dickies work shirt. Compared to his fellow dwarves, he was a veritable giant, towering just over five feet tall.

"As for where you are, this is Conegar," he said stonily. "Keep your hands where I can't see 'em, Kymeran. Try pointing any fingers at me and I'll Taser your ass faster than you can make a fist. Now, what are you doing in my warren?"

"Please forgive our trespassing, Officer," Hexe said humbly, placing his hands in the small of his back, "but we need to get to Golgotham as fast as possible. It's a matter of life or death."

"It's Chief Constable, if you please," the dwarf said pointedly. "And who are *you*, Kymeran?"

"My name is Hexe, son of Syra, grandson of Eben."

"You're Lord Eben's grandson, eh?" The chief constable stroked his beard with his free hand. "I knew him, in his day. He did the dwarf folk fair." He took the pickax off his shoulder and nodded for his deputies to follow suit. I heaved a small sigh of relief. "The name's Brock Fardigger," the dwarf lawman said, offering Hexe a broad, hairy hand. "How can I be of service?"

"We need to use the Sub-Rosa to get to Golgotham, Chief Constable," Hexe explained. "As I said, our friend's life hangs in the balance."

"Are these your creations?" Fardigger asked Hexe, eyeing the metallic figures grouped behind us.

"No, I made them," I replied.

Fardigger raised a bushy eyebrow in surprise. "Nice metalwork, girl," he said, rapping his knuckles against the Cyber-Panther's steel hide. "Impressive. Nowhere near dwarf quality, of course, but *very* good for a human."

"Thank you, sir," I said, blushing at the compliment. Dwarves are famous for their metallurgical skills, so the chief constable's comment was high praise, indeed. Since I was sure to be savaged by the critics after tonight's "walk out," it was probably the last compliment my art would ever receive.

The Sub-Rosa Subway Station was located on one of the deeper levels of the warren, and it was accessible only through a pair of heavy metal doors just slightly taller than Hexe and me. Through them we passed into a short tunnel, which divided into two branches. We followed the chief constable down the right-hand tunnel, which led to an elegant Edwardian-style saloon, more than a hundred feet long and fourteen feet wide. The floor was covered with Persian carpets, and the walls were hung with pictures of what I assumed were famous dwarves, with an expensive-looking ornate clock in the center. At the far end of the salon were two doors. Hexe and I had to duck to keep from becoming ensnared in the elaborate crystal chandeliers that huge from the low-slung ceiling. Several dwarves sat on upholstered settees, smoking pipes and reading newspapers as they awaited the arrival of the next car. It looked more like the lobby of a posh fin de siècle hotel than a subway platform.

"This is the waiting room for the downtown tube," Chief Constable Fardigger explained. "There's an identical room on the other side for the uptown tube. Your ride should be here any second."

As if on cue, there was a loud chiming sound and the left-hand door at the far end of the salon opened, and several dozen dwarves in heavily soiled work clothes, filed into the waiting room. They were wearing hard hats and clutching metal lunch pails. The dwarves who had been sitting on the sofas quickly gathered up their things and made for the right-hand door. Hexe and I, accompanied by the chief constable, fell into line behind them.

Descending a half-dozen steps, we found ourselves upon the railway platform, near the portal of the tunnel, and in full view of the vast machinery used to propel the passenger cars. The pneumatic "blower" resembled a cross between a giant blacksmith's bellows and a river paddleboat, and it sounded like the world's largest asthmatic. The tunnel was round and six feet in diameter; the top was surmounted by a keystone of pressed brick, over which was carved a series of runes in the dwarf language. At either side of the tunnel, set atop twin pedestals, were bronze figures of scantily clad dwarf women holding aloft gaslight torches.

From where I stood on the platform, I looked into the tunnel and could see that it curved slightly before straightening back out. The walls were lined with a network of gracefully curved iron ribs, while the track was secured by bracings of hardwood and fastened crosswise at intervals by flat girders of cast iron.

The passenger car was itself circular in shape and made of wood, and ran on wheels provided with separate axles and springs. A dwarf dressed in an old-fashioned conductor's uniform stood at the entrance of the car, collecting fares from the passengers.

"Here you go," Fardigger said. "All you have to do is ride it to the end of the line. You'll come up near the Fly Market."

"We appreciate your help, Chief Constable." Hexe smiled.

"No problem—just don't do it again, okay?" the dwarf said with a gruff chuckle. "Oh—and good luck with your friend!"

"Tickets, please," the conductor said, holding out his hand.

I reached inside my purse. "You take U.S. dollars?"

"Of course we do," the conductor replied, rolling his eyes. "We're in America, ain't we?"

"Yeah, of course," I replied, handing him a five-dollar bill. "Give me two tickets to the end of the line."

"Doncha mean *seven*, Long Tall Sally?"

"Where'd you get that number from?" I frowned.

"They're with you, ain't they?" the conductor asked, pointing at the statues standing patiently in line behind me.

"Yeah, but they're not really *alive* ... " I protested.

"They got keisters on 'em, don't they? If they can sit down and take up a seat, they gotta have a ticket.

Them's the rules, lady. But seeing how I'm such a swell guy, I'm gonna let the cat ride for free."

The interior of the passenger car was relatively cramped, by human standards. Hexe and I had to hunch down to keep from bashing our skulls on the ceiling. The statues, however, didn't seem to mind whacking their metal noggins against the various overhangs, causing them to ring like gongs.

Once we had taken our seats on the long, upholstered benches that ran the length of the passenger car, the conductor closed the door and threw a switch mounted on the wall, triggering the release of air into the tunnel. The passenger car shot forward, carried along like a sailboat on the wind.

"Are you okay?" Hexe asked.

"I just feel like I'm trying to deposit loose change at the drive-up teller, that's all," I said, glancing nervously at the statues, unsure how the change in air pressure might affect their welds. Ariadne was seated beside me, as serene as she was beautiful, the Cyber-Panther curled at her feet like an adoring house cat. If her seams and joins were giving her any problems, she kept it to herself.

True to the chief constable's word, we emerged from the Sub-Rosa Subway's final stop at the corner of Perdition and Water streets, about four blocks up from the Fly Market. I automatically heaved a sigh of relief upon seeing a satyr trotting down a side street, pulling a rickshaw full of drunken leprechauns.

Where the appearance of six animated metal sculptures on the streets of West Chelsea had triggered screams and cars plowing into buildings, in Golgotham we barely rated a second look.

Thank God I'm home, I thought to myself.

Only a block in length, Duivel Street was one of the shortest thoroughfares in Golgotham. However, it made up for its brevity by being the most notorious street on the island of Manhattan. Since the Revolutionary War, Duivel Street had served as a red-light district, and was home to the rowdiest taverns, the sleaziest strip clubs, and the bawdiest brothels. Because of that, it was famous throughout the eastern seaboard for being the perfect place to fuck or fight, depending on your mood. Much of Golgotham's reputation for being dangerous had to do with this twenty-four/seven party zone.

The only establishment on Duivel Street that *wasn't* a bar, whorehouse, or cootchie club was Ghastly's, a hole-in-the-wall diner famous for some of the worst food in Golgotham, which, considering the typical Kymeran cuisine, was really saying something. For some reason, this was where Lukas's abductors had taken him.

We joined the steady stream of individuals, human and otherwise, that thronged the sidewalks. Although nowhere near as crowded as Witch Alley, Duivel Street was just as chaotic, with hundreds of patrons roaming in and out of the numerous clubs, clutching plastic go-cups full of alcohol.

As we headed up the street toward our destination, the steel skin of the walking sculptures reflected the lurid neon signs advertising Madame Messalina's, the Golden Flagon, and Club Eros. On the other side of the street, a scantily clad huldra rode back and forth on a swing affixed to the front fire escape of Le Boudoir, next to a multicolored neon sign promising TABLETOP DANCING AT MODERATE PRICES, her long cow tail tickling the scalps of passersby.

Hexe pointed to a group of boisterously drunk

middle-aged men in rumpled business suits, their ties
pulled askew, no doubt visiting CPAs out on the town,
sampling whatever sins the Big Apple had to offer. They
were about a hundred feet ahead of us. As we watched,
they ducked inside a pair of glass doors with skulls
painted on them, the hollow eyes illuminated by lights
shining inside the café.

"I'd heard rumors that Ghastly's was a Malandanti
front, but I never realized exactly what for until now,"
Hexe said.

"What are we going to do?" I asked. "Do you have a
plan besides just walking in and demanding they hand
Lukas back to us?"

"Yeah, but it hinged on our reinforcements being
here by now," Hexe admitted anxiously. "Lukas doesn't
have a lot of time. Boss Marz is going to make an example of him to the other pit fighters, as to what they
can expect if they try to escape. If we wait for Hildy and
Lyta to arrive, it may be too late."

"That's what I thought you'd say." I sighed. "So I guess
we'd better get our butts in gear, huh?" I motioned for
my welded warriors to follow me. "C'mon, gang—let's
get some chow!"

The first thing I noticed upon entering Ghastly's Diner
was the stink of boiled cabbage and stale tobacco. The
second thing I noticed was that the drunk businessmen who had entered just before us were nowhere to
be seen. The booths and tables of the diner were empty,
and the only sign of life was the waiter standing behind
the counter, idly drying a plate with a greasy rag. He was
tall and gaunt, with grayish skin and lank hair parted
down the middle of his skull, staring eyes that looked

like a pair of hard-boiled eggs, and an upturned nose like a bat's.

"Where's Ghastly?" Hexe asked curtly.

"In the kitchen," the waiter replied, gesturing with his rag.

Hexe and I pushed through the metal swinging door, the statues following at out heels. The stench that permeated the front of the restaurant grew even stronger, becoming as tangible as the walls and the floor. The diner's owner, the same kind of snub-nosed humanoid as the waiter, stood in front of a commercial gas stove. Dressed in a badly stained apron, he was stirring a large pot of foul-smelling stew, a lit cigarette dangling from his lip.

"Employees only!" the cook snapped.

"Tell me where they are," Hexe demanded stonily.

"Are you nuts or something?" Ghastly growled, sending the ash from the end of his cigarette into the pot he was stirring.

"How do we get to the kennels from here?"

"I don't know nothing about that," the cook replied, returning his gaze to whatever was in the pot. "You got the wrong place, buddy."

I pointed my finger at Ghastly, and the Dying Gaul stepped forward, bringing his sword to the cook's throat. Ghastly's protruding eyes popped out even farther from their sockets.

"So I lied," the restauranteur said nervously. "You go in through the storage room. There's a cupboard in the corner that's really a door. There's a tunnel behind it that leads to a converted warehouse behind this building, facing Shoemaker Street. That's where they hold the pit fights."

"Any guards?"

"Two. They're stationed just before the door at the other end of the tunnel."

"Thank you for being so forthcoming," Hexe said. "I have just one final question, and then you're free to go—what's in the pot?"

Ghastly gulped so hard it looked as though he were trying to swallow his own Adam's apple. "W-werewolf stew."

"That's what I thought."

The moment the Dying Gaul's sword moved away from his jugular, Ghastly heaved a sigh of relief and raised a trembling hand to his pallid brow—and kept it there.

"What the hell *is* this guy?" I asked, staring into the diner owner's frozen eyes.

"He's a ghoul," Hexe replied, grimacing in disgust. "I have to hand it to Boss Marz, though—he figured out the perfect way to dispose of the evidence from his barbaric little enterprise."

My stomach flip-flopped as what Hexe said sank in. "I think I'm gonna be sick," I groaned.

"Hey! What did you do to Ghastly?" The waiter was standing in the doorway of the kitchen, still holding his rag in one hand. As Ariadne and the Cyber-Panther turned to face him, the dishrag dropped to the floor. The ghoul opened his mouth to call out for help, only to freeze in midshout. I could see the pinkish gray slug of his tongue and double rows of tobacco-stained teeth.

The storage room was at the very back of the kitchen, beyond the dish pit. It wasn't hard to figure out which cupboard was actually the secret door, since the drunks ahead of us had not bothered to close it, revealing a brick-lined tunnel lit only by low-wattage bulbs strung from a crumbling ceiling.

Hexe took his scrying egg from his pocket, fogged it with his breath, and held it up to the dim light. Inside the crystal I could see a pair of Malandanti goons shooting craps at the end of the tunnel. They were so engrossed in their game that they didn't hear the sound of rapidly approaching, rattling metal until my welded warriors were almost on top of them.

The first Malandanti—a heavyset Kymeran with a cobalt blue brush cut—jumped to his feet, gesturing frantically with his left hand. A fireball, which he hurled at Ariadne, instantly filled his palm. The fire immediately obliterated the papier-mâché mask that served as her face and then spread to her silver lamé gown, none of which stopped her from wrapping her articulated typewriter-key fingers around his throat. The blue-haired croggy shrieked as the hellfire he had summoned spread to his own body, sending him to whatever unpleasant afterlife awaited him.

The second Malandanti, who wore his lime green hair in dreadlocks, was knocked to the ground by the Cyber-Panther. The Lovers moved forward in tandem, crushing his hands under their metallic feet. The goon cried out in agony as his fingers broke, robbing him of what magic he might possess.

Hexe knelt beside the dreadlocked Malandanti, grabbing his face so he was forced to look directly into his eyes. "Tell me where the kennels are."

"Bang off, fecker," the croggy groaned through clenched teeth.

"I can make the pain go away," Hexe promised, tightening his grip on the other man's face. "But you have to tell me where the kennels are."

"He'll kill me if I tell you," the dreadlocked goon moaned.

"He's going to kill you, anyway, for not stopping us," Hexe countered.

The Malandanti guard closed his eyes and nodded, surrendering to Hexe's logic. "On the other side of the door you'll see a stairway to your left and a door to your right. The door leads to the kennels. There—I told you what you wanted to know. Now make the chuffin' pain go away."

From his breast pocket Hexe removed the copper tube he'd used to anesthetize Lukas and shot a fine white powder into the wounded Kymeran's face. Within seconds the Malandanti's eyes rolled back in his head and his body went limp.

"Is he dead?" I whispered.

Hexe shook his head. "I placed him in an induced coma until he gets to a healer or a hospital. I might despise the Malandanti and all they stand for, but I'm not a sadist."

"What about him?" I asked, pointing at the other Malandanti, whose charred body lay tangled with Ariadne's.

"He's beyond any mortal help," Hexe said grimly. "He was doomed the moment the flames spread to him."

The Cyber-Panther nudged the amorphous glob of melted metal and plastic that used to be his companion piece's head with his muzzle, like a mother cat urging a sickly kitten to its feet. To my surprise, Ariadne's partially fused fingers began to twitch, and she managed to raise her upper torso a few inches, only to collapse once more. The Cyber-Panther touched the pile of scrap with his paw, but this time Ariadne remained still.

"She's gone," I explained, placing my hand atop the Cyber-Panther's sleek skull. "The heat was too intense. It melted her joints and destroyed her welds."

On the other side of the tunnel were the staircase and

doorway the guard had described. Hexe put a finger to his lips as muffled footsteps and muted voices floated down from the floor above. From the sound of their laughter, it did not appear that the battle in the tunnel had been overheard.

Hexe opened the door that led to the kennels, keeping a wary eye on the stairway in case someone came down to check on the tunnel guards. I shooed the remaining sculptures in ahead of me. The last one across the threshold was the Cyber-Panther, but not before he cast a final glance in the direction of his fallen mistress.

On the other side of the door was a huge, dimly lit room with row upon row of large enclosed steel cages, with narrow channels cut into the floor to drain away the waste generated by the inhabitants. There was a low, persistent hum, which I recognized as the sound of electrified fencing. The air was so rank, my eyes watered and I had to breathe through my mouth.

"Mother of God!" I groaned in disgust. "It smells like the lion house at the zoo!"

"There's a reason for that," Hexe said dourly, pointing to the occupant of the nearest cage.

An African lion, its ribs visible under its tawny pelt, paced back and forth, regarding us with a fiercely burning look. Upon seeing the Cyber-Panther, the lion bared its fangs and growled. The metal cat responded in kind, making a noise that sounded like squealing brake drums. Startled, the malnourished king of beasts retreated to the far corner of its prison.

The lion was not the only captive in Boss Marz's kennels. A cursory glance revealed a half-starved grizzly bear and a hungry Sumatran tiger on the first row alone.

"They probably keep the beasts separated from the

shape-shifters and half-men," Hexe said. "At least that's the impression I got from Lukas."

"Where do they *get* these things?" I wondered aloud.

"Probably from private zoos or circuses," he replied. "It would be easier to buy captive animals from inside the country than to run the risk of having them smuggled in."

"What about this one?" I asked, pointing to the unicorn. A tennis ball had been jammed onto the end of its razor-sharp horn, like the button on a fencer's rapier. The unicorn glared at me with its ruby-red eyes and bit the air with its teeth.

"*That* was definitely a smuggler job. Don't get too close—its hooves are as sharp as its horn," he warned, pointing to the beast's cloven feet. "If it lands a kick through those bars, it'll cut you to the bone."

"Where do you think he is? This place looks like the warehouse in *Citizen Kane*. . . . There are hundreds of cages down here!"

"Maybe our friend there can help point the way," Hexe said, nodding to the Cyber-Panther. "Lukas served as the model for the sculpture. I've noticed that he seems to be more aware than the others. Perhaps there is a sympathetic connection between the two?"

"I thought you said they weren't alive?"

"They aren't. But there's something *unique* about this one. Maybe it's because it was actually modeled on another living being. Perhaps a spark of Lukas is in there?"

"There's only one way to find out if you're right." I leaned down and whispered into the Cyber-Panther's ear, "Go to Lukas."

The metal feline jumped to his feet and ran down one of the rows like a cheetah going after a gazelle. Hexe cursed in surprise and sprinted after the Cyber-

Panther as the figure sped through the dimly lit maze of caged animals. I hurried after him, the remaining sculptures in tow, but he had already crossed the border into shadow and disappeared into the darkness beyond the feeble glow of the overhead lights. A few seconds later, I found myself at a crossroads formed by two intersecting aisles of cages, trying to figure out which way they had gone.

I didn't want to shout, for fear of alerting any Malandanti that might be lurking about in the kennels, so I stood in the middle and turned around and around, hoping to catch a glimpse of the Cyber-Panther's steely hide.

Suddenly I heard the sound of tiny bare feet slapping against the concrete floor. I looked in the direction of the noise and saw the *cutest* little monkey, dressed in a red velvet vest and matching fez, scamper out from between the cages. Upon catching sight of me, the tiny primate froze and began to chatter in fear. Sucker that I am, I felt sorry for the damned thing. You would have thought the last time I found myself lost in a maze would have taught me something.

"Poor little thing . . . What are *you* doing down here?" I asked, talking in that high, slow voice reserved for small animals and the mentally handicapped. I crouched down on one knee, motioning for it to come closer. "It's okay, little fella. . . ." The squirrel monkey made a high-pitched chirping noise as it nervously washed its hands. After looking about fearfully, the squirrel monkey took a couple of cautious steps toward me. "That's a good boy." I smiled. "I'm not going to hurt you. . . ."

"Tate! No!"

I looked up to see Hexe standing in the aisle opposite me, a bruised but otherwise unharmed Lukas alongside him and the Cyber-Panther. The horror on both their faces told me something bad was happening. I turned back toward the cute little monkey in the cute little fez, only to find it had been replaced by a hideous demon-ape.

It was six feet long from snout to tail, and stood five feet high at the shoulder, with greenish yellow fur. It looked like a mutant combination of mandrill baboon and hyena, with long forelegs and short, backward-sloping hindquarters. Huge, menacing spikes grew along its spine, like those of a dinosaur. Its head, which hung low between its hunched shoulders, was hairless, with a prominent brow and patches of bright blue ribbed skin marking its cheeks, as well as a long, bright scarlet snout. It still had on the fez and matching vest it had worn in its squirrel-monkey aspect, which somehow made it all the more terrifying.

Bonzo, the familiar of Boss Marz, opened his jaws in a terrifying yawn that split his head from brow to breast-bone, revealing curved fangs the size of steak knives as he charged right for me.

And then everything went black.

Chapter 21

I was surrounded by shadows, shadows that shuttered my eyes and sealed my ears, rendering me blind and deaf. The shadows also lay heavily across my arms and legs, making it difficult for me to move. Although I could not see or hear anything, I somehow knew there was something dangerous hidden in the void.

As I struggled to look around, it felt as if my body were mired in fresh tar, and the faster I tried to move, the more enmeshed I became. I looked up and saw, far above my head, a pale, shimmering gray smear, like the moon hidden behind storm clouds. As I fought my way toward the distant glow, I became aware of the sound of muffled voices in the distance. Although I could not make out the words, the tone was angry. Yet there was something about one of the murky, dimly heard voices that made my heart leap and spurred me toward the rapidly expanding halo of light.

Suddenly I was awake, gasping like a swimmer tossed onto some nameless beach by an angry sea. I was on my side, my hands bound behind me. The nap of the Persian carpet I was lying on was pressed against my cheek. My body ached as if I'd just been in a collision, but I did not feel any sharp pain in my bones or flesh.

"Ah-ha! It looks like your lady friend is finally awake," Boss Marz said. He was seated behind a very large, very imposing desk, and was smoking an equally oversized cigar. He seemed to be enjoying himself immensely.

As I focused my eyes, the first thing I saw was Boss Marz's familiar, still in its demon-ape aspect, leaning over me. I gasped and tried to recoil when it poked me in the ribs with its leathery finger.

"I swear by the sunken cities, Marz, if that baboon of yours hurts her . . ."

It was the voice that had summoned me from the shadows back to the land of the living. I turned my head and saw Hexe kneeling a few feet from where I lay, his hands encased in metal globes chained together at the wrist. Behind him stood Boss Marz's lieutenant, Nach, and a tall, lean man dressed in matching leather pants and jacket, with dirty blond hair and the unibrow of a shape-shifter.

"You'll do *what*?" the crime lord sneered as he leaned back in his chair and put his feet up on his desk. He rolled his cigar between his thumb and magic finger, savoring the moment. "You're hardly in a position to threaten me, 'Serenity.'"

"I'm okay, Hexe," I said, trying to sound braver than I felt. "Just a little sore, that's all." I looked around, but there was no one else in the room. "What happened to Lukas?"

"Allow me to answer that question, my dear," Boss Marz said as he moved to sit on the corner of his desk nearest Hexe and me. "I sent your feline friend back to his rightful place in the kennels. But you needn't fear— you'll be seeing him again quite soon enough. And as for your ragtag army of welded warriors—I took the opportunity to dismantle them while you were unconscious." He gestured with his cigar to a pile of scrap metal heaped just inside the door. "Pity, really. Their construction was quite artful."

I gasped aloud as if I'd been punched in the gut upon espying the Dying Gaul's sword lying bent into a steel pretzel. A second later I spotted Lover Number Two's torso, her aluminum funnel breasts pointed at the ceiling, and one of the Thinker's arms amid the tangled wreckage. The sight of my creations lying there, mangled and tossed aside like so much junk, genuinely shocked me. It was like discovering several close friends slain in a drive-by shooting. Although they had not been truly alive, neither had they been simple automatons. I had put something of myself into each of them, and seeing them demolished was as if a part of me had been violated several times over. As I looked at Boss Marz's smug, self-satisfied face, I was overcome by a loathing so profound it erased all vestiges of fear.

"You'll pay for destroying them, you bastard," I growled.

"I sincerely doubt that," Marz said, blowing a lungful of smoke into my face. He then turned his attention to Hexe. "I must say, 'Serenity,' you disappoint me. I gave you credit for being smarter than this! Invading a Malandanti operation with nothing more than a human girl and a handful of overglorified marionettes?"

"We still managed to take out your guards and breech your defenses, didn't we?" I said defiantly.

"And see how well that worked out for you," Boss Marz replied condescendingly.

"How did you know I was harboring Lukas?" Hexe asked.

"It wasn't that difficult to figure out, really," Marz admitted. "I knew you were the only healer in all of Golgotham who would dare to defy me. Then a mutual acquaintance told me that he had seen you at a party in the company of a young man with an unusual five o'clock shadow." He smiled as he tapped the space between his brows. "But I realized it would not be . . . *prudent* . . . of me to kick open your front door and demand the return of my property. So I had to wait until the most opportune time to make my move. When you left the security of Golgotham, and the protection of your mother's skirts, to travel uptown, that's when I *knew* I had you. Still, my primary goal was simply to recover my chattel. It never occurred to me that you would deliver yourself to my care so soon. Now you and that were-cat bastard will learn at the same time what happens to those who disobey me."

"Am I supposed to be *scared*, Marz?" Hexe asked, his words dripping with contempt. "You're nothing more than a parasite, sucking the blood of the Kymeran people!"

"Mind your tongue, hedger!" Nach snarled, cuffing Hexe hard enough with his metal hand to knock him to the floor.

"Keep your hands off him, you candy-colored asshole!" I shouted as I struggled to get to my feet. The shape-shifter Phelan stepped away from Hexe to push me back down with his boot.

"Leave her alone!" Hexe snapped.

Nach and Phelan exchanged glances and snickered in amusement, but neither one touched me again.

"You and your kind have helped keep our people locked in the ghettos by perpetuating the stereotype of witches and warlocks as the willing accomplices of murderers and rapists." Hexe spat in disgust. "It is bad enough that you help others justify their mistrust of our race, but you have preyed on your own people far worse than any witchfinder."

"Those are *fine* words from the descendant of the greatest traitor to ever bear twelve fingers!" Boss Marz retorted, his cheeks turning bright red. "If it weren't for the Malandanti, thousands more of our people would have died in the Sufferance. Ours is an ancient and noble organization, and we have much to be proud of. Who are you to stand in judgment? Your precious royal ancestor surrendered our rights as a sovereign people by agreeing to the disarmament and dispersal of the Dragon Cavalry. He turned a proud and feared race into nothing more than common charm peddlers and potion pushers."

"It is because of the Malandanti that the humans felt justified in persecuting us to begin with!" Hexe replied hotly. "By following the Left Hand Path, you do nothing but invite enmity from the humans. . . ."

"Enough!" Marz abandoned his seat on the edge of the desk. His eyes had a fiercely burning look, as cold and distant as the farthest star. "I will not be preached to by a dexie! Your uncle is right—you *are* a dunderwhelp. What do you think you're proving, using only Right Hand magic?"

"That I'm better than you, for one."

Moving with amazing speed for a man his size, Marz backhanded Hexe, bloodying his lip.

Hexe did not flinch or cry out, but instead glared at the Malandanti. There was no fear in his eyes, only defiance. As I looked at him, I felt my heart swell as it had that night at the Two-Headed Calf when he held my hand and looked into my eyes. A voice in my head spoke as clearly as if someone had whispered in my ear, *I love this man.*

"You know what I do with idiots stupid enough to offend me?" Marz hissed. "I toss them in the pits and tell them if they can kill whatever's thrown at them, they get to walk away, free and clear. Simple as that. Do you know how many of those idiots have been able to do so?" He touched his index finger to his thumb. "And since you love your bastet pal so chuffing much, I've decided *you* can be his object lesson on what happens to bad kitties who run away from their owners." He reached inside one of his desk drawers and retrieved a silver-bladed bowie knife and tossed it on the carpet in front of Hexe. "You and the were-cat will fight to the death in the pit. You're going to fight him using that. You'll be tonight's main attraction. And to make sure you don't use one of those wussie passive-aggressive dexie spells, like suspended animation, your right hand will be literally tied behind your back the whole time. If you want to live, you'll have to either stab the bastet to death or use Left Hand magic to defeat him."

"I will *not* fight my friend," Hexe said determinedly, shaking his head. "I would rather die than hurt him."

"Fine. I can assure you that your precious Lukas will have no such problem." Boss Marz sneered. "You see, I've created a potion that summons forth the beast within shape-shifters, no matter what the circumstance. Once injected, they lose control and become ravaging animals, and the madness doesn't recede until they have tasted blood."

"Be that as it may, I refuse to kill or use Left Hand magic, even if it's to save my own life."

"Oh, but I think you will, my friend." Marz grinned.

"Because if you *don't* fight, I'll give the girl to my familiar to do with as he likes. You'd enjoy that, wouldn't you, Bonzo?"

The demon-ape hooted in glee, flashing those terrible fangs as he bobbled his head in agreement with his master. The familiar moved to stand over me, lowering his head to sniff my hair. I bit my tongue and quickly looked away so I wouldn't scream. Although I could not see the look in Bonzo's eyes, there was no way I could avoid smelling the creature's reek of brimstone and monkey house.

"You win, Marz," Hexe said, dropping his gaze. "I'll do as you wish. I'll fight in the pit."

"No!" I wailed, throwing myself at Boss Marz's feet. As much as the threat of becoming Bonzo's plaything terrified me, the possibility of losing Hexe forever was a hundred times worse. "Please! Don't let him do it!" I begged. "I have money—more than you can imagine. I'll pay you to let us go. We won't tell anyone about what you're doing here, I swear. Just. Don't. Hurt. Him."

Boss Marz stared down at me as if I were some strange and vaguely interesting insect of which he had heard tell but had never seen before. "I appreciate the offer, my dear. And I shall admit to being somewhat tempted. But this goes beyond mere money. It's now a matter of honor. He has conspired against the Malandanti by harboring the bastet Lukas, and now he must pay the price. To turn a blind eye to such an affront would make me look weak. And I cannot allow that. Phelan—take him downstairs and prepare him for his fate."

"As you wish, Boss," the werewolf growled. He bent down and retrieved the silver knife, carefully holstering it in a leather sheath affixed to his belt. He then grabbed the chains dangling between Hexe's wrists and yanked him to his feet. "C'mon, 'Serenity'—your public awaits."

As Phelan dragged Hexe from the room, I wanted to run to him, wrap my arms about him, and tell him how much I loved him and how sorry I was for not being brave enough to admit to myself what my heart had known since the moment I first met him.

As he was being hustled out the door, Hexe met my gaze and gave me a reassuring smile. "Don't worry, Tate—everything will be okay."

"*Sure* it will, bub," Phelan snarled.

As the door slammed shut behind them, the tears I had stifled finally spilled, unbidden, down my cheeks. This wasn't how it was supposed to end, damn it.

"Come now, Ms. Tate," Boss Marz said, clucking his tongue. He fished a silk handkerchief from his breast pocket and offered it to me.

Upon realizing my hands were still tied, he motioned for Nach to free them. I stared at the offered hanky as if it were a sleeping cobra while I massaged the circulation back into my wrists.

"Please take it," he insisted, his voice oddly apologetic for someone who had just threatened to feed me to his baboon. "I may be a cold-blooded killer at times, but that doesn't mean I cannot be a gentleman."

I grudgingly accepted the handkerchief, but only because my nose was really starting to run. I took a perverse pleasure in blowing a huge wad of snot into it, and handing it back to him.

"So, what do you think of my skybox?" Boss Marz smiled, gesturing to his surroundings with a delicate wave of his hand.

I realized for the first time that the office was actually a lofted room suspended over the warehouse, with a wall made of windows that looked out onto the floor below. Now that I was free to look around, I was surprised to discover the walls were hung with original Warhols and Harings. A bronze statue of Shiva the Destroyer, garlanded in skulls and snakes, sat in a recessed alcove.

"This is where I come when I weary of the twunts down below. I can retire up here and check my market portfolio while enjoying a hot-oil massage."

Rather than dwell on the mental image of Boss Marz receiving a rubdown, I looked out the windows. On the ground floor was a large octagonal hole, ringed with razor wire, over which was suspended a set of boxing ring lights. Grouped around the pit was a set of raised bleachers, three tiers high, jammed full of swearing, screaming, yelling men frantically waving fistfuls of cash at one another as they watched as whatever hapless creatures below them battled to the death.

I turned back to stare at Boss Marz, who was puffing on his cigar. It did nothing to mask the odor of scorched metal that radiated from his body.

"How can you do this?" I asked. "You're a man of sophisticated tastes. I can tell that by the works of art on display here. How can you appreciate things such as these and then turn around and pit those poor creatures against one another?"

"I do it for money, of course," he replied matter-of-factly. "What do you think *paid* for these paintings? Nothing gets the twunts more excited than blood sports. It gets their juices flowing, makes them wager big. They pay a cover to get in, and the house gets a cut of every wager, win or lose, on top of that. As for the creatures that fight in the pits; in the end, they're just dumb beasts— who cares if they die here or in the slaughter yard?"

"'Just dumb beasts'?" I shook my head in disbelief. "What about Lukas and the other shape-shifters? They're sentient, thinking creatures, with families who love them."

"Don't kid yourself, girl," Boss Marz said with a humorless laugh. "Shape-shifters carry beast blood in their veins. It swims in their DNA. That makes them no different than pit bulls or fighting cocks, in my book, except that they can talk and have thumbs. I'll grant you that they're smarter, savvier fighters in the ring than the true beasts—but they're also more savage. The twunts love shape-shifters because they know they'll get their money's worth out of them. And I'm all about giving my customers what they want."

I looked away, in case the crime lord saw the disgust in my eyes and took offense. Despite his fondness for tailored suits and his taste in art, Boss Marz was a bigger beast than any of the creatures he kept locked away in his kennels. As my gaze fell on yet another Warhol, I reminded myself that the Nazis had appreciated art as well. It didn't make them kinder, gentler beings; it just meant they were murderous assholes with stolen Old Masters hanging in their studies.

"Come, Bonzo," the Malandanti leader said, motioning for his familiar to join him. "It's time we joined the rabble."

The hell-ape grunted and jumped onto the desk, changing into his tiny squirrel-monkey aspect. The transformed familiar scampered up Boss Marz's arm and took his place on his master's left shoulder.

"Nach will show you downstairs," Boss Marz said as he fished a pistachio from his pocket and handed it to Bonzo. "You certainly don't want to miss your friends' big fight. I've arranged ringside seats for you—that way you're sure to see *everything*."

While Nach escorted me out of Boss Marz's "sky-box," I paused to look one last time at the ruins of my own artwork, which lay heaped beside the door. As I stared at the jumble of dismantled sculptures, I realized something was missing from the pile of mangled pistons, typewriter keys, and repurposed transmissions.

Where was the Cyber-Panther?

Chapter 22

As Nach led me down the wooden staircase from Boss Marz's private "skybox" to the open floor below, my mind was racing, desperately trying to figure out a way to get out of what was, without a doubt, the worst clusterfuck of my entire life.

As screwups went, this one left the time I got busted joyriding in my dad's BMW in the dust. Enduring my mother's tongue-lashing and my father's icy stare seemed like absolute heaven in comparison to what I had to look forward to. Despite the danger I was in, I was more worried for Hexe and Lukas than for myself—especially for Hexe. The thought of losing him tugged at my heart like a fishhook.

The first floor of the warehouse was filled with stacks of crates, save for the open area in the back where the pit was located. It was a huge open space, with high ceilings, exposed rafters the size of railroad ties, and a pyramid-style skylight high overhead. Bleachers were set up on each side of the pit, rising high enough so that the paying customers crowding about could get an unobstructed view. The place smelled of blood, animal waste, sweat, and death. A pall of tobacco smoke hovered above the assembled gamblers, adding to the general miasma.

The "twunts" as Boss Marz called them, were a mix of coked-up wannabe-thugs decked out in Affliction T-shirts, Jager-bombed Bridge and Tunnel douche bags in Ed Hardy gear, overweight middle-aged men with shaved heads and graying goatees wearing Tap Out shirts, Triad gang members in flashy Hong Kong suits, and older, well-dressed businessmen with three-hundred-dollar haircuts. Those in the last category creeped me out the most since they didn't shout and hoot like the others, nor did they seem intoxicated. Instead, they intently watched the carnage taking place before them, eyes shining like wet stones in otherwise unreadable faces.

The audience wasn't composed entirely of humans, as I first thought. I spotted several Kymerans and other paranormals sprinkled throughout the stadium seats, including a smattering of ghouls and the inevitable leprechaun or two. The only other woman in the room besides me was a sloe-eyed maenad dressed in a moth-eaten leopard skin, selling warm beer and cigarettes to the crowd from a tray slung about her neck. A dozen Malandanti croggies, dressed in the prerequisite boxy suits and dark sunglasses, prowled the makeshift stadium, ensuring the twunts didn't get too rowdy between matches. A couple of seedy-looking satyrs were working the crowd, giving odds and taking wagers.

All of the bleachers had three tiers of stadium seating, save one, which was outfitted like the emperor's box in the Roman Colosseum, with a huge thronelike chair draped in silks and embroidered tapestries. As Nach pushed me up the risers that led to the grandstand, I

looked down into the octagon, the top of which was
wreathed in razor wire.

The pit was at least twenty feet deep with wooden
walls, its floor covered in sawdust. A couple of Kymerans dressed in janitorial jumpsuits were removing the
carcass of the lion I had seen earlier. There was a fist-
sized puncture wound in the big cat's chest and a somewhat smaller exit wound on its back, as if someone had
rammed a pike—or a unicorn's horn—through its heart.
A third flunky tossed shovelfuls of sawdust onto the
floor to absorb the gore from the previous battle and
provide a fresh playing surface for the next fight.

I was forced to stand beside Boss Marz's throne while
Nach kept an eye on me in case I made a break for it.
The moment I stepped onto the bleacher, the twunts
began shouting obscenities at me. I realized I was still
wearing my sexy black dress, the one I had picked out
for my gallery show. No doubt the mouth-breathing
knuckle-draggers thought I was just another victim of
Boss Marz's come-hither spell. I was nothing more
than meat to them, no different than the creatures that
fought and died for their pleasure. A minute later Boss
Marz ascended the grandstand, followed by the werewolf Phelan, and the catcalls changed into cheers. All
hail the patron of the feast.

A door in one side of the pit opened, and Hexe was
shoved into the arena. He was stripped to the waist and
the metal globes removed from his hands in exchange
for an elaborate bondage-style harness that kept his
right arm securely strapped behind his back. In his left
hand was the silver knife. He raised his knife hand, using
his forearm to shield his eyes against the glare from the
overhead lights. I knew he was looking for me. I stepped

forward to call out to him, only to be yanked back by
Nach.

I desperately searched the crowd for some sign of surprise or shock on the faces in the bleachers, but all I saw
was bloodlust. These men had already witnessed several
murders that night—what was one more to them? For
a second I thought I spotted a glimmer of recognition
in the eyes of an older Kymeran, but there was so much
going on, I couldn't be sure. One thing of which I was
certain was that if there was any help to be found, it was
not coming from anyone who had paid handsomely to
see things die.

As I looked down at Hexe, my heart ached as if there
were an iron fist inside my chest slowly squeezing the
life from it. A cold, numbing dread spread through my
body, as if I had been dipped into ice water. The spit in
my mouth dried up and as much as I did not want to see
what was about to happen, I could not look away.

"*Quiet down, you bastards!*" Boss Marz shouted,
holding up a beringed hand for silence. After a second
or two, the cheering died down to a ragged murmur.
"This man before you conspired to keep me from what
was rightfully mine! By offending me, he has offended
the ancient order of the Malandanti, we who proudly
walk the Left Hand Path! He thought, because of the
accident of his birth, he could flaunt the will of the
Malandanti without fear of repercussions! But tonight,
all of Golgotham shall learn that no one—prince or
pauper—is immune from our vengeance! Release the
beast!"

A panel on the other side of the arena slid open and,
accompanied by an angry roar, Lukas came bounding
out on all fours. He was almost entirely puma, with no

human attributes, and the shock collar was once more around his neck. I involuntarily flashed back to the night he chased me through the garden maze. There was no sign in those burning green eyes of the sweet, goofy teenager I had come to know—only that of a ravening animal. Despite myself, I gasped and cringed in fear at the sight of my friend.

The moment Lukas hit the sawdust, the gamblers crowding the ringside began to yell even louder and wave even more money at the satyrs, who dashed back and forth, hurriedly taking bets. Lukas warily circled Hexe, who was careful not to let the were-cat get behind him. Lukas flattened his ears against his tawny skull and hissed at the sight of the silver knife in his friend's hand. Although the drugs in his system had erased his human inhibitions, he still recognized danger. Lukas swiped at Hexe with his forepaw, but he was able to quickly sidestep his friend's razor-sharp claws.

"I told you to *fight*, not dance!" Marz bellowed. "You know what happens if you don't give me a show. Now mix it up!" Bonzo screeched and leaped from his master's shoulder onto me, clawing my face and pulling my hair with his tiny, filthy paws.

Startled by the unexpected attack, I screamed and tried to swat the familiar away, only to have the little bastard bite my fingers with his needle-sharp teeth. Spurred by the sound of my shrieks, Hexe lunged forward and slashed at Lukas with the knife. Lukas countered by raking his claws across Hexe's exposed torso, knocking the weapon out of his hand. A second later, four long streaks of wet red suddenly blossomed on Hexe's left side. Lukas screamed in excitement as he caught the scent of his opponent's blood and quickly placed himself between Hexe and the knife.

Boss Marz prodded me in the ribs, pointing at Lukas. "See what I mean about the shape-shifters putting on a better show?" he said excitedly. "A true mountain lion wouldn't have the brains to put itself between its opponent and a weapon."

I watched in horror as Hexe lunged for the knife, only to have Lukas pounce on him like a house cat going after a mouse. The moment the were-cat landed on his back, Hexe dropped to the ground and curled into a ball like a hedgehog. He tucked his chin in, grabbing the back of his neck with his left hand to protect the top of his spinal column, while drawing his knees to his chest to keep from being disemboweled. Ironically, the leather harness used to restrain Hexe's right arm behind his back provided him at least a modicum of defense from the tearing fangs and slashing claws of his attacker.

Although there was no way I could possibly stop what was happening before me, I had to try, no matter the cost. I could not stand by and watch the man I loved being savaged by the friend I held as close as a brother. Wresting myself free of Nach's grip, I threw myself against the railing that separated the grandstand from the pit.

"*Lukas! Stop it! He's your friend!*" I screamed. "*Hexe is your friend!*"

To my surprise, Lukas stopped his attack on Hexe and turned his head in my direction. His green-gold gaze locked with mine, and I saw recognition flicker in his eyes, if only for the briefest moment. I had definitely caught the were-cat's attention, but I had no way of knowing if he understood me.

"Get away from there, you crazy nump," Nach snarled. Lukas hissed angrily upon catching sight of the Malandanti goon as Nach grabbed my arm and brusquely yanked me back in line.

"Keep that stupid bitch quiet," Boss Marz snarled.

Nach nodded his head and clamped his metal hand over my mouth. I winced in pain as the overlapping fish-like scales bit into my flesh. I cried out in protest, only to have my cry reduced to a muffled moan.

Hexe began edging away from the distracted were-cat and crawling toward the knife. Lukas caught the move-ment at the corner of his eye and spun back around, swat-ting Hexe hard enough to flip him onto his back. Hexe lifted his head from the sawdust, keeping his eyes on Lukas. He knew the second he looked away the were-cat would be on him. Although his opponent seemed completely helpless, Lukas slowly edged forward, as if wary of a trap.

While he kept Lukas's attention fixed on his face, Hexe slowly . . . slowly . . . slowly stretched out his left arm toward the dropped knife. Lukas took a cautious step forward, then another, head held low, ears flattened against his skull. Hexe's fingertips brushed the handle of the knife and, with nightmare slowness, pulled the hilt into his palm. Lukas stood directly over Hexe's prone body, dripping fangs inches from his exposed throat as his fingers twined themselves about the blade.

The wagering grew even fiercer as the twunts bet on whether Lukas would bury his fangs into Hexe's throat before Hexe plunged the knife into Lukas's chest. The smart money was that they would die together. I tried to block out the sound of the gamblers taking odds, as hot, salty tears spilled from my eyes and trickled down Nach's cold metal hand. All I wanted was to break free of my captor and leap into the pit alongside my friends. It would be better to die alongside them than to be forced to endure the torment of watching them kill each other.

Just as Lukas was about to sink his fangs into his opponent's throat, the were-cat suddenly stopped in mid-snarl and began to sniff Hexe's body. I could see Hexe lying there, bleeding, his outstretched arm holding the knife trembling, while he debated on whether or not to plunge its blade into his friend's body.

Please wake up, Lukas, I prayed silently. *I know you're in there. Just please wake up.*

As if in answer, the were-cat leaned in close and began to lick Hexe's cheek, his growl down-clutching into a purr. Hexe burst into relieved laughter and dropped the knife. He wrapped his free arm around Lukas in an awkward embrace and buried his face in his friend's furry neck.

The onlookers' response to this heartwarming show of loyalty was to boo and start throwing beer cans and bottles, empty or otherwise, at both the fighters in the pit and the grandstand.

Boss Marz leaped from his makeshift throne, his face dark with rage. "Damned dexie! I told you I wanted a good fight! Nach—kill them! Kill them all!"

"Even the girl?"

"What part of 'kill them all' do you not understand, nitwitch?" Marz growled. "Phelan—I need you to kidnap the old were-tiger and his pretty little daughter. Perhaps they'll provide better sport when pitted against each other."

Lukas roared in anger and launched himself at Boss Marz, sinking his claws in deep as he fought to scale the steep sides of the pit. The lord of the Malandanti flinched and took a step back from the railing.

Hexe got to his feet, pressing his free hand over his

bleeding wounds. "Marz! You gave me your word! You said you wouldn't hurt her!"

"No, I said I wouldn't hand her over to Bonzo," Boss Marz replied. "I didn't promise I wouldn't let Nach kill her. But first, I'll have him get rid of you and your mangy friend."

As Nach handed me over to Phelan for safekeeping, I thought I saw a familiar silhouette moving along the rafters overhead. I looked again to make sure, but the glare from the arena lights made it impossible to see anything besides blobs of pulsing shadow.

The pink-haired Malandanti stepped forward, holding aloft his metal left hand as he summoned forth the hellfire that would turn Hexe and Lukas into unrecognizable lumps of carbon.

As the first tongue of flame began to flicker in the hollow of Nach's palm, the Cyber-Panther jumped onto his back from its hiding place in the warehouse rafters, knocking him over the railing and into the nest of razor wire surrounding the upper lip of the pit. Nach screamed in agony as the wire sliced through his clothes and into his upper body, while his legs dangled into the pit. Roaring in triumph, Lukas made a second running jump, only this time his claws sank into flesh, not wood.

As the were-cat pulled the shrieking Malandanti down into the pit, the audience began to panic. There was a horrific scream as Nach dropped to the sawdust with a heavy thud, leaving his prosthetic left arm behind in the razor wire perimeter. The panic turned into full-fledged chaos as the spectators filling the bleachers began climbing over one another in a desperate attempt to escape.

I don't know how the Cyber-Panther had escaped the destruction of his fellow sculptures, or how it was able to move about on its own. Perhaps Hexe was right and that a part of Lukas was inside the sculpture. Perhaps I had created a doppelgänger instead of a piece of art. Whatever the reason, I couldn't have been happier to see it if it was Santa Claus, James Bond, and Elvis rolled into one.

The Cyber-Panther, his unblinking gaze fixed on Boss Marz, made a noise that sounded like a buzz saw ripping into a tin roof. As it stepped forward, Marz snatched me from Phelan, shoving me in front of himself like a shield. The Cyber-Panther halted its advance, its segmented metal tail lashing back and forth in consternation.

"Tell it to back off!" Marz snapped.

"Like hell I will," I snapped. "Sic him, kitty!"

Bonzo leaped from his master's shoulder, transforming in midair into his demon-ape aspect. He struck the Cyber-Panther full force, carrying them both off the grandstand and onto the concrete floor below.

Although fashioned from steel the same thickness of an automobile body, the Cyber-Panther was still, essentially, a work of art, not a war machine. He didn't stand a chance against a demon spawned in the bowels of hell. Bonzo pinned the Cyber-Panther to the floor and effortlessly ripped his head from his shoulders. Whooping in triumph, the familiar held aloft his trophy. My heart sank as the light faded from the Cyber-Panther's LED eyes.

From somewhere on the other side of the warehouse there came a thunderous thumping sound, as if a giant were knocking on the side of the building. One of Marz's croggies ran up onto the grandstand, looking extremely nervous.

"Are you okay, Boss?"

"I'm fine. What in seven hells is that noise?"

"There's a seven-foot-tall woman with one eye banging on the loading dock door with the biggest chuffin' hammer I've ever seen in my life!"

A look of alarm crossed Boss Marz's face. "Bonzo!" he shouted, pointing toward the pit. "Kill Hexe and the were-cat! Do it now!"

Before Bonzo could do his master's bidding, there was the sound of something shattering overhead, followed by a rain of broken glass. Shielding my eyes, I looked up to see Scratch, in full demonic aspect, drop down through the skylight, dragon wings spread wide and talons extended. The familiar hit the ground pissed off, knocking a Malandanti goon halfway across the warehouse with a lash of his crocodilian tail.

Bonzo jumped onto Scratch, biting and clawing the invading familiar viciously, only to have Scratch return the attack in kind. Locked in infernal combat, the familiars rolled about on the floor, knocking over bleachers and slamming into the fleeing spectators. The noise the demons made as they battled each other was like something from a Godzilla movie. It was so loud, in fact, I didn't realize the loading dock door had been breached until I heard the sound of approaching motorcycles.

The Golgotham Iron Maidens MC, two-dozen strong, came roaring through the warehouse, Hildy and Lyta leading the charge on a Harley Trike. The Amazon was hunched over the handlebars, while the Valkyrie rode pillion, wielding a thirty-pound sledgehammer to bash Malandanti who got in their way.

Boss Marz's men, already spread thin trying to control the mass exodus of frightened spectators while staying clear of the battling familiars, were unable to defend themselves from the unexpected attack. As they fumbled with their spells, desperately trying to summon forth hellfire or some other form of magical weapon, the lesbian bikers tore into them with war axes, crossbows, and chains, their voices raised in an ululating war cry.

Boss Marz grabbed Phelan's arm, a look of genuine fear on his face. "Get me out of here—now!"

"The secret tunnel to Ghastly's is gonna be jammed," the werewolf said. "But we can escape through the kennels."

I tried to make a break for it, hoping all the excitement might distract my captors, but Boss Marz grabbed my upper arm, nearly yanking it out of its socket.

"You're staying with *me*, nump," he snarled. "Just in case I need a little 'insurance' down the line."

Skirting the melee taking place between the Malandanti and the Iron Maidens, Phelan led Boss Marz to a door behind one of the bleachers. As we hurried past, I glanced down into the pit, but all I saw was Nach's savaged body lying in the bloody sawdust. There was no sign of Hexe or Lukas.

Just then there came an earsplitting roar, and Scratch and Bonzo, still locked in their unholy grudge match, rolled through the razor-wire perimeter and toppled into the pit. Too bad the twunts all beat cheeks back to Ghastly's, because they were missing one hell of a fight—literally.

The stairs led down to a different section of the vast underground kennels I had been in earlier, although it smelled just as bad and was just as poorly lit. As Boss Marz dragged me down one of the aisles, I saw a minotaur sitting in a bed of filthy straw, a shock collar about his thick neck. Upon spotting Phelan, the man-bull lurched to his feet, snorting in anger.

"Calm down, you!" the werewolf snarled, fishing the

remote for the shock collar out of his pocket. "You want to get zapped, Elmer?"

The minotaur fell silent and stepped back, but the hatred smoldering in his big dark eyes did not diminish. On either side of his cage were other half-beasts and beast-men, like the yeti and wingless sphinx. All had about their necks the same kind of shock collar as the minotaur.

Farther down the aisle were the cages reserved for the shape-shifters, who were recognizable by their unibrows. Some were bastet, like Lukas, while others were lycanthropes, and there were even a couple of heavyset berskirs. Whether were-cat, werewolf, or were-bear, they all shared the same slave-collar about their throat and resentful look in their eyes. As Boss Marz and Phelan hurried past, they hissed, barked, and growled at the werewolf who had sold them into slavery and the warlock who held them captive.

Suddenly the figure of a man stepped out of the shadows, blocking Boss Marz's escape route. The figure raised its right hand, commanding them to stop. Although he was ragged, bloodied, and bruised, I would have recognized that silhouette anywhere.

"Hexe!" I cried. I tried to break free of Boss Marz's grasp and run to him, but the crime lord's grip was stronger than iron.

Marz and Phelan turned, as if to flee back the way they came, only to have Lukas slink out of the shadows behind them. The were-cat stood up on his hind legs, adding his voice to the chorus of growls and hisses from his fellow gladiators. He held up the mangled remains of his shock collar, the hated symbol of his captivity, in one taloned hand.

"So much for your Left Hand Path," Hexe said, tossing what was left of Nach's metal left arm at Marz's feet. "Let her go, or I'll make you."

"You and what army?" Marz sneered, tightening his hold on me until I grimaced in pain.

"This one," Hexe replied calmly, pointing his right hand at the lock of the nearest cage.

A finger of blue-white lightning shot forth, short-circuiting the electric current and making the door spring open. The magic then jumped from lock to lock up and down the row of cages, like St. Elmo's fire, until every cage was no longer electrified and every door hung open.

The captive shape-shifters slowly got to their feet and exchanged glances with one another, unsure whether or not what they were seeing was truly real. The first one to take a tentative step toward freedom was a burly man with dark brown hair.

Phelan pointed the remote control at the were-bear, who grimaced in agony and began clawing at the collar encircling his neck. "Get back! Get back or I'll fry each and every one of you!" the werewolf shouted.

Suddenly there was a loud, bellowing sound as Elmer the minotaur came charging up the aisle, head lowered. Before Phelan could react, he found himself tossed into the air by the man-bull's horns. The remote control flew from his hand, to land at Lukas's feet. The were-cat snatched it up and smashed it against the bars of a nearby cage.

Phelan yowled in terror as he fell to the ground, transforming from man to wolf in less time than it took me to blink. The werewolf scrambled to his feet and ran, yelping, past Hexe. The captive shape-shifters, roaring in unison, cast aside their human skins and gave chase to their tormentor, like hounds going after a blooded fox. Lukas shrieked in delight and dropped onto all fours, joining his fellow prisoners in the hunt.

Boss Marz raised his left hand and hurled a fireball at Hexe. Hexe raised his right hand, moving it in a clockwise pattern, as if wiping a window, and the fireball splattered harmlessly against the invisible shield like a paintball.

"Let her go, Marz," Hexe said. "Once they finish with the werewolf, they'll be back for you. You'll have a decent head start if you leave now. . . ."

As Boss Marz tried to decide whether holding me hostage against Hexe was worth being torn to shreds by a pack of furious were-men, I spun around and kicked him in the shins as hard as I could.

"Take that, you creepy bastard!" I yelled as I broke free of his sweaty grasp. "Nobody makes *my* friends fight to the death!" I ran to Hexe, who quickly stepped in front of me, shielding me with his body.

"Don't think this is over between us, 'Serenity,'" Boss Marz shouted over his shoulder as he headed back the way he came. "I'll *never* bend my knee to a nump-loving dexie—and I'm not the only one!"

He probably had a couple more villainous threats to hurl at us before making his escape, but he was cut short by Hildy stepping out from between the cages and hitting him like a piñata with her sledgehammer. The crime boss dropped to the floor like a poleaxed steer.

"Did I kill 'im?" Hildy asked as her partner came forward to hog-tie the fallen Malandanti.

"No such luck," Lyta replied as she wrapped the hemp rope around Boss Marz's ankles and wrists.

Hexe turned to me, his golden eyes darting over my body. "Are you all right?" he asked. "Did he hurt you?"

I shook my head. "I'm okay."

"Thanks to all the gods in every heaven," he whispered, cupping my face in his right hand. "I don't know what I would do if anything bad ever happened to you."

He wrapped his arms around me, pressing my body tight against his own, as his warm, pliant lips found mine. I eagerly returned his kiss, like a woman dying of thirst drinking a glass of cold, clear water. I had come so horribly close to losing this amazing man forever, I never wanted to let him go.

But as we broke our first kiss, Hexe's eyelids fluttered and his face went deadly pale. I caught him in my arms as he fell into a swoon. It was then I realized just how badly he'd been wounded in his battle with Lukas. His naked torso was covered with deep scratches and bite marks, and when I gently cradled his back as I helped him to the ground, my arms came back bloody.

"What's wrong?" Lyta asked.

"Hexe has been hurt," I explained, trying to keep my fear at bay. Bursting into tears at that moment wasn't going to do either one of us any good. "He's lost a lot of blood. He needs a doctor!"

"Will I do instead?" Lady Syra asked, smiling down at me as I held her injured son in my arms. She knelt and removed a small jar of ointment from her Prada purse, which she then rubbed over Hexe's wounds. Within seconds the bleeding stopped and the cuts and bites began to close.

"What are *you* doing here?" I gasped.

"Don't look so surprised, my dear. Apparently there was at least *one* fan of this horrific blood sport still loyal to the royal house." She returned the ointment to her purse and removed a flask of greenish liquid, which she tipped into her son's mouth, causing him to spit and sputter. "I received an anonymous text message, informing me of what Marz was up to."

Hexe's eye fluttered open. "I should have known you were involved, Mom." He smiled ruefully. "You're the only other person who can let Scratch out of the house."

"Yes, when I learned what was happening, I lost no time setting your familiar free and sending him ahead of me. Imagine my surprise," Lady Syra said, nodding in the direction of Hildy and Lyta, "when I arrived to find the cavalry loitering in front of Ghastly's Diner."

"Yeah, sorry about getting here so late, guys," Hildy said apologetically. "We were on our quarterly ride to Woodstock when I got your text. We got back as fast as we could."

"What about Scratch?" Hexe asked as he got back on his feet. "Is he okay?"

"He's fine, son," Lady Syra said reassuringly. "Marz's familiar decided to dematerialize rather than risk being killed on the mortal plane. I've already sent Scratch home to lick his wounds. You should do the same. That healing is fresh, and I don't want you tearing it back open." She shook her head in disgust as she looked at the squalor of the kennels. "I took the liberty of calling the Paranormal Threat Unit just before I arrived. They should be here any minute to mop things up. I would recommend that you and your friends make yourselves scarce. The New York City justice system takes a dim view of vigilantism—even in Golgotham."

"Your mom's right," I said as Hexe and I slipped our arms around each other's waists. It felt so incredibly natural, as if we had been holding each other for years.

"She usually is." He smiled. "You'll find that out soon enough."

"C'mon, you two!" Lyta said, motioning for us to hurry up. "We'll give you a ride home."

I looked around, suddenly realizing we were missing a member of our group. "Where's Lukas?"

"Don't worry about him." Hexe smiled. "You know how cats are. He'll show up at the house when he's hungry. Besides, he has no reason to hide anymore."

I took Hexe's six-fingered hands in my five-fingered ones and kissed them. "Before we go riding off into the night with a bunch of lesbian road warriors, there's just one thing I wanted to tell you. . . ."

"Yes, Tate? What is it?"

"Don't you *ever* nearly get yourself killed trying to save my life *ever* again! Not that I don't appreciate the gesture, mind you. . . ."

He grinned and leaned in for another kiss. "You know what they say—'No pain, no gain.'"

I rolled my eyes at that last part, but I kissed him anyway.

Chapter 23

After a week spent recuperating from his near miss in the fighting pit, Hexe was finally taking me on our first real date. And, as promised, he wasn't taking me to the Calf.

Lukas was standing in the door of the kitchen as I came down the stairs in a strapless black sequined lace cocktail dress and a pair of Jimmy Choo open-toe sling-back pumps. Now that he was no longer a fugitive from the Malandanti, the teenaged were-cat had transitioned from refugee houseguest to paying boarder, thanks to his new job delivering prescriptions and medicinal meals via bicycle for Dr. Mao.

"What are *you* all dressed up for?" he asked.

"Hexe has reserved a table for us at the Golden Bowery," I explained as I finished swapping out my stainless steel hoops for sparkling pear-shaped diamond drop earrings.

"You two are going out?" he groaned. "Why didn't anyone tell me before I went out and bought a large pizza to celebrate my first paycheck?" He pointed to the pizza box sitting on the kitchen table, the top of which was emblazoned with the Strega Nona logo—a witch riding sidesaddle on a pizza peel.

"Why don't you invite Meikei over?" I suggested. "After all the times she's brought you food, it's about time you returned the favor."

Lukas's eyes lit up. "That's a great idea!"

"You're welcome, kiddo."

"I just got a call from Kidron," Hexe announced as he leaned over the second-floor balustrade, still fussing with his tie. "He's waiting for us at the curb." His golden eyes widened upon seeing me. "Wow! You look amazing."

"And *you* look like you're not ready yet," I chided.

" 'Tis merely an illusion, I assure you." He snapped the fingers of his right hand, and the tie about his neck looped itself into the perfect Windsor knot. He trotted down the stairs to join me, adjusting the cuffs of his Ralph Lauren suit along the way. "What do you think? Am I presentable?"

"You clean up pretty good." I smiled. "If I didn't know better, I'd think you were a male model. Although I'll admit I never would have guessed you owned a suit like that when I first met you."

"I didn't!" he laughed. "My mom bought it for me when I told her where I was taking you for dinner. I think she was afraid I'd show up in front of the maître'd in a sports coat and a Panic! At the Disco T-shirt."

"Something tells me she didn't need a crystal ball to see *that* in your future," Scratch sniffed from his perch on the ground-floor newel post. His hairless body still bore the fading scratches and bite marks from his brawl with Bonzo.

"So, if you two are going out on the town, who's gonna feed me?"

"Lukas will take care of that, won't you, kid?" I replied, catching the were-cat's eye.

"No problem," Lukas answered.

"And you'll make sure our young friend here stays out of the liquor cabinet while we're gone, right Scratch?" Hexe said pointedly.

"Awww, c'mon Hexe ... " Lukas groaned.

"Emancipated minor or not, you're still just sixteen," Hexe reminded him. "And while you're living under my roof, you abide by the rules. And the rule is 'no drunk underage were-cats.' I have enough headaches as it is without adding that to the list."

Hexe wasn't kidding. Thanks to Roger's big mouth, once he had unfrozen, everyone now knew I was the heiress to the Eresby fortune. So now Derrick Templeton, Roger, and the taxi driver who plowed through the plate glass window when the Cyber-Panther ran out in front of his cab had all filed civil suits against Hexe and me for everything from breach of contract to pain and suffering to supernatural assault. It looked as though for the foreseeable future most of my trust fund payments would be going to pay my lawyers.

Luckily, though, Lady Syra's connections had kept us from getting into real hot water with the authorities. Once the PTU realized the extent of the Malandanti's pit-fighting operation, they could have cared less about finding out who put Boss Marz in the hospital with a broken sternum, or how Nach ended up with *both* arms ripped off.

Marz could have dropped the dime on us himself, of course, once he regained consciousness, but all that would've netted him were a couple charges of kidnapping and attempted murder on top of the RICO charges he was already looking at.

"Don't worry, boss," Scratch assured his master. "I'll keep an eye on things while you're away."

Having bid our housemates good night, Hexe and I gathered up our belongings and headed for the door.

"Here, allow me," Hexe said, helping me into my coat.

"How Continental of you!" I teased.

"Yes, but in my case the continent is at the bottom of the sea." He opened the front door with a grand flourish, motioning for me to exit ahead of him. "Milady, your chariot awaits."

As I stepped out onto the front stoop, I gasped in surprise at what stood waiting at the curb. Instead of the usual hansom cab he piloted, Kidron was harnessed to a Victorian carriage, like the ones in Central Park. The trim of the carriage was decorated with a garland of interwoven red roses, and there were flowers woven into the centaur's mane and tail.

"Do you like it?" he asked hopefully.

"It's *beautiful*," I replied.

"You deserve to be surrounded by beauty," he said as he helped me into the carriage. "If it were in my power, I would make every day from here on in perfect, so you would never be unhappy again."

I leaned back and rested my head on his shoulder, staring up at the few brave stars strong enough to pierce the night sky over Manhattan. The sound of Kidron's hooves clip-clopping against the pavement was almost hypnotic. Hexe slipped his arm about my waist, pulling me even closer.

"As long as you're with me, I don't think I *can* be unhappy," I whispered.

"Me, too," he replied.

*   *   *

The Golden Bowery was located on Green Man Lane, a relatively short dogleg street that connected Maiden Lane with Liberty Street. I don't know if it would be fair to call it a "throwback" to the halcyon days of the Stork Club and the Copacabana, because it predated them. Since the Roaring Twenties, the Golden Bowery had mixed the sophistication of the "smart set" with the allure of the exotic into a potent cocktail of power, money, and glamour, in every sense of the word.

Although its exterior was relatively nondescript, it boasted a pair of huge doors cast from bronze and gilded in fourteen karat gold. On either side of the entrance were huge African lions carved from marble. The twin statues were said to be enchanted and would come to life should anyone be foolish enough to try and steal the establishment's trademark portals.

After dropping off our coats with the hatcheck station, which was run by a young woman with four arms, we went to see about our reservation.

"Name, please?" the headwaiter asked without looking up from his seating chart.

"Hexe. Party of two."

The maître d', an older Kymeran with a scrying-glass monocle screwed into his right eye, snapped to attention as if he'd been goosed with a cattle prod. "Of course, sir!" He picked up a couple of heavy leather-bound menus and motioned for us to follow him. "Your table is right this way, Serenity."

The Golden Bowery's main room was supported by Grecian pillars and hung with velvet drapes the color of good wine. Vines wrapped themselves around the pillars, creating a living canopy through which strands of colored lights were cunningly woven. On the ceiling overhead painted nymphs frolicked with fauns bearing clusters of ripe grapes. In the middle of the room was a large parquet dance floor. The chandelier hanging overhead from the ceiling was made of stained glass, which cast a rainbow of light onto the crisp white tablecloths below.

At least half of the clientele was human, and I recognized several famous actors, influential politicians, and wealthy socialites. The other half was a mixture of Kymerans, leprechauns, huldrefolk, and various shapeshifter species—all as elegantly dressed and carefully groomed as their human counterparts. These were the Beautiful People of Golgotham, not unlike those I had been raised among on the Upper East Side.

Our maître d' led us to a raised section overlooking the dance floor, opposite the swing era–style band box. As we wound our way through the other diners, the Golden Bowery's Kymeran patrons fell silent to watch us, only to start talking again, in hushed voices, once we had passed.

A bottle of champagne was already awaiting us at our table, nestled inside a silver bucket full of ice. Hexe held out my chair for me as the maître d' set about uncorking our wine, which he then poured into delicate crystal flutes, the rims of which were chased in twenty-four karat gold.

"Everybody's staring at us," I whispered.

"Let them go ahead and stare," he replied. "It's time certain things changed in Golgotham. Here's to our first night out as a couple." He touched his glass to mine. "And many more ahead."

"I'll drink to that." I smiled. "Here's to the right kind of change—for both of us."

"You know my people can read auras, right? That means we can see the energy those around us give off, both positive and negative. Do you know what I saw the first time I met you?"

"A nump?"

"You have *never* been a nump in my eyes—and you never will be," he said emphatically. "No, what I saw was a beautiful halo about your head. It looked like a hybrid of a sunflower, a stained glass window, and a mandala, and it spun and pulsed like a kaleidoscope. I've never seen anything like it before. That's why I automatically assumed you were a psychic or a medium. When you said you weren't, something inside me said, *This woman is worth knowing.* I knew right then and there, no matter what, you and I were destined to be together."

"That is the most romantic thing I've ever heard. Most guys would just say, 'I thought you were really hot.' "

"Well, that, too," he said, winking at me over the rim of his champagne glass.

The bandleader—a dapper-looking huldu with a gray goatee—gave a short downstroke, directing his ensemble with the cow's tail hanging from the special vent in the back of his dress pants. The band promptly launched into an up-tempo Glenn Miller cover orchestrated for panpipes, lyre, aulos, bodhran drum, and didgeridoo. It should have been an unholy cacophony, but somehow it worked. Several couples got up from their seats and headed for the dance floor.

"Would you care to dance?" he asked.

"I'd love to," I replied, offering him my hand.

He gallantly wrapped my arm about his and escorted me to the open dance floor. He watched the dancing couples as they twirled past, waiting for an opening, then quickly stepped in to join the crowd, drawing me in after him. He pulled me close against him, resting his hand against my hip as we circled the floor, the other dancers pressing in against us. I could feel him burning against my thigh like a banked coal, so I moved so that my own heat pressed against him. It was as if we were locked together below the waist, joined at heart, hand, and loin.

No wonder I'd had such lousy luck in the romance department in the past—all my previous lovers had been human. And not one of them would have been willing to die to save my life; of that I'm certain. Hell, most of them couldn't be bothered to put the toilet seat down. Although, to be fair, I probably wouldn't have jeopardized my life for any of them, either. But as I looked up into his golden eyes, shimmering like twin suns, I knew there was nothing I would not dare for my warlock prince.

We began undressing each other the moment we entered the door. I hungrily kissed his face and neck as I loosened his tie, while he reached behind me and fumbled with my zipper.

"It's about *time* you two got back," Scratch commented acidly from his guard post atop the liquor cabinet. "Lukas took Hello Kitty out to the movies."

"Beat it, Scratch!" Hexe said, flapping his tie at the familiar. "Scat!"

"I *beg* your pardon?" the familiar sniffed.

"You heard me! Go sleep in Lukas's room tonight."

"Oh, you're doing *that* again, huh?" Scratch said, rolling his eyes in disgust. "You mortals and your revolting mating habits!" With that, the familiar snapped open his batlike wings and flapped out of the room.

"Your place or mine?" I winked, kicking off my Choos.

"Mine." He grinned. "I have my own bathroom."

"I *knew* there were perks to fooling around with the landlord!"

Before I was halfway to the stairs, Hexe scooped me up in his arms, taking the risers two at a time, both of us whooping and laughing the whole way. I was impressed by his strength and how effortlessly he carried me, as if I were a doll.

Hexe's bedroom was at the very end of the second-floor hallway, overlooking the garden. He gave the door a kick with his foot, and it swung open to reveal a room twice the size of mine. In the center of the room was a king-sized four-poster, with bedknobs shaped like owls.

As he set my bare feet back onto the floor, I gave him a deep, wet kiss, lolling my tongue around in his mouth. We stumbled toward the bed, our clothes falling along the way, and we tumbled onto the sheets, giggling like children at play.

He raised himself on one elbow and looked down at me, smoothing my hair out of my face with his wizard's hand. I, in turn, ran my fingers over his shoulders, his neck, and across his hairless chest, exploring his physique with my sculptor's touch.

Where my mother would look at Hexe and view him as "inhuman" or "deformed" because of his cat-slit pupils, extra fingers, and strangely colored hair, I exulted in his otherness. I didn't set out to fall in love with Hexe; yet here I was, trembling in his arms as if I had never been with a man before in my life. I wrapped my five fingers about his six.

He seemed to know exactly how far I needed to go, and he steered me there as slowly as he could, making my desire double up against itself, until I was writhing beneath him, hanging suspended from a precipice. I gave voice to something between a laugh and a moan as

I dissolved into ecstatic relief, wrapping my legs about him while he buried his face in my hair.

When it was over, he rolled onto his back and pulled me to him, so that my head rested on his bare chest. He gestured with his right hand, and flowers leaped from his fingertips. Slowly they drifted through the air, filling the room with their delicate perfume. I watched in quiet amazement as the blossoms slowly dissolved, their beautiful colors fading like a rainbow in the sun, until they became lacy whiffs of pale gray smoke. We lay like that, our limbs loosely wrapped about each other, for the rest of the night, exchanging whispers and kisses, until the morning star was lost in the lightening sky.

I awoke the next day to find myself staring up at a painting on the ceiling depicting a group of beautiful young Kymeran women draped in diaphanous veils, dancing among rose tendrils. Comets shot across the blue sky above the carefree dancers, while at the very epicenter was a dragon, rising from a pillar of flame.

Hexe lay curled beside me, his naked body as pale and pure as marble in the early-morning light. I sat there for a long moment and watched him sleep, drinking in the sight of him. Now that I was able to view his naked body in full daylight, I was pleased to see that all his hair was the same shade of purple as that on his head. His splendid physique would make a wonderful subject for a statue. . . . With a start, I realized that Hexe's body was an exact flesh-and-blood double for that of the original *Dying Gaul.*

How strange I should find myself in bed with a man who bore such a strong resemblance to the statue that first sparked my imagination and curiosity, all those years ago, and inspired me to become the artist I had now become. Then again, Golgotham was the place for strange things. And there was nothing stranger than love. Although we were born of wildly different cultures, there was something in our hearts and brains that drew us together and kept us there. I could no more cease to love him than I could cease to breathe.

Since it was still relatively early, I thought I would surprise Hexe by making breakfast. I remembered the Mexican clay-pot coffee he'd made for me, and I decided to return the favor. I went back to my own room and slipped into a T-shirt and jeans, then headed downstairs.

A quick inventory of the kitchen pantry informed me we were out of coffee and milk. The nearest corner market was Dumo's, two blocks away on the corner of Horsecart Street and Beekman. I could get there and back in plenty of time before Hexe woke up. I grabbed my coat—still crumpled on the floor from the night before—and headed out on my grocery run.

It was a beautiful fall day in the city. It wouldn't be long before winter would arrive, muffling the streets under blankets of slush and snow. But until then, the sky was blue and clear, the air crisp and refreshing. I tilted my head back, luxuriating in the simple pleasure of sunshine on my face. It was funny how being in love made everything seem just a little bit special, as if the world had been washed clean for my benefit, and presented to me sparkling new.

Due to the nocturnal habits of the majority of my neighbors, the streets at that time of day were largely empty, save for the Teamsters making their deliveries to the various restaurants and other businesses. That was why it took me only five minutes to find and buy the ingredients I needed at Dumo's.

As I stepped out of the store, I happened to glance across the street where I saw a chestnut centaur hitched to a delivery wagon and recognized the burly upper torso of Kidron's brother, Rowdy. Judging from the furniture on the back of the wagon, he was either moving someone in or out of one of the row houses lining Horsecart Street.

I was about to call out a greeting to the centaur when I spotted yet another familiar face. It belonged to Greer Bartholomew, aka Bartho, the photographer I'd met at my art opening. He was talking to Sylvester, the ipotane, directing him as to the order in which he wanted his belongings removed from the wagon. From the look on Syl's face, Bartho was going to be damned lucky if, by the end of the day, he could sit down on anything without it collapsing. I turned and hurried back in the direction of home. I didn't want Hexe to wake up and find me gone.

Upon returning, I set about preparing a fresh batch of Mexican clay-pot coffee and tried not to dwell on what the arrival of another artist—and fellow human—in my immediate neighborhood signified. On the upside, the leprechauns would have someone else to throw beer bottles at. But what was the downside? Maybe Uncle Esau was right, after all. Perhaps I *was* the harbinger of destruction.

"There you are! I thought I heard someone rattling those pots and pans."

Hexe, his hair still tousled from the bed, was standing in the doorway of the kitchen, dressed in a silk dressing gown the color of wine and embroidered with dragons.

"I wanted to make us coffee," I explained, pouring the fragrant mixture through the strainer. "I *was* going to serve it to you in bed, but since you're already up . . ."

"I can think of better things to do in bed than drink coffee." He gave me a languid smile. "I *could* use a little pick-me-up after last night, though." He stepped behind me, nuzzling the nape of my neck. I leaned back, relishing the feel of his strong arms encircling my waist. "Is something wrong? I saw you frowning when I walked in."

I shrugged my shoulders as I poured out two steaming cups of the delicious brew. "It's nothing. There's a storm coming, that's all."

"Really?" Hexe glanced out the kitchen window at the clear autumn sky. "I don't see any clouds...."

"It's still in the distance, but it's on its way. I can feel it."

"I love lying in bed on a lazy, rainy day." He smiled. "Besides, as long as we're together, it doesn't really matter what's going on outside my door. I don't care if the world comes to an end, as long I'm with you."

Had that speech come from anyone else's mouth, I would have snorted and said something snarky. Instead, I wrapped my arms about him, resting my head against his chest. I could feel his heart beating, just for me, as mine now beat only for him. Whatever the future held for us, I knew that as long as it involved my loving him, and being loved by him, there was nothing to fear.

"You're right," I said as we headed back to bed with our coffee. "There's no point in worrying about something that hasn't happened yet. Who knows which way the winds will blow? Perhaps the storm will pass us by altogether."

Golgotham Glossary

Abdabs: The frights/terrors; any number of creatures known for harassing/frightening humans. Used in Kymeran slang to connote annoyance, as in "Bloody abdabs!"

Ambi: Someone who practices both Right and Left Hand disciplines.

Bastet: A shape-shifting race taking the form of different big cats, such as tiger, lion, and panther. Also known as the Children of Bast.

Berskir: A race of shape-shifters taking the form of various species of bear, such as grizzly, black bear, and polar bear.

Centauride: A female centaur; also known as a centauress.

Charmer: A wizard who creates charms for a living.

Chuff/Chuffing/Chuffed: Euphemism for sexual intercourse.

Come-hither: A spell that calls a man or woman against

his or her will, often during sleep or in an altered state of consciousness. Because of this, the subjects of come-hithers rarely have any memory of what happened to them once the spell is lifted. This spell is a favorite of date rapists and stalkers.

Client: Humans who pay to consult Kymeran witches and warlocks for any number of reasons.

Croggy: A subordinate or acolyte.

Crossed: Also known as cursed, afflicted, hexed, jinxed.

Dexter/Dexie: Someone who practices Right Hand magic, such as lifting curses and curing ailments. Right Hand magic is protective/defensive, as opposed to Left Hand magic, which is malicious/offensive.

Dowser: A psychic who specializes in finding lost things or locating fresh water.

Dunderwhelp: A stupid or unwanted child.

Dysmorphophilia: An inflicted preference for ugly sexual partners. A favorite curse among ex-wives whose former husbands have dumped them for a younger woman. Considered a nuisance curse.

Fecker: A contemptible person.

Glad Eye: The opposite of the Evil Eye. A charm that casts good fortune and success, especially in love and business.

Hamadryad: A shy, seldom-seen nature-spirit who lives inside one particular tree, such as an oak, birch, ash, or sycamore. Because of the urban nature of New York City, only a handful of hamadryads live in Golgotham.

Hamble: To cripple an animal, supernatural or not, by cutting out the balls of its feet for the purpose of fighting. This mutilation guarantees that the animal cannot physically back down from a fight because it lacks the ability to move backwards without falling.

Hambler: One who specializes in crippling animals for the fighting pit.

Heavy Lifter: A well-regarded banisher; one who can lift malignant curses.

Hedger: Short for "hedgewitch" or "hedge doctor"; a wizard specializing in herbal treatments of various illnesses.

Huldra: Female member of the huldrefolk, one of the supernatural races living in Golgotham. They resemble beautiful young women, except for the cow tails growing from the base of their spines. The males of their kind, known as huldu, appear as handsome men, except for the tails of bulls growing from the base of their spines.

Imbulbitation: A spell that makes the afflicted defecate whenever they are wearing pants.

Inflicted: The state of having an illness or spate of misfortune that's supernatural in origin.

Inflictions: A number of spiteful/socially embarrassing medical illnesses and physical conditions that are the result of supernatural agents. These curses mimic genuine physical and mental illnesses, such as cancer or schizophrenia, and require a diagnosis by a Kymeran healer. If the illness is natural in origin, the client is referred to a doctor. Also referred to as afflictions.

Ipotane: One of the supernatural races found in Golgotham. Humans from the waist up, they are horses from the waist down. Unlike centaurs, they have only two legs. They are often mistaken for satyrs, much to their disgust.

Juggler: Someone who is known as a competent practitioner of both Right and Left Hand magic.

Lifter: A witch or warlock who specializes in lifting curses.

Ligature: Magical binding using knotted cords that prevents someone from physically doing something.

Lubbard: An idle person who can work but does not.

Maenads: One of the supernatural races living in Golgotham. Maenads are female followers of Dionysius, the Greek god of wine. They go into ecstatic frenzies during which they lose all self-control and engage in sexual orgies, ritualistically hunt down wild animals (and occasionally men and children), tear them to pieces, and devour the raw flesh.

Micturition: Infliction of excessively frequent urination.

Misanthrope: An antihuman bigot.

Nimgimmer: A healer who treats venereal diseases.

Nitwitch: An incompetent wizard.

Nump: A fool. A derogatory racial slur directed at humans.

Numpies: Slang for human yuppies.

Numpsters: Slang for human hipsters.

Peddler: Short for "charm peddler"; a wizard who specializes in selling charmed objects for commercial gain.

Pikey: An itinerant wizard who sells magic on the streets.

Pissing Contest: A magic battle between drunken wizards.

Power Lifter: A well-respected banisher.

PTU: Short for Paranormal Threat Unit, a separate branch of the NYPD in charge of policing Golgotham and responding to paranormal/supernatural events throughout the triborough area.

Pusher: Short for "potion pusher"; a wizard who specializes in selling love potions, untraceable poisons, etc., for commercial gain.

Satyr: One of the supernatural races living in Golgotham. Satyrs are humans from the waist up, goats from the waist down. They also sport horns on their heads. They are notorious for being prone to gambling, drinking, and kidnapping beautiful women. Female satyrs are called fauns.

Talent: A natural magic ability, applying both to humans and Kymerans.

Twunt: Slang for a paying customer who visits Golgotham's red-light district.

Widdershins: The direction in which a curse must be turned in order to undo it.

Devon Monk

MAGIC TO THE BONE

Using magic means it uses you back, and every spell exacts a price from its user. But some people get out of it by Offloading the cost of magic onto an innocent. Then it's Allison Beckstrom's job to identify the spell-caster. Allie would rather live a hand-to-mouth existence than accept the family fortune—and the strings that come with it. But when she finds a boy dying from a magical Offload that has her father's signature all over it, Allie is thrown back into his world of black magic. And the forces she calls on in her quest for the truth will make her capable of things that some will do anything to control...

"Fiendishly original."
—#1 *New York Times* bestselling author
Patricia Briggs

Also in the series

Magic in the Blood
Magic in the Shadows
Magic on the Storm

Available wherever books are sold or at
penguin.com

R0031

NIGHTLIFE

by

ROB THURMAN

*When the sun goes down,
it all goes down...*

Welcome to the Big Apple. There's a troll
under the Brooklyn Bridge, a boggle in
Central Park, and a beautiful vampire in a
penthouse on the Upper East Side—and
that's only the beginning. Of course, most
humans are oblivious to the preternatural
nightlife around them, but Cal Leandros is
only half-human.

**"A roaring rollercoaster of a read...
[it'll] take your breath away."**
—*New York Times* bestselling author Simon R. Green

R0010

Caitlín R. Kiernan

THRESHOLD

Chance Matthews is drawn into a battle between angels and monsters because of something in her possession—a fossil of a creature that couldn't possibly have ever existed.

But it did.
And still does.

ALSO AVAILABLE
Silk
Low Red Moon
Murder of Angels
Daughter of Hounds
The Red Tree

**Available wherever books are sold or
at penguin.com**

THE ULTIMATE IN SCIENCE FICTION AND FANTASY!

From magical tales of distant worlds to stories of technological advances beyond the grasp of man, Penguin has everything you need to stretch your imagination to its limits.

penguin.com

ACE

Get the latest information on favorites like
William Gibson, T.A. Barron, Brian Jacques,
Ursula K. Le Guin, Sharon Shinn, Charlaine Harris,
Patricia Briggs, and Marjorie M. Liu,
as well as updates on the best new authors.

ROC

Escape with Jim Butcher, Harry Turtledove, Anne Bishop,
S.M. Stirling, Simon R. Green, E.E. Knight, Kat Richardson,
Rachel Caine, and many others—plus news on the
latest and hottest in science fiction and fantasy.

DAW

Patrick Rothfuss, Mercedes Lackey, Kristen Britain,
Tanya Huff, Tad Williams, C.J. Cherryh, and many more—
DAW has something to satisfy the cravings of any
science fiction and fantasy lover.
Also visit dawbooks.com.

*Get the best of science fiction and fantasy
at your fingertips!*